W9-DGA-414

A Place for for Murder

by EMMA LATHEN

A KANGAROO BOOK
PUBLISHED BY POCKET BOOKS NEW YORK

A PLACE FOR MURDER

Macmillan edition published 1963

POCKET BOOK edition published June, 1972

4th printing ....December, 1976

This POCKET BOOK edition includes every word contained in the original, higher-priced edition. It is printed from brand-new plates made from completely reset, clear, easy-to-read type.
POCKET BOOK editions are published by
POCKET BOOKS,
a division of Simon & Schuster, Inc.,
A GULF+WESTERN COMPANY
630 Fifth Avenue,
New York, N.Y. 10020.
Trademarks registered in the United States
and other countries.

ISBN: 0-671-81116-9.
Library of Congress Catalog Card Number: 63-14188.

This POCKET BOOK edition is published by arrangement with Macmillan Publishing Company, Inc. Copyright, ©, 1963, by Emma Lathen. All rights reserved. This book, or portions thereof, may not be reproduced by any means without permission of the original publisher: Macmillan Publishing Company, Inc., 866 Third Avenue, New York, N.Y. 10022.

Cover illustration by Roger Kastel.

Printed in the U.S.A.

"PEGGY LINDSAY DOESN'T COME INTO THIS HOUSE EXCEPT OVER MY DEAD BODY,"
said the elegant Olivia Austin in an unusual burst of fury. (She was willing to let her husband go, but not the house.)

"I'll die before I let Olivia get away with this," said Peggy Lindsay. (She planned to marry Olivia's husband, and the house went with the deal.)

All this talk of dying was not idle, as it turned out.

If John Putnam Thatcher hadn't been spending a reluctant weekend with the president of the Sloan Guaranty Trust, he wouldn't have become involved. Nor would he have had to attend that disastrous Development Committee Banquet.

But when it's a matter of murder and the bank's president is held for questioning, Thatcher is deeply involved. Even *he* doesn't suspect the truth until a night of unseemly celebrating after the local dog show....

Books by Emma Lathen

Accounting for Murder*
Ashes to Ashes*
Banking on Death*
Come to Dust
Death Shall Overcome*
The Longer the Thread*
Murder Against the Grain*
Murder Makes the Wheels Go 'Round*
Murder to Go*
Pick Up Sticks*
A Place for Murder*
A Stitch in Time*
Sweet and Low*

*Published by POCKET BOOKS

*Are there paperbound books you want
but cannot find in your retail stores?*

You can get any title in print in **POCKET BOOK** editions. Simply send retail price, local sales tax, if any, plus 35¢ per book to cover mailing and handling costs, to:

MAIL SERVICE DEPARTMENT
POCKET BOOKS • A Division of Simon & Schuster, Inc.
1 West 39th Street • New York, New York 10018

Please send check or money order. We cannot be responsible for cash.   *Catalogue sent free on request.*

Titles in this series are also available at discounts in quantity lots for industrial or sales-promotional use. For details write our Special Projects Agency: The Benjamin Company, Inc., 485 Madison Avenue, New York, New York 10022.

A Tender of Particulars

MUST VACATE: Unusual place near an unspoiled village with rare community spirit, an open hunting season, and responsible officials nearby. Convenient to New York, a magnificent estate with pleasant neighbors, and many interesting views. An opportunity for dog lovers and gentlemen farmers. Easy commuting to downtown financial district from this spacious dwelling with varied scope for activities, indoors and out. Refreshment of spirit for the discriminating close to the beauties of nature. Inquiries invited.

Contents

1 "Must Vacate . . ." 11

2 ". . . Unusual place" 20

3 ". . . near an unspoiled village" 29

4 ". . . with rare community spirit" 38

5 ". . . an open hunting season" 46

6 ". . .and responsible officials nearby." 53

7 "Convenient to New York, . . ." 62

8 ". . . a magnificent estate" 70

9 ". . . with pleasant neighbors" 78

10 ". . . and many interesting views." 86

11 "An opportunity for dog lovers . . ." 95

12 ". . . and gentlemen farmers." 101

13 "Easy commuting . . ." 108

14 ". . . to downtown financial district" 116

15 ". . . from this spacious dwelling" 127

16   ". . . with varied scope for activites"   139

17   ". . . indoors and out."   149

18   "Refreshment of spirit for

the discriminating . . ."   161

19   ". . . close to the beauties of nature."   170

20   "Inquiries invited."   180

A Place
for
Murder

I   "Must Vacate..."

THE BURDENS OF HIGH PLACE—AS ONEROUS ON Wall Street as elsewhere—include certain mandatory public appearances. Accordingly, one fine October day John Putnam Thatcher, senior vice-president of the Sloan Guaranty Trust (as well as head of its Trust Division and acting head of its Investment Division) found himself dutifully involved in a rather poor lunch at the Security Analysts' Luncheon Committee and, unfortunately, an even poorer speech by a member of the President's Council of Economic Advisers.

"Some Thoughts on the Price-Cost Spiral" were inaudibly whispered to the assembly; after hearing them, Thatcher, who believed in giving every man a fair chance, did not hesitate to ignore inviting gestures from the powerful personages at the head table. Sketching a wave, he unashamedly propelled himself away from the security analysts toward Broad Street.

There, he stood for a moment savoring the chill breeze and hard sun. Then, inhaling deeply, he set off through the scurrying lunchtime throngs toward Exchange Place and the Sloan. The perils of what the speaker called "upward oozing prices" did not occupy his thoughts; instead, he considered with pleasure the prospect of a bracing afternoon devoted to clearing his desk of its accumulation.

Not even the grandeur of the Sloan lobby dissipated this sense of vigor. Thatcher, essentially a conservative, never entered the Crystal Palace that was the New Sloan without a twinge of regret for the Old Sloan which had been decently reticent and dignified. But time was dulling his response to copper latticework and nightmare murals; he contented himself with a commiserating nod at the elevator starter. More conservative than Thatcher, Billings had never recovered

11

from the loss of a grill to be ceremoniously pulled open for a vice-president. As Thatcher was borne up to the sixth floor, he dismissed the failures of modern architecture and concentrated on his own immediate plans. With an uninterrupted afternoon, with a short Investment Committee meeting tomorrow morning—why, he might very well take advantage of the magnificent autumn weather to drive up to Connecticut for the weekend. In the years since he had become a widower, John Thatcher's life had been essentially urban— but he did have a new grandson to inspect, and the trees would be turning russet. . . .

As was to be expected, the moment the elevator doors slid open, he found one part of his large staff assiduously typing, filing, conferring—a secretary had reported his energetic stride—and the other part eager to put a spoke in his wheel.

"John," said Everett Gabler, braking at the elevator door. "Glad I caught you. I'd appreciate a moment if you've got one."

"I haven't," said Thatcher firmly. "My afternoon is taken up."

In the subsequent exchange, Gabler, one of the senior trust officers, succeeded in wringing from his superior only the promise of a brief meeting on Friday morning. Thatcher resumed his passage down the long corridor that led to his suite with a slight feeling of relief. Just then, another subordinate issued from one of the offices on the hall.

"Good!" said Charlie Trinkam, catching sight of him. "Just been talking to Miss Corsa. Now John, these Handasyde reports . . ."

"Charlie," said Thatcher, without stopping, "I've got an important appointment. Bring them in tomorrow morning."

Charlie wavered on the brink of expostulation, then shrugged. "OK, but they're important," he said. To Thatcher's back.

Rather pleased with himself, Thatcher continued into his offices. "That's the stuff to give the troops," he thought.

Miss Corsa looked up from her typing. "Mr. Thatcher, Mr. Gabler and Mr. Trinkam have both been looking for you. And Mr. Robichaux called . . ."

"I've already taken care of Gabler and Trinkam," said Thatcher, quietly triumphant. "Won't have time for them this afternoon. Make appointments for them tomorrow—short appointments. I'll call Tom Robichaux later. Now Miss Corsa, I want to be undisturbed this afternoon. Got a lot of work to do. You can bring your book in at three-thirty."

"And," said Miss Corsa without visible response to this show of force, "Mr. Withers would like to see you this afternoon. If," she added, seeing him halt on his way to the inner office, "if it is not inconvenient." Her voice was devoid of sarcasm.

"Hell!" said Thatcher.

Bradford Withers, president of the Sloan Guaranty Trust, could scarcely be relegated to tomorrow, however richly he deserved it. He was an amiable, diffuse man who wisely delegated the nonceremonial aspects of his august position to subordinates; courtesy as well as kindness demand that he be treated with kid gloves. Thatcher grudged him nothing but time; Bradford Withers invariably took time.

He found Miss Corsa regarding him sympathetically. "I suppose you didn't suggest that I had a good deal . . . no, no, of course not."

"He did say that it was important," said Miss Corsa. "And if you would just step upstairs when you got back from lunch."

A realist, Thatcher wrote off his plans for the afternoon. "I'll go right up," he said gloomily. "And Miss Corsa, we might as well satisfy Trinkam and Gabler. Tell them I can see them later this afternoon."

He strode back to the elevator and savagely punched the button. Withers thought the damnedest things were important, things like public relations firms, the decor of the executive dining room, new ways to economize on stationery. Thatcher profoundly hoped that he was not being diverted from his work for yet another discussion of the Employees' Thanksgiving Party.

"Oh good," said Miss Prettyman when he reached a room that looked like an outpost of the Museum of Modern Art. "Go right in, Mr. Thatcher. Mr. Withers has been hoping you would get there in time . . ."

"Not the Thanksgiving Party," Thatcher muttered, turning to find the president himself at the door, relief shining from his mild eyes. Bradford Withers was not the man to show strong emotion; he had a well bred, vacuous face and a bland embarrassed manner. He reserved his enthusiasm for his quite remarkable series of athletic feats, performed at

13

great cost in inaccessible areas of the world. Until a few years ago, he had been a four-goal man in polo.

"John," he said warmly. "Glad you could make it. We have a problem—oh, Miss Prettyman, will you make sure that we're not disturbed for the next hour? Come in, John. You know Gil Austin, don't you?"

Thatcher shook hands with Gilbert Austin, a tall solid man with a shock of dark brown hair who was just levering himself out of a complex leather contraption that Withers apparently regarded as suitable seating for his visitors.

"Of course," said Thatcher. They had met at the Witherses' city apartment on Beekman Place. Searching his memory he recalled that Austin was a partner in a well known firm of consulting engineers and—that was it!—the husband of Mrs. Gilbert Austin who was Withers' sister.

"Good to see you, Thatcher," Austin said, looking very grave. Withers circled his desk. "Helluva thing," he said audibly.

Thatcher cautiously sat down and awaited enlightenment. Austin looked at him. "I asked Brad to call you in, John, because I thought you might help us get this thing moving. We've wasted a lot of time. . . ." He had a pleasant, deep voice, and unlike his brother-in-law an eye for the effect of his words. Correctly reading Thatcher's practiced look of polite incomprehension, he flushed slightly, then said, "Didn't Brad tell you? It's the divorce. Olivia and I are getting a divorce."

"Oh," said Thatcher, prey to two distinct emotions. One was surprise, and he hoped it did not show. Gilbert and Olivia Austin—the noted and beautiful Mrs. Gilbert Austin —were a decorative as well as an ideally suited couple. Certainly they had been married for more than twenty years.

His second emotion was irritation with a society that presented him with such announcements without providing suitable rejoinders.

"I didn't know," he said, after clearing his throat.

Withers leaned forward. "Didn't mention it to people, Gil," he said earnestly. "Didn't think you'd want me to, and then I thought—that is to say, I hoped . . ."

"No," Gilbert Austin said, looking embarrassed. "I guess not. Well, we're getting a divorce, Olivia and I, and I don't have to tell you that Olivia is being wonderful about it, John. But there's this delay—I'm planning to remarry, you know, and I want to get the property settlement cleared up so that we can get the divorce over with."

His pleasant voice, which had risen slightly, returned to normal. Without emotion, he outlined the situation to Thatcher. There was a good deal of property owned jointly by Olivia and Gilbert Austin, some of it held in trust by the Sloan. Before the divorce was undertaken, some agreement on the division of this property was necessary.

"Everything," said Austin, "is quite clear. Olivia is wonderful about everything—but this little disagreement has arisen . . ."

"What little disagreement?" asked Thatcher shortly. Notwithstanding some sympathy for Austin, who was determinedly businesslike, and for Bradford Withers, who looked disconsolate, he could not help feeling that men like himself who had managed satisfactory marital careers should be spared the divorce proceedings of others.

Austin flushed. "Peggy—that's Peggy Lindsay who I'm marrying—seems to feel . . . that is. . . ."

Surprisingly, Withers clarified the point. "Peggy and Olivia don't agree about the value of that house in Shaftesbury, John. You remember that Gil and Olivia have a place next to mine. Farm and kennels as well. Peggy's a local girl. . . ."

His snobbery was unconscious but not unnoticed. Gilbert Austin looked moderately displeased at this description of his affianced, but he did not protest as Withers continued, "She seems to feel that Olivia is being unfair."

"We all agree that Olivia is behaving very well," said Austin, reluctant to intrude the personal element. "But we can't seem to agree about the Shaftesbury place. I thought that if we could get an independent opinion and agree to abide by it, we can get on with the property settlement and the divorce. It's just a formality."

Here, at least, was safe footing.

"Certainly," Thatcher said briskly. "And if you and Olivia are parting, we should start reviewing your holdings anyway. If you want us to check your records on the Shaftesbury property, we will. And then we'll get in touch with the lawyers. I don't see any difficulty."

Austin nodded gratefully, but it was Withers who spoke, and mournfully. "I was hoping that we wouldn't . . . that we

15

wouldn't . . . that we could settle all of this without a lot of formalities."

Thatcher was tempted to ask precisely what this piece of euphemism meant but Austin rose impatiently.

"God knows, you can't feel worse than I do, Brad," he said with suppressed violence. "But there's no use waiting. I don't want things dragging on, this way. It's hard on all of us. If we can get things moving, then get the divorce settled. . . ." He broke off, took a breath, then turned to Thatcher. "Well, Thatcher, if you'll get the machinery going, I'd appreciate it."

Thatcher was matter-of-fact. "Don't worry, Austin. We'll start this afternoon. After we send somebody up to value the property, you should be able to settle things through lawyers."

Austin nodded. "Thank you," he said. He looked across the desk toward his brother-in-law. "And Brad . . . thanks." He smiled briefly, then strode quickly from the room.

He had gone before Thatcher could wish him good luck. Under the circumstances, he reflected, this was just as well. Gilbert Austin's forthcoming nuptials did not, at a glance, seem to be a matter of immediate happiness.

"Terrible thing, this divorce," said Bradford Withers dolefully.

"Well, it won't be complicated," Thatcher said quickly, hoping to avert confidences on the subject. "We'll run a review of the trust. Then we'll check the Shaftesbury records and send up an appraiser later on. If Olivia isn't raising difficulties, the lawyers shouldn't have too much trouble."

"Olivia is admirable, admirable," her brother said heavily. "She's sticking her heels in about Ridge Road Farm, but I don't say that I blame her about that. As a matter of fact, I'm more upset than she is. And Bud, too, of course."

"Bud?"

"Gilbert, junior. He's twenty-two, you know. In his first year up at the Harvard Business School. We may have a place for him here at the Sloan."

Listening to his superior's flow of complaint, Thatcher let himself think about Olivia Austin, a tall woman with superb presence and a gracious composed intelligence. Hardly surprising that she should cope with the divorce better than her brother.

". . . and after twenty-five years," said Withers who had switched to another train of thought. "What on earth has gotten into Gil? He and Olivia have always gotten along . . . been proud of her . . . beautiful home. Dammit, I've always liked Gil—still do, for that matter—but I simply don't understand this."

"He mentioned remarriage," Thatcher said drily.

Withers got up, jammed his hands into his pockets and snorted. "Remarriage! He's divorcing Olivia to marry that Lindsay girl. Doesn't make sense! Oh, don't misunderstand me—Peggy's a nice enough girl—but compared to Olivia. . . ." Words failed him.

"I gather," said Thatcher, feeling that he might be treading dangerous waters, "I gather she is younger than Olivia."

Withers relieved his qualms. "Gil isn't the type to run after a youngster," he said, dismissing Thatcher's comment. "Peggy Lindsay is younger than Olivia, but that's all. She's plain and she shows dogs. You know the kind. That's how she met Gil. She was showing some of the Austindale Dobermans . . . well, I tell you I don't understand the whole thing, John."

Miss Corsa had once showed Thatcher a three-page spread in *Vogue* entitled "New York Beauties at Home" in which "Mrs. Gilbert Austin, the well known hostess, sportswoman and supporter of the arts" figured. But youth, so cavalierly dismissed by Bradford Withers, is often enough. Thatcher did not say so.

"And besides," said Withers with another unexpected flash of shrewdness, "does Gilbert Austin strike you as the man to lose his head over a woman? Does he even look happy?"

Gilbert Austin did not, Thatcher agreed as he rose, but he had no desire to prolong the discussion. "Bear in mind, Brad, the fact that few of us would look our best while we discussed divorce with our brother-in-law," he said, belatedly recalling Mrs. Withers. Possibly the remark had been tactless. "Well, I'll be going."

He was not destined to escape so easily.

". . . and embarrassing, I don't mind confessing," Withers grumbled. "Then on Sunday we have some damn fool committee meeting about the Dog Show where Gil and Olivia and the Lindsay girl and half of Shaftesbury will turn up. I tell you, John, Olivia may take all this sort of thing in her stride but it's hell on poor Gil and me. You know . . ."

He stopped, and looked keenly at his vice-president. "You should look over the Austin place—Ridge Road Farm."

Thatcher had seen this coming. He replied promptly that if

17

the farm were a bone of contention, a professional apppraiser was what was needed.

"No, you could talk to Olivia," Withers said, growing moderately animated, "and Peggy. . . ."

Thatcher was chilled by the prospect.

"Then, there's the Shaftesbury Inn," Withers said persuasively. "Remarkable woman has taken it over. Really, remarkable. Best French cooking in northern Connecticut. There was an article in the *Times*."

"I'm a steak and potatoes man," said Thatcher uncompromisingly.

"John," said Bradford Withers, "I don't like to impose on you, but frankly, it would be a big help for me if you could come up for the weekend. Carrie is in the Bahamas, you know, and that leaves me with the whole mess on my hands. . . ."

"I am spending the weekend in Shaftesbury, Connecticut," John Thatcher informed one of the junior trust officers later in the afternoon.

"That sounds extremely pleasant, sir," replied Kenneth Nicolls.

Thatcher had gladdened the hearts of Charlie Trinkam and Everett Gabler by attending to the matters that concerned them; he was now redressing the balance by assigning to a staff member a chore that would certainly entail overtime work, if not Saturday attendance at the Sloan. "I should get the major provisions of the Austin-Withers portfolio summarized by Saturday noon," Nicolls continued in formal tones.

Reading Nicolls' mind with no difficulty, Thatcher turned to a paper on his desk, an awe-inspiring expression on his face. "Since," he said, "I have pointed out that I am required to spend my weekend in the midst of this divorce, Nicolls, I am not prepared to sympathize with your natural irritation at this disruption of your weekend plans." He looked up. "And if any difficulties arise, you can call me at the Withers place."

He waved dismissal, then relented. "And send my apologies to Mrs. Nicolls. How is she?"

Nicolls, abashed by this comprehensive right and left, turned fiery red, murmured something disjointed and fled—to sink his teeth into the Austin-Withers trust documents, no doubt. Thatcher watched him depart in some confusion.

"She's expecting," explained Miss Corsa, eyes modestly downcast, when he demanded enlightenment.

"Expecting what?" asked Thatcher, examining a file on her desk.

Miss Corsa was outraged. "A baby!"

"Well, the Austin divorce will keep his feet on the ground," Thatcher said unsentimentally. "But don't let us forget to send a cup."

Miss Corsa, who had already noted the need for a christening cup some six months ago, followed him into the inner office, and settled herself with her dictation book while Thatcher circled the desk. But once he was seated, he did not give his preliminary cough. Instead he looked up.

"Miss Corsa," he said suddenly, "how would you feel if you had been happily married for twenty-five years, and your husband left you for a younger woman?"

Miss Corsa disapproved of Mr. Thatcher's frivolities; nevertheless she gave this serious consideration.

"I wouldn't like it," she said finally.

"I thought not," Thatcher muttered. "Well, let's see. Dear Sweeney . . . Your letter. . . ."

But even as he turned his attention to the president of a small Massachusetts firm who fondly thought that he was going to dilute an equity held by the Sloan Guaranty Trust, part of his mind was still upon the recent interview. Both Shaftesbury, Connecticut, and Olivia Austin had faded a little in his memory. By the time the weekend was over, both would no doubt be a good deal clearer in his mind.

2   ". . . Unusual place"

SHAFTESBURY, CONNECTICUT, IS NOT SUBURBAN
Connecticut. In Shaftesbury there are no spirited struggles
over four-acre zoning, no petitions for better commuter
service, no interest at all in the local school system (which
exists primarily to serve the need of the servants' children).
Instead there is a sense of calm and plenty, a sense of spreading fields, and a sense of remote detachment from the business
office, which is visited on a voluntary basis for an occasional
review of the activities of junior partners. Unfortunately, from
John Thatcher's point of view, a farm is a farm anywhere.

"Yes," he was saying unenthusiastically, "yes, he looks like
a splendid specimen."

The Black Angus returned his melancholy stare with an
equal lack of enthusiasm. Olivia Austin, prodding expertly,
made a technical comment about hindquarters.

It was Saturday afternoon and things were not going well.
Six years had dimmed Thatcher's memories of Shaftesbury,
Connecticut. Now it was all coming back. Magnificent foliage,
exhilarating air—and everlasting talk about livestock. Brad
Withers had picked him up at the railroad station that morning
in artfully dilapidated clothing, apologized for the absence of
his wife, summoned Olivia to preside at the luncheon table
and then announced firmly that John would like to look
around the farm.

John had now been looking for two hours. The only relief
in sight was his appointment with Peggy Lindsay some forty-
five minutes hence. He was to "talk some sense into the girl."
Meanwhile, he seemed doomed to inspect Black Angus.

In deference to his guests' urban proclivities, Withers had
emphasized the financial aspects of raising beef cattle in Connecticut.

"Look at them," he urged, gesturing proudly at the green-sward dotted with black figures. "Every one of them is a walking tax loss!"

Thatcher sidestepped with care. Privately, he thought that tax losses could be achieved without exposure to animal droppings.

And furthermore he wanted briefing on the quarrel about the property settlement. His lunchtime attempts to get one had been remarkably unsuccessful. At the first mention of the Austin divorce, Bradford Withers, indicating distaste, plunged into discussion of the local hunt. Olivia Austin, less transparent than her brother, referred to her husband's plans with calm, expressed pleasure and gratitude to Thatcher for undertaking an informal negotiation of the property settlement, then talked agriculture.

She did it gracefully. But then, she was always graceful. It was the first thing one noticed about Olivia Austin. A beautifully balanced body that rose to a long slender neck and a fine-boned head almost too fragile to support the luxuriant mass of dark hair twisted into a chignon. She had a trick, during thoughtful pauses in conversation, of bowing her head and lowering the outer corners of her eyelids so that her large gray eyes were half hidden from view.

Yes, thought Thatcher, eyeing his hostess resentfully, she was a beautiful woman. Unfortunately, to beauty she added maturity and reserve—presumably not traits presently attractive to Gilbert Austin off in pursuit of his nymphet. But none of this gave Olivia Austin the right to inflict more pastoral scenes on him.

He flourished his watch. "I should be thinking of going down to the village, Olivia," he said.

"Yes," she replied. "We'll have time for you to look over the kennels and have a drink before you go."

"A drink would be fine," said Thatcher meaningfully; but he was not surprised to find himself following Olivia Austin across the road to the Austindale Kennels. She had made it abundantly clear, since Withers had tactfully left them an hour earlier, that a heart-to-heart talk was not on her agenda. It was a decision that Thatcher not only respected but applauded. In the course of his life, too many would-be divorcees had victimized him with detailed revelations. On the other hand, he had been summoned from the comfort of his home to the foothills of the Berkshires to discuss property settlements, not to look at kennels. It would be helpful if somebody gave him some information. Irritably he looked at the Austin Number One field; it looked like the Withers Number One field.

"The kennels," said Olivia briskly, pointing out an enclave of buildings and dog-runs that looked extremely efficient.

Beyond the wire netting, twenty-seven Doberman pinschers effortlessly assumed "At the Ready" positions and eyed Thatcher keenly.

"They look very intelligent," he said. He did not add that intelligence unaccompanied by amiability was no recommendation to him in the animal world. A Chesapeake retriever met in the course of a Maryland duck hunt remained his ideal of doghood.

Olivia, who had opened the door of the kennel office and was peering into its empty interior, replied absently.

"They're very intelligent. But it is difficult to take a Best in Breed with Dobermans. The competition is tremendous. Oh good. Here's Roger."

A small, compactly built man rounded the corner of the kennel office, a fair-haired young woman at his side. They were introduced as Roger and Cynthia Kincaid. Roger, it developed, was the Austin farm manager.

"What do you think of the dogs?" he asked Olivia after a round of greetings. "We should have a good entry for the Westminster. That last litter is coming along nicely."

"And a good entry for the local show too, I hope," Olivia replied spiritedly.

Roger smiled. "Now don't rip me up, Olivia," he said laughingly. "I've already agreed to go along with you. You'll have your display of hometown spirit. But it still doesn't make sense to waste your big guns on a small show."

"Of course you're right from a business point of view, Roger. It's just that—" Olivia hesitated with uncharacteristic self-consciousness. "Oh, well, you know how it is."

"Yes, I know," he said comfortably. And when Olivia suggested that the Kincaids come up for a drink, he tucked Olivia's arm into his own and bore her off along the path chatting about their possible entries.

Obviously a tactful man. Just what he was being tactful about eluded Thatcher until Cynthia Kincaid took him into her confidence.

"It's the Housatonic Dog Show," she explained in a low

voice. "It's an outdoor show held someplace different in Connecticut every year. Last Christmas Olivia and Gil and Peggy Lindsay talked the Shaftesbury Development Committee into inviting the show to be held here. That, of course, was before Gil and Olivia started having trouble." Cynthia looked cautiously up the path. Convinced that her words were inaudible, she proceeded. "Now we're all stuck with the situation. Olivia is damned if she'll retreat one inch and is insisting on full participation. Her attitude is that *she* has nothing to be ashamed of. Peggy is the biggest dog handler in New England, so she can't retreat, and Gil is handling the business end. Tomorrow night," she concluded grimly, "should be absolute hell."

"Tomorrow night?" asked Thatcher curiously. "I thought we were having some sort of dinner at the Shaftesbury Inn."

"We are," said Cynthia gloomily. "The first public meeting of all three of them. For the Development Committee Dinner to hear the reports on the show. To make things even worse, the three of them are the only people in town even remotely interested in dogs. Except for Roger and me, of course. We're attending to provide some dilution. I expect that's what you're here for too," she ended on an uncompromising note of candor.

Thatcher decided that a Pollyanna tone was necessary. He was not prepared to spend the next twenty-four hours confidently awaiting a social catastrophe.

"I am looking forward to tomorrow night," he said firmly. "I'm told that the Shaftesbury Inn is famous for its dinners."

But Cynthia Kincaid, preceding him through the doorway of Olivia Austin's home, had the final word. "Oh, the *food* will be all right," she said with sinister emphasis.

It was with some relief that Thatcher joined Roger Kincaid and Olivia. His Cassandra-like companion was beginning to irritate him. He suspected a hidden relish in disaster. In fact, now that he came to think of it, Cassandra had probably made herself obnoxious to her Trojan colleagues by the morbid joy she experienced in predicting the fall of Troy. He turned his attention to Olivia.

"John will have to hurry off," she was explaining. "He has an appointment with Peggy."

Cynthia Kincaid shook her head, indicating that she expected no good from the interview. Her husband, however, was puzzled. "I thought you were from the Sloan," he said.

23

"John is handling the property settlement for us," said Olivia easily.

"But so soon?" asked Roger, his pleasant, sunburned face crinkling into a distressed expression.

"It had to come some time," said Olivia.

Roger Kincaid was no happier about the Austin divorce than Bradford Withers. "But you and Gil have hardly had time to try to work things out," he said.

"Gil isn't interested in working things out, Roger," said Olivia sadly. "It's his decision, and he's insisting on a quick settlement. Let's not talk about it. . . . What can I get for you?"

Thatcher settled back and reflected that, while he was under the disadvantage of knowing very little about the issues involved, he would approach Miss Lindsay with one card up his sleeve: as an experienced negotiator, he knew that the side insisting on speed is at a disadvantage. What you need is a leisurely attitude suggesting you are ready to dicker for at least a year.

Not until drinks had been passed did Olivia resume the discussion, this time on a brisker note. "In any event," she said, "it's time that somebody lays down the law about this house to Peggy. I'm glad that John is going to do it."

Cynthia was blank. "This house?"

"Yes," Olivia twisted her face into a rueful grimace. "Having taken my husband, now she wants my home!"

Roger Kincaid put down his drink and shifted unhappily.

"Now Olivia," he protested, "that's not altogether fair. I know that Peggy is involved in the fuss about the valuation of this house for the property settlement but she's not trying to turn you out. She only . . ."

"Oh, for heaven's sake!" Olivia exclaimed, impatiently. "Don't be blind, Roger. I know that you're fond of Peggy. I was too before Gil fell in love with her. But that doesn't change the facts."

Thatcher leaned forward hopefully at the word "facts."

". . . she's incurably romantic and she has some vision of living here and queening it over the village. Well, she's not going to!"

"Gil has always loved this house," Cynthia contributed broodingly.

"Gil is very adaptable in his loves," Olivia retorted contemptuously.

24

Roger Kincaid merely shook his head.

"I gather that Gil is willing to accept any agreement that we can reach with Miss Lindsay," said Thatcher, hoping to lower the emotional level.

"Yes," Olivia told him grimly, "and my position is clear. Peggy Lindsay doesn't come into this house except over my dead body!"

"I'll die before I let Olivia get away with this," said Peggy Lindsay half an hour later. "It isn't fair! It's Gil's property and she thinks she can take it away from him by acting like a tragic heroine." Her chin came forward mulishly. "Well, I won't let her."

Heroic proclamations, John Thatcher concluded, require appropriate settings. Olivia Austin's vow to die before letting Peggy Lindsay usurp her home had been made in a large, apple-green and white living room, with sunlight streaming through French windows onto a variety of artfully blended styles of furniture. The atmosphere at Ridge Road Farm was one of great comfort, quiet distinction and, unmistakably, wealth. On the whole, it made her vehemence sound rather melodramatic.

But Peggy Lindsay was breathing an equal willingness to sacrifice herself in surroundings that lent some force to her declaration. Thatcher was sitting in the Victorian living room of a gabled white house just one street off Shaftesbury green. The room was crowded—with fringed lamps, gold-framed pictures, small stools, uncomfortable heavy furniture, dark draperies, photographs, mementos—and people.

For two persons nodded defiant agreement with Peggy Lindsay. Thatcher had not expected his interview to take place before her mother and brother. He was not particularly pleased at this development. Nor, he suspected, was Peggy Lindsay. Upon his arrival she had made several abortive attempts to persuade the masterful dowager to retire. To no avail.

"Peggy is a dear sweet child," announced Mrs. Lindsay authoritatively. "She does not want Gilbert to lose anything because of his marriage." She settled back in her chair with an air of finality.

It was a moment before Thatcher realized that the marriage she had in mind was the forthcoming union between her daughter and Gilbert Austin. His own opinion, admittedly old-fashioned, was that the less said the better about a woman taking a man from his wife and children, particularly with respect to losses.

"Oh, Mother!" Peggy burst out, "that's not it. It's just that I can't stand to see Olivia twisting Gil around her little finger. She talks about her home being all that she has left! She looks dark and tragic—and all the time she's trying to cheat him! Can you imagine what it will be like when we're married? She wants to sit up on the hill at the farm with the kennels—and have everybody in Shaftesbury saying how well she's behaving! Well, I'm not letting her get away with it!"

She thrust a strand of light brown hair from her forehead and ignored her mother's monitory frown. Thatcher had abandoned thought of nymphets upon meeting Peggy Lindsay. Gil Austin might be the typical middle-aged man seeking one last fling, but he was indulging himself in a manner far removed from the stereotyped. Peggy Lindsay was younger than Olivia, it was true. In her late twenties, she preserved the gaucherie of the uncertain teen-ager with none of the morning-of-the-world radiance that should accompany it. Her indeterminate coloring, her healthy vigor and her sudden bursts of enthusiasm could, no doubt, be attractive when she was not scowling with vexation. But she was not an Olivia and she never would be.

"Peg's right, you know," Donald Lindsay interjected, leaning forward to tap his cigarette holder against an ashtray. "The well known Mrs. Austin just won't admit that she's been beaten. Gil is leaving her—and it's ridiculous for her to think that she can go on being the great lady of Ridge Road Farm. All that is over." He delivered this dictum complacently while his mother regarded him with admiration. Clearly Donald Lindsay, although several years younger than Peggy, was accustomed to uncritical reception of such superior explanations.

Thatcher inhaled happily. Peggy Lindsay, laboring under a quite reasonable desire to leave her mother's house and ensconce herself at Ridge Road Farm, was an object of pity; Mrs. Lindsay roused no emotion other than a wish to remove from her presence; Donald Lindsay, on the other hand, was completely and thoroughly objectionable. "I am afraid," he began, "that you do not fully understand the nature of a joint tenancy. . . ."

During the next ten minutes, he provided a lovingly detailed description of such a tenure, including exhaustive discussion of Olivia Austin's rights. He saved his blockbuster for the end: "And of course, if you and Mr. Austin insist upon a judicial separation of the realty, it can be obtained. But, in that case, I think you should reconcile yourself to a considerable delay in the actual divorce."

This provoked a storm. Mrs. Lindsay proclaimed magisterially that an extended delay was out of the question. The dear children were anxious to be married. And her daughter's position in Shaftesbury was not comfortable. Donald Lindsay, becoming more languid by the moment, advised his sister not to let impatience betray her into making any concessions. If her position was uncomfortable, Olivia's was more so. Fight it out if it takes all summer. Olivia had no staying power. Peggy, flushed with annoyance, mutinously maintained her position. She wanted a quick divorce and she wanted Ridge Road Farm.

"Don't be a fool!" snapped Donald. "Dig your heels in. You don't have to give in on anything."

"Oh, leave me alone," wailed Peggy, tears bursting to the surface. They were not attractive tears. Thatcher had felt certain that they would not be. "I don't want anything that isn't right. You're trying to turn me into a little schemer. You none of you undersand." Muffled in a handkerchief, she fled from the room.

Thatcher felt no remorse. So far as he could tell, Peggy was suffering more from the exacerbations inflicted by her relatives than from his own dry-as-dust monologue. All in all he was satisfied with the first round. Given two irreconcilable positions, it was folly in this initial interview to attempt anything other than the creation of a more malleable frame of mind. As a kind of bonus he had also sown dissension in the ranks of the enemy. At this point a prudent man would retire.

Naturally Bradford Withers did not share this satisfaction. Upon hearing Thatcher's report, he looked at his vice-president with touching disappointment. It was, he said, a fine state of affairs when Gil Austin engendered so much turmoil just because he didn't know how to have a fling. Thatcher, who had been privileged to witness a few elephantine flings by Withers, agreed gravely.

"And tell me, John," Withers insisted, "now that you've met Peggy, do you understand this idiocy of Gil's any better?"

Thatcher answered truthfully. "No. Now that I've met her, I don't understand anything at all."

3 "... near an unspoiled village"

THE SECOND MORNING OF JOHN THATCHER'S weekend in Connecticut promised to be no improvement on the first. It started with breakfast, a combination of splendid provender and extended complaint.

". . . we have to go to this damned Founder's Day Parade this afternoon," Withers grumbled, dispiritedly spooning marmalade. "Here, try some of the ham. Then, there's the Development Committee Dinner tonight and that's going to be pretty dreadful, let me tell you."

After breakfast, Thatcher donned a disreputable jacket, refused the offer of a car, and started to walk to Shaftesbury for an interview with Gilbert Austin. Naturally, he was not in the best of spirits as he set off down the long driveway leading from the Greek-revival portico; Ridge Road Farm, the bone of contention, was nestled behind a white cross-barred fence, a feather of smoke hanging motionless against the cloudless sky.

"Very handsome," said Thatcher sourly, turning toward Ridge Road. The weather was magnificent with a hint of smokiness in the air, but as he passed the Kincaid home, with carefully tended fields, Black Angus, and in the distance, the Austindale Kennels, Thatcher was not stirred by the undeniable beauty of the scene. He remained similarly unmoved by the sun-gilt foliage of the woods through which Ridge Road led him, by the splendor of the distant Berkshires and by the charm of the rustic stream meandering along near the road.

Shaftesbury was a riot of careful, tax-deductible delights, a spiritual sister to Dutchess County. Unimpressed, Thatcher strode along, first past great estates, then past white houses with trim shutters and neatly kept front yards. His goal was Shaftesbury Inn, where Gilbert Austin was maintaining temporary residence. It fronted on the green, as did a white-spired church gleaming in the sunlight. Across from the church was a massive white building that Olivia had pointed out as the Shaftesbury Grange. No doubt local cultivators, outfitted by Abercrombie & Fitch, gathered there frequently to discuss livestock.

"Humph," said Thatcher disagreeably, allowing himself a moment to contemplate Shaftesbury green because he was not eager to cross the street to the inn. As he stood there, a station wagon passed; in it, a sober young man, four children, one dog, and in the back, two garbage cans. These pretentious communities are always a little short on community services, the banker told himself, just as a subdued burst from the church indicated that the congregation was launched into song. It sent Thatcher into the inn.

Shaftesbury Inn, like all inns, was dark, redolent of smoke and liberally adorned with artifacts. Gilbert Austin was easy enough to locate. He sat in the living room, looking out at the green with tired eyes. Happily, he had his emotions under iron control; he listened to Thatcher's suitably expurgated accounts of his discussions with Olivia and Peggy, expressed indifference to the ultimate fate of Ridge Road Farm and agreed that the sensible thing to do was to put the whole thing into the hands of the lawyers. If anything, he sounded uninterested in the whole sorry mess. Under the circumstances, Thatcher thought this admirable.

"I'd drive you back," said Austin, escorting him to the reception hall, "but I want a word with Peggy."

"Thank you," Thatcher replied. "Olivia is going to pick me up."

"Good," said Austin. "Oh, have you met Giselle? Madame Dumont, the magician who transformed Shaftesbury Inn from a simple rural hostelry to a famous gourmet experience."

"You joke," said the woman at the registration desk, "but it is true. How do you do, Mr. Thatcher?"

Rarely had Thatcher seen anyone less appropriate to a Colonial setting than Giselle Dumont, an opulent Mediterranean Valkyrie, built on heroic lines. For Shaftesbury, she exuded a remarkable amount of unmistakable womanliness.

"Church is out," said Austin. "Will you excuse me?"

Thatcher was ready to make his farewell and follow Austin when Madame Dumont said, "Poor Gil! He is not happy."

"Er . . . no."

"You are here with Brad Withers about the divorce," she said turning large, but by no means melting, eyes on him.

"Yes. It has been a pleasure . . ."

"Foolishness!" Giselle Dumont said disapprovingly. "They are all in . . . a fuss!" Nothing, said her tone, ever put her in a fuss. "They do not have the temperament for this sort of thing. Ah, are you lunching here?"

Alarmed, Thatcher hastily disclaimed such intentions, but she had been talking over his shoulder to a little clutch of newcomers bustling in.

"We read about it in the *Times*," said a portly man who was shepherding a large party.

"I simply insisted," came the voice of Donald Lindsay, who was escorting his mother after the portly man's party. "Oh, hello there, Thatcher."

Quelling a purely instinctive desire to kick Donald Lindsay, Thatcher greeted his mother while Giselle, Donald and the newcomers engaged in talk at the door to the sitting room.

"And will we see you at the Development Dinner tonight?" Mrs. Lindsay asked archly, her eyes never leaving Donald who was gracefully propped against a desk, surveying the party of *Times* readers (from New Jersey it developed). "Even Donald says the food and the atmosphere at the inn are really remarkable."

Thatcher, an eye on the mature but handsome Giselle, thought he could understand that.

". . . he's in the theater, you know, and *so* sensitive. He's simply dropped everything to come up and support us during Our Difficulties. He's been a pillar of strength."

Her gracious tone dropped, Mrs. Lindsay turned to look narrowly at Thatcher. Foreseeing another excruciating exchange with her, he cravenly let himself get nudged out of her way by another group of newcomers who were hurrying in to lunch. Smiling an apology, he nodded pleasantly and escaped.

The green, he discovered when he made his way out of the inn, had come to life. Churchgoers were still eddying forth while small groups inspected the Civil War Memorial and the grandstands. From nowhere, it seemed, cars—many with out-of-state licenses—poured into the inn's parking lot. Station wagons, each furnished with children and garbage cans, glided by.

Thatcher checked his watch. He was to meet Olivia Austin in front of the church in ten minutes. He decided to fortify himself with a *New York Times,* and set off across the green to Central Street. The newspaper shop, which adjoined the railroad station, was a half-block walk and, he discovered when he reached it, another community gathering place. The long narrow room, presided over by a bad-tempered dotard, was a crush of Shaftesburyites, their attire indicating a morning in church (suits, flowered hats, gloves) or a morning at the garbage dump (sweaters, slacks, sneakers). Thatcher struggled through several animated conversations, snatched a paper—finding to his irritation that it would cost thirty-five cents—and was in the process of extracting himself from the crowd when he heard a familiar voice.

"Donald and Mother are at the inn, Gil, and I said I'd join them. Then, I have to go over there early tonight to set up the table. You know Giselle doesn't have the remotest notion about place cards—oh, hello, Mr. Thatcher."

Thatcher greeted Peggy Lindsay and Gilbert Austin who were wedged into a corner of the store near the front window. Courtesy required some conversation, and while he had no particular desire to talk with either of them, he was forced to admit that Peggy Lindsay was probably at her most attractive this morning. Although she would look better in casual tweeds than in the prim navy blue suit she affected, her mouse-colored hair had been tossed into a pleasant aureole by a slight breeze, her eyes were bright and a delicate color bathed her face. Austin smiled down at her.

"Well, for God's sake, Peg, be careful of what you do at the dinner table with the seating," he said, nodding to Thatcher. "Things are bad enough . . ."

She gave a gurgle of laughter. "I love the feeling of power," she said gaily to Thatcher. "I'm seating the whole Shaftesbury Development Committee. Now, let me see—you're coming as Brad's guest, aren't you? You see, I could place you anywhere."

"Put me next to Madame Dumont," said Thatcher. Austin looked amused, while Peggy laughed aloud, oblivious to the covert glances their group was attracting. "Unless," Thatcher continued, "there's a Monsieur Dumont."

"He's a symphonic cellist," Peggy told him. "He's never around."

"Fool," said Thatcher. Peggy grinned at him.

"Unless my palm is greased you'll go—let's see—between somebody who will lecture you on compost gardening . . ."

"My God!" said Thatcher, genuinely horrified.

". . . or old Mrs. Walworth who's deaf as a post."

"Now you can do better than that," he said earnestly.

Peggy looked as if she might carry the joke further, but some slight change in Gil's manner checked her. "All right," she said smiling, "I'll put you near—oh, let's see—the Kincaids or—or Olivia. . . . No, they'll be at the head table. . . . Well, somebody financial or professional, anyway."

Peggy Lindsay had the rather heart-rending exuberance of the adolescent, with all of its awkwardness and uncertainty. Could Gilbert Austin really prefer it to Olivia Austin's smooth poise?

"Speak of the devil," Austin was saying sociably. "Hello, Cynthia. I haven't seen you lately."

"Hi!" said Mrs. Kincaid, struggling through a crowd to join them, the small girl she clutched rendering her passage difficult. "I just thought you might like to know that Olivia's coming in," she said in the voice of doom.

In view of the chins-up attitude publicly adopted by the principals, Thatcher could only feel that these conspiratorial tones were unnecessary, but they effectively banished Peggy Lindsay's smile, and brought back Austin's air of constraint.

"I don't need to be warned that Olivia is coming in, Cyn," Peggy replied more loudly than necessary. Austin suddenly became conscious of the faintly perceptible pause of curiosity that hushed the voices around them.

"I should hope not," said Olivia Austin who stood in the doorway. "Hello, Gil, Peggy," she said with a bright smile. Whether by design or art she wore black; framed by the sunlight she looked superbly soignée. Without waiting for reply, she advanced into the store, nodded to some acquaintances, picked up a paper, and without pausing, unhurriedly walked out to the Jaguar double-parked on Central Street. As they watched, she swept into a U-turn. She left an embarrassed silence in her wake.

And John Thatcher.

"There goes my ride home," he remarked acidly. It was perfectly obvious that Olivia Austin was going to sweep out

Ridge Road; there was no place in this bravura performance for a delay at the church steps.

"We'll give you a lift. Bye, Peggy, bye, Gil—and don't worry!" This last was in a whisper that did not seem to hearten either of them, but Mrs. Kincaid pulled her daughter and Thatcher along with her to the sidewalk. "Roger is picking me up—oh, there he is! Come on."

She darted into a Buick station wagon as Thatcher, a prey to deepest foreboding, followed her.

Kincaid greeted him, directed his daughter to join her mother in the back seat, and listened to Cynthia's account of the encounter. "It's going to be hell, tonight," she concluded emphatically. "Just pure hell."

"That's fine language for a minister's daughter," said her husband good-naturedly. He drove around the green carefully before adding, "We're all upset about this divorce, Mr. Thatcher."

"So I gather."

"It's always hard," Cynthia said from the back seat. "I mean when you're friends of everybody concerned."

Thatcher agreed that divorce is an inconsiderate imposition on one's friends.

"I guess the best thing we can do is to forget it and hope for the best," said Kincaid. "Have you seen the Hebert place? It's one of the biggest operations in Shaftesbury."

They drove to the Withers mansion without reverting to the Austins. Just as Roger Kincaid stopped the car, Olivia Austin hurried out of the house.

"John!" she exclaimed ruefully. "I simply forgot. Will you forgive me? And Roger—thank you! Come in for a drink . . . no? Well, thanks again. And I'll see you this afternoon."

With a friendly honk, Roger Kincaid headed back to his own house while Olivia tucked an arm into Thatcher's and led him to the library where Bradford Withers sat with a drink. "What must you think of me?" she asked.

"I think," said Thatcher, regrettably ungallant, "that you can get me a Scotch." He deposited *The New York Times* on the library table next to two of its unsullied fellows. One of the perils of the emotional life—or possibly it was simply the remoteness of northwest Connecticut—was that he had found it impossible to read a newspaper. Although, he thought, accepting the drink that Olivia poured him, it was to be hoped that if war broke out news of it would penetrate to Shaftesbury—sooner or later.

". . . pretty foolish," Withers was saying judiciously. "I don't say that I don't admire you, Olivia, because I do—and Carrie does too, for that matter. But you are making it hard on yourself. Take this dinner tonight."

Olivia, sinking gracefully onto the divan, toasted her brother. "So much good advice," she said sweetly. "You, and Roger and Cynthia, and John here—and Bud is driving down this afternoon to tell me what he thinks of his parents' behavior."

Thatcher did not like the inflection in her voice. "I saw Gil," he said hurriedly. "He doesn't really seem to care . . ."

"Ha," and Gil's wife disagreeably.

". . . about Ridge Road Farm, so I feel the best thing to do is to call in a Sloan appraiser and get a firm valuation. Then you're going to have to let the lawyers worry it out."

"Peggy Lindsay is not getting Ridge Road Farm," said Olivia Austin.

"Now, Olivia," Withers harrumphed.

"Don't 'Now Olivia' me," she said. "It's my house, it's where I raised my children—and I intend to keep it."

Thatcher sipped his drink and remained silent. There was no immediate value in pointing out to Olivia that it was quite possible that the lawyers would counsel differently. Unhappily, Withers was not the man to let such considerations deter him.

"But what if the lawyers insist?" he said in a voice that sometimes led business acquaintances to assume Machiavellian cunning since such innocence was inconceivable. His sister was under no such misapprehension.

"They won't," she said, with a faint echo of his own stubbornness.

In the silence, the houseman entered the room with small dishes of olives. Thatcher helped himself, a fleeting moment of regret for his normal Sunday morning in New York.

". . . just wants to show me," said Olivia Austin levelly.

"Why should she want to show you?" her brother asked.

"I don't know," she said. "I must confess that Peggy Lindsay has surprised me. First—Gil. Then all of this—malevolence about the house. After all, I gave her her start."

"Start?" Thatcher was surprised into demanding. Surely Olivia was not the woman for *double-entendre*.

"Certainly," she said with a rueful smile. "She had her first important dog handling assignment at the Austindale Kennels—and she's gone on from there. You knew that, didn't you?"

"Somebody did mention that she was a dog handler," Thatcher admitted. "It's not the sort of thing I tend to remember."

"Well, she's very much in demand," she explained. "I'd be surprised if she didn't make at least twenty-five thousand dollars a year."

"Good heavens!" That, of course, was the sort of thing Thatcher remembered.

"Oh, yes, she supports the old lady and that good-for-nothing brother—well, I'm sorry for her, but she's got Gil and that's enough. She's not stealing my house."

"Still think you're making a mistake," Withers said.

Olivia ignored the repetition. "Anyway, I haven't apologized to John for stranding him that way in the middle of town," she said turning to Thatcher with imperative appeal.

Clearly diversionary tactics were in order. "Don't give it another thought. The Kincaids came to the rescue, and I enjoyed the ride. Cynthia was filled with dire predictions." He prepared himself to be long-windedly anectodal.

"That's the early Calvinist training showing through." Olivia picked up the ball neatly. "She's the daughter of the old Presbyterian minister in Shaftesbury."

"Good people, the Kincaids," Withers grunted. He was always easily distracted. "It's hard to find good farm managers at a price these days. And Roger's from a Vermont farm, too. Half these fellows don't know a thing about New England farming, you know."

This would have surprised no financier except Bradford Withers, reflected Thatcher, considering that New England farming has been unprofitable since 1870. Himself a native of Sunapee, New Hampshire, Thatcher had seen his future elsewhere at a very early age.

"We jumped at the chance to have them when Cynthia said they weren't taking to life in New York. And we were right," Olivia encouraged her brother.

"Yes. It makes a difference having people who fit in to Shaftesbury," Withers agreed with simple social snobbery. "Shame we don't have a chance to get in some duck hunting, John. Roger's a fine shot."

Thatcher reminded himself that, agriculturally speaking, Shaftesbury was a very different kettle of fish from New Hampshire. Meanwhile Withers was winding up to a conclusion indicative of the superiority of singlemindedness to intelligence.

"And dammit, Olivia," he said returning to his grievance, "even Roger says there's no point in being stubborn with Peggy about the house if the lawyers . . ."

But a lifetime of experience had provided Olivia with more than one weapon for dealing with her brother's waywardness.

"If you don't mind," she said with tightened lips, "we'll just forget about it for the time being. Bud will no doubt lecture me enough. Tell me, John, are you going down to the parade?"

Thatcher cocked an inquiring eyebrow at his host who, for some reason, flushed warmly. "I don't know—are we, Brad?"

"I may be late getting there," Withers replied. "If you want to be sure to see it, you might go early. That is, I have to drive into Winsted for the antlers."

"Antlers?" said both Thatcher and Olivia.

"Happened to notice the stag's head at the inn was a little motheaten," Brad said fluently. "Got that fine head I shot in Scotland last year. Told Giselle, Madame Dumont, that is . . ."

"Brad!" Olivia said accusingly.

Her brother, looking shaken, ignored her. "If you'd care to come along with me, John," he said, without enthusiasm.

"Don't worry about me," said Thatcher cheerfully. Clearly, Olivia Austin's emotional turmoil, and some new Withers folly—comparison of Giselle with Carrie Withers made the thought inescapable—had left him a loophole. "I'm going to spend the first part of the afternoon reading the newspapers."

They looked astonished.

4   ". . . with rare community spirit"

PARADES VARY IN SIZE, CONTENT AND DEGREE of solemnity. They may be large or small; conduct themselves with military precision or ambling informality; progress at a dirgelike pace behind a flag-draped coffin or step out briskly under a hail of ticker tape. Sound effects may be supplied by a virtuoso brass section or by a handful of amateur drummers producing erratic bursts of noise calculated to add a sense of excitement to the proceedings rather than to impose a disciplined tempo on the participants. Tanks, horses, cars, floats, planes and fire engines can take part in all possible combinations and permutations.

But all parade-watching crowds look the same. Half an hour before the parade is scheduled to pass (and an hour before it will pass) two policemen speed down the road on motorcycles—looking superior for no apparent reason. At the same time policemen looking harassed extend their arms and start to herd the crowds back onto the sidewalk, bringing to the task equal dedication whether the local Boy Scout troop is turning out in honor of Groundhog Day or Khrushchev is proceeding from the Hotel Commodore to the Russian Consulate amidst hostile Hungarians. (In the latter event, of course, the reason for the dedication is all too apparent: one rotten egg on target would mean Staten Island for life.)

After the police come the entrepreneurs. The Good Humor man takes up a strategic position and does land-office business regardless of temperature. The grandstand, hastily erected the night before to the imminent peril of all passing traffic, remains empty until the critical moment with the solitary exception of an unknown middle-aged couple seated quite far back who return the stare of *hoi polloi* with massive self-consciousness. Dogs appear from nowhere and prance across the street in defiance of regulation under the benevolent gaze of authority. Children elude parents, balloons are sold, people shout, flags fly. Nothing happens.

John Thatcher, to whom nothing had been happening for some time, was becoming increasingly weary of the annual Shaftesbury Founder's Day Parade. The trouble with the country, he thought from his post near the grandstand, was that it was so difficult to get away from people. In the city you could always plead an urgent appointment to have a drink with somebody at the Plaza. But in Shaftesbury one was driven to wilder flights of fancy. Shortly after lunch Olivia had left and a red-faced Brad Withers had embarked upon an incredible rigmarole designed to explain why he wished to visit the Winsted taxidermist in private. Thatcher, noting the glassy glaze of determination accompanying this preposterous speech, had firmly kept himself from examining the possibilities inherent in the *tête-a-tête* presentation of a stuffed stag head to Giselle Dumont (and a less suitable recipient it was difficult to imagine) and had tactfully removed himself from the house. The price of this tact had had been an early arrival at Shaftesbury green and an opportunity to inspect the arrangements for the parade in exhaustive detail. He had seen the memorial on the green gradually become obliterated from sight by a swarming crowd of urchins. He had seen the road around the green first become dotted with cars, then crowded and finally swamped. The eye of the financier was quick to note the absence of children over thirteen or fourteen and quick to assign a reason. In Shaftesbury the boys were all at Exeter and the girls were all at Miss Porter's.

Four-thirty, the appointed hour for the festivities to commence, came and went with no immediate result other than the arrival of Mrs. Lindsay who took up a commanding position near the grandstand. By sheer force of personality she managed to maintain a small clearing in which she was now holding court with her customary regal composure. Given the satisfied smile which wreathed her face as she graciously acknowledged greetings and the animation she displayed in talking to those who stopped, Thatcher was not surprised by the snatches of conversation which came his way:

". . . a lovely couple. You must be so proud. . . ."

". . . probably a winter wedding. Gil is so impatient."

"How nice for you she's marrying somebody from Shaftesbury. Not like Joan Small's girl. . . ."

". . . in strictest confidence. Of course, Elvira, we haven't announced it yet . . . just a few friends. . . ."

Nobody seemed to be mentioning the word divorce. Scarcely surprising. Mrs. Lindsay had adopted the official role of mother of the bride. No coarse reality would be allowed to dim the luster of that part, the bridegroom's age and marital status being majestically ignored by Mrs. Lindsay and her attendant acolytes. The one called Elvira seemed to be something of a problem with her frequent assurances to newcomers that "it" was practically settled and the wedding could now go forward, but Thatcher felt confident that Mrs. Lindsay would bring her henchwoman under control before exposing her to the perils of the Development Committee dinner that was to follow the parade. That dinner was assuming new aspects of horror since Thatcher had met the principal characters. Mrs. Lindsay, he felt sure, would regard the occasion as suitable for a show of power.

Under the circumstances he could only sympathize when he saw Gilbert Austin emerging onto the green with what seemed to be the entire staff of the Shaftesbury Inn. Austin cast one disgruntled look at the group surrounding his future mother-in-law and hastily steered a course in the opposite direction. Thatcher shook his head. Tactics like that were all very well on a temporary basis, but a more decisive policy would be required if Austin seriously contemplated extended residence in the same town as Mrs. Lindsay. He might of course plan to spend more time as a consulting engineer and less time as a gentleman farmer.

Parking places had long since disappeared, but an unending stream of vehicles continued to enter the square, only to cruise about dejectedly before searching farther afield in the roads behind the inn and the Grange Hall. Among the passing motorists Thatcher recognized the figure of his host, back from his strange errand. A wave failed to attract his attention. Withers, who seemed to be sharing the front seat of the Lincoln with some monstrous object whose ramifications extended out through the window, had his eyes glued

40

to the roadway as he covered the course around the green and back toward the inn. A short way behind him Roger Kincaid had succeeded in bringing all traffic to a halt while he decanted his wife and daughter from a battered old pickup truck. Horns honked, fists were clenched, voices shouted as Roger leaned over the side to signal a hasty farewell to Cynthia, firmly detached his daughter's plucking fingers from the tarpaulin covering the load in the back, brayed an incoherent apology over his shoulder and at last set himself—and a long line of indignant vehicles—once more in motion. His face betrayed the anxiety endemic to motorists participating in modern public festivities.

Thatcher considered joining Cynthia Kincaid but at this moment the first blare of a trumpet came to his ears, the street that lay between them became engulfed by the advancing legions of the Shaftesbury Volunteer Fire Department complete with fife and drum corps, and his attention was claimed by a woman at his side.

"Ah, Mister Thatcher, you do not remember me? I am Madame Dumont from the inn. We met this morning." Dark eyes invested their meeting with hidden significance.

Thatcher assured the lady that he remembered.

"So, you have come to watch our parade. It is well. In a village of this size, one must partake of community activities. All of my staff is watching too. It makes a good impression."

Her timing, Thatcher said, had been perfect. The staff emerges and, behold, the parade starts! Madame Dumont said it was nothing but observation. Always the parade was half an hour late. If the authorities set four-thirty as the official time, she set five o'clock as the time for the inn staff to present itself in a display of civic spirit. Everybody was happy. While this little dialogue wound through its rather stately course of compliment, refutation and countercompliment, Thatcher became uneasily aware that he had not captured Madame Dumont's attention to the exclusion of other interests. Throughout she maintained a watchful eye over his left shoulder; and now as someone approached, she bade him a hurried goodbye with the assurance that she would see him at the dinner that night and moved away.

"Hello, Thatcher."

Austin greeted his wife's representative with resigned

gloom. The gloom, however, seemed general and in no way attributable to Thatcher's official position.

"Afternoon," grunted Thatcher. "I'm just watching your parade. Fine turnout."

Austin assented abstractedly as the 4-H Club float passed unseen before him.

"Do you know if Peggy has said anything to Brad?" he asked abruptly.

"Peggy? No, not to my knowledge. That is, not up until I left for the village anyway. Why?"

Thatcher found it hard to visualize a less likely couple than Withers and Peggy Lindsay. Surely the whole purpose of his trip was to insulate Withers from contacts of that sort.

"Well, he just came out of the inn and I started to join him, but he shuffled off. I think maybe he's avoiding me." Gilbert Austin sighed heavily. He was not a man used to a burden of guilt, but when he did something he did it thoroughly. Obviously one of the problems that Shaftesbury society would have to cope with in the forthcoming months was a morbid sensitivity to imagined slights by Austin. No doubt he would hasten to compound everyone's embarrassment by admitting that he deserved to be slighted.

"Oh, I don't think so," said Thatcher kindly. "Brad's been off on some junket of his own all afternoon. Why should it have anything to do with Peggy? Where is she anyway?"

"I don't know, and I don't care," Austin replied shortly with a jaundiced glance across marching Campfire Girls toward Mrs. Lindsay.

So that's it, thought Thatcher. If Peggy were a more experienced home wrecker, she would have taken care to shelter Gil Austin from any prolonged exposure to her redoubtable mother and her even more repellent brother. But, being the kind of girl she was, she had probably assumed that intimacy between her intended husband and her own family was inevitable. After all, she was remarkably helpless in protecting herself from their demands. It was not to be expected that a sudden display of efficiency on her part could hide from Austin the kind of relatives he was acquiring.

Thatcher decided that a discussion of the Lindsay ménage, however veiled, could only lead to an increase in Austin's dejection and his own discomfort.

"The dinner tonight," he said, falling back on his standard conversational sedative, "will be my first experience with the

Shaftesbury Inn. I gather that it's become famous since Madame Dumont took over."

Gil Austin laughed harshly. "Oh, Giselle's a born innkeeper. And tonight will be a real challenge to her. We're all going to be there, you know. The Lindsays, the Austins, and a good large audience."

The occasion, Thatcher agreed, would tax anyone's social powers. But would Madame Dumont feel that the gaiety of the event was one of her responsibilities?

"She will. She's quite magnificent at soothing difficulties. If anybody can make things better Giselle can. Peggy . . ." he broke off, then added in hollow tones, "I tell you if I had the nerve, I'd junk the whole thing."

"Well, you don't," said Thatcher brutally, "so you might just as well grin and bear it. By tomorrow morning it will all be over. Look here, as soon as the American Legion is out of the way, why don't we go over and join Cynthia Kincaid. She seems to have her hands full."

Austin obediently looked across the street where Cynthia had her left hand firmly hooked into the belt of her daughter while she was being harangued by a bespectacled young man carrying an attaché case. Her head was rotating with clockwork regularity between the two objects competing for her attention as she controlled the child's spirited attempts to join the parade and directed a series of short remarks, no doubt lugubrious, to her companion.

"Dammit!"

"What's the matter?"

"You can go if you like. That's my son with Cynthia." Gilbert Austin seemed completely disgusted by this development. "And I can just imagine what he's saying. I'll get enough of that tonight."

Thatcher could readily believe it. While he waited for the last section of the parade to pass, Austin quietly melted back into the crowd and left him to make his approach alone. Cynthia seemed to be rapidly losing control of the situation, throwing distracted glances to the right and left, as the young man grounded his case in order to provide gesturing accompaniment to his increasingly loud remarks. Happily at this juncture support arrived in the form of Roger Kincaid. Interposing himself between his wife and Bud Austin, he laid a persuasive hand on the boy's shoulder and launched into a low-pitched, placatory rumble.

It was not particularly effective. Just as Thatcher took advantage of the straggling finale of the parade to cross the street to join them, the hand was impatiently shaken off.

"He can't do this to us!" Heads were turning toward the young man.

"Now, Bud, wait a minute. Don't go off half-cocked," pleaded Roger. "You don't understand."

"I understand plenty." Bud Austin had turned an apoplectic crimson. "Dad never thought of this himself. Oh, what's the use? Leave me alone." Happily, three noisy little boys drowned these remarks.

He turned and angrily thrust his way through the crowded sidewalk, leaving Roger looking resignedly at his still outstretched hand.

"Well, if that isn't the limit," said Cynthia indignantly. "There's no need for him to snap at you."

"The thing that's really upset him," Kincaid said, "is that Olivia agreed to meet him here and didn't show up. He also saw that little performance of Gil's. Wants to know why his parents are avoiding him."

Thatcher said that it was a pity Bud Austin was so young. The boy was scarcely at an age to recognize his parents' plight. Cynthia tartly remarked that if Bud were any older his father would be beyond the age of making a fool of himself. Unbelieving silence followed this statement. The three of them had been deserted by the rest of the crowd which was streaming toward one of the memorials on the green to listen to the speeches which would accompany a wreath-laying ceremony.

Roger finally roused himself to remark that the important thing was to provide some sort of buffer between Bud and his parents at the forthcoming dinner. Things would be bad enough without an adolescent display of prudery. He looked hopefully at Thatcher who had no hesitation in declaring his unavailability. It seemed to him that Kincaid had been destined from birth to be a buffer.

"Oh, all right," said Kincaid fatalistically. "Then I suppose I'd better take Fanny home and get my clothes changed so I can catch Bud right at the start of this shindig. Cyn, I'm going to borrow your Pontiac, the station wagon's got a flat."

Thatcher, who had now absorbed the fact that although her husband was in work clothes Cynthia was in high heels and pearls, felt that he should make a push to be helpful.

Preferably in an area which would cause him as little personal discomfort as possible. Accordingly he suggested that Cynthia join him in watching the tail end of the ceremonies at the memorial while Roger pursued his domestic tasks. Cynthia seemed suitably grateful at being assured an escort in the first rush for cocktails. Fanny displayed no more than the normal dissatisfaction of a ten-year-old pulled away from a public ceremony by her father, and the group split up.

Thatcher's estimate of a tail-end speech was, it developed, unduly optimistic. He underrated the staying power and wind of the local state legislator who saw in the difficulties attendant upon the settling of Shaftesbury a powerful analogy with the perils facing modern America and called upon his audience for a display of the same qualities of hardihood, dedication and self-sacrifice—at length.

Not until six o'clock did release finally come, an even division of time having been achieved between parade and oratory—half an hour for each. It was not an allotment likely to recommend itself to anyone not running for elective office, thought Thatcher. A restive impatience in the audience was manifest as the speaker approached his peroration. By then Thatcher and Cynthia had been joined by Olivia Austin. She appeared at their side during a compelling portrayal of the first winter in Shaftesbury ("And did our forefathers falter? They did not!"). During a *sotto voce* exchange of remarks she seemed her normal composed self, although she confessed to Cynthia's charge that she had deliberately avoided her son Bud on his arrival.

But as the trio prepared to enter the inn and launch themselves on the horrors so clearly in store, she stiffened slightly. Thatcher noted her jaw harden and her voice assume an aggressive cheeriness quite alien to the Olivia Austin he had thus far known.

"I must tell you about the letter I got from the man who's going to judge terriers at the show," she began relentlessly. "It was really quite funny. He thought that we should . . ."

An ominous beginning. Thatcher's heart sank and he hurried his charges toward the bar. He was going to need a drink.

5   "...an open hunting season"

EVEN EXCELLENT LIQUOR CANNOT SALVAGE some occasions. At seven o'clock, John Thatcher gloomily took another Scotch and water, looked about the crowded Shaftesbury Inn living room and decided that the Development Committee Banquet was one of them. Crowded around him, smoking, drinking, chatting, waving, were the local luminaries. Those known to him were in the grip of powerful emotional turmoil, those unknown to him were hearty and agricultural.

"I beg your pardon," he said, bending to catch Cynthia Kincaid's remark.

"You have to admire Olivia," she repeated.

Thatcher glanced over the crowd to Olivia Austin animatedly talking to a depressed looking couple. From the moment that her lovely chin had lifted upon entering the inn, Olivia had been gracious enough to depress almost anybody. Sourly, he said as much.

"Well," countered Cynthia, "she's putting on a better show than Gil. I'm surprised at him."

It was true that nobody, at the moment, could possibly have described Gilbert Austin as gracious. He stood silent, a remarkably forbidding frown on his face, next to his son. Bud was doing the talking.

On the other hand, thought Thatcher fair-mindedly, Austin had been severely tried since he entered the room. Cynthia Kincaid was by no means the only admirer of his wife's fortitude. The room fairly rang with comments uniting respect for Olivia and deprecation of her husband's callous insensitivity. In addition, Austin had suffered from the proprietary instincts of Mrs. Lindsay who tended to display him to the company with a thin triumphant smile. At first she had been joined in her triumph by her son. But Donald Lindsay's smile had grown steadily weaker as Peggy's absence continued, and he was now drinking steadily. For a man to be outshone by his wife, lectured by his son, made a fool of by his fiancée, dangled as a trophy by her mother and toadied by her brother is enough to cast anyone into the dumps. Somebody, mused Thatcher, ought to declare Gilbert Austin a disaster area and send relief.

At that moment Roger Kincaid came to the rescue. Suitably attired for a social event, he stood in the doorway, scanned the room briefly, and advanced on Bud Austin. Within moments he had not only detached the boy from his father but integrated him relentlessly into another group.

"Poor Roger," moaned Cynthia viewing her husband's martyrdom. "What a day this is turning out to be! We've been in such a stew about the dinner tonight, he forgot about the parade. I just dragged him away from his work without giving him a chance to change—we promised Fanny the parade—and he said why didn't I go, but I said no, we've got to turn up and stand by Gil and Olivia and Peggy, too, of course, and so he had to go back and change and now he has to fend off Bud somehow, and if Peggy really doesn't turn up, it's going to be simply ghastly."

As far as Thatcher was concerned, it already was ghastly. Nor did he have much sympathy to spare for Roger Kincaid. After all, his own employment at the Sloan was involving him in much the same horror as did Kincaid's employment at Ridge Road Farm. And without the same justification.

Some acquaintances claimed Cynthia Kincaid's attention and Thatcher tried to edge his way toward the fireplace. There stood Bradford Withers with the air of a man trapped in a bargain basement. Since Madame Dumont, notable in flowing crepe, was at his side Thatcher assumed a genuine irritant.

"I can't understand it," Withers was saying in unusually testy tones as Thatcher approached. "I certainly put them on the hall table."

"No doubt they are somewhere," Madame Dumont replied absently, a vigilant eye on the passing waiters.

"Dammit," Withers expostulated, "I tell you that they're

valuable, Giselle. And . . . oh, hello there, John. Didn't see you. Helluva thing . . ."

"What is?" inquired Thatcher cautiously as Giselle Dumont delivered Withers into his hands with a practiced smile.

Her impressive departure deflected the Sloan's president for a moment. "Marvelous woman," he said, watching her. "Marvelous. But, of course, women don't understand . . . dammit, I made a special trip into Winsted for the antlers and now Giselle says she can't find them."

Thatcher, who had always felt the presentation of the antlers was ill-omened, applied himself to the task of being soothing just as Olivia Austin, inspired by some impossible ideal of gallantry, swept up, an edgy Donald Lindsay in tow.

"Brad!" she cried, implacably gay. "Are you still fussing about those antlers? Well, you've got to stop and come and meet Mr. Craley. He'll be at the head table with us, you know."

Having accomplished her purpose, a public display of the civilized relations between the Lindsays and the Withers, she gathered up Withers, still muttering: "I shot that stag in Scotland. And now it's gone and nobody seems to care." This left Thatcher with the baby.

Donald Lindsay and the vice-president of the Sloan exchanged wary glances. The temptation was too much for Thatcher.

"Don't believe I've seen your sister yet this evening," he began cordially when his inquiry was forestalled.

"Don, where the hell is Peggy?" Gilbert Austin had shouldered his way to the side of his brother-in-law elect.

"She's around somewhere, Gil," Donald replied nervously.

"What do you mean, somewhere? She's an hour late already," snapped Austin.

"Now, take it easy, Gil," advised young Lindsay, running a tongue over dry lips and signaling the waiter for a drink. "She came early to fix the place cards, you know. Anyway I saw her things in the hallway. Probably some snafu over flowers or something."

"By God, if she's left me to face this mess . . ."

"Nothing of the sort," blustered Donald as Austin, favoring him with one last suspicious look, yielded to the beckonings of a group in the corner.

Donald drowned his drink in one convulsive gulp. "If that

48

fool queers the pitch now," he whispered to himself half-desperately.

"Young man," said Thatcher crisply, "you'd better pull yourself together." Lindsay glowered defiantly as he retreated.

"He's drinking too much," explained a woman in red taffeta who had listened unashamedly to their exchange. "That's the trouble with these amateur drinkers. No prudence. Look at Roger Kincaid. He always watches it in public. Sensible man."

"Indeed?" Thatcher said courteously.

"Good for old Roger," said her consort owlishly. "Just goes off and has himself a good blowout in private. Drink has been the downfall of many a good man. Don't you agree, sir? By the way, don't believe we've met. The name is Wrenn. And Mrs. Wrenn."

"Nelson," said Mrs. Wrenn unresentfully, "you're sozzled."

"Never," he said, horrified.

Mrs. Wrenn regarded him tolerantly as she led him off. And well might she look tolerant, thought Thatcher. Those were real pearls wrapped negligently around her thin neck.

"I see you got saddled with Donald," said Cynthia Kincaid materializing out of the crowd. "He's in a terrible state about Peggy's not showing up! If you ask me, Peggy is fed up with him. I saw her this afternoon and she was simply livid. I have a feeling there's something wrong there."

"What's wrong where?" asked Roger Kincaid, appearing at her side. He looked quite sober if harassed. "I've lost track of Bud," he explained. "Just when that damned kid is ripe for murder."

"Oh," said Cynthia, pleasurably apprehensive. "Well, I was talking about the way Peggy looked this afternoon. When she passed the house, she didn't even say hello. Just walked on, with her head down and her jaw all clenched. I thought there had been some sort of fight."

Roger Kincaid did not share his wife's enjoyment of the dramatic. "Yes," he said heavily. "She stomped past me too. I thought she was out for some sort of row—but good Lord! Even if she's had a real fight with Don she doesn't have any right to stand Gil up this way. It makes him look like a fool." He looked around the crowded room with troubled eyes.

"Oh, it's no excuse, but still . . ."

"Dinner!" cried a waitress.

"Thank God!" said Thatcher, surfeited with the drama of Shaftesbury's emotional life.

He found he had been premature.

The arrangement of the dining room accentuated this very drama. A head table invites attention when surrounded by smaller groupings, even when its occupants are not involved in deep and serious conflicts.

Happily Thatcher found he was sitting at one of the other tables. Giselle Dumont, telling him she had seen his name, pointed it out, then turned to Withers. "And you, Mr. Withers," she said insinuatingly, "for you, the Head Table, of course. . . ."

She banished Withers' peevishness for all of five minutes, Thatcher saw amusedly, as he threaded his way to his seat and greeted three strangers.

"Dr. Cooper," an elderly gentleman informed him. "Mrs. Cooper and Miss Finchley who is our librarian."

Thatcher greeted the ladies, one cushioned and one angular, and prepared for another conversation centering upon Olivia's nobility, Gil's bravery, or Peggy's absence. He discovered, however, that his companions were indifferent to the drama swirling around them. After a few perfunctory remarks about the cultural development of Shaftesbury (about which Dr. Cooper was profoundly skeptical and Miss Finchley timidly hopeful) the conversation centered on a common passion—organic gardening.

"No, living as I do in the city . . ." Thatcher began.

"Disgraceful," Dr. Cooper told him happily. "Terraces . . ."

"No doubt . . ."

"Pure vegetable matter . . . best thing in the world. . . ."

Thatcher swiftly discovered that the cuisine of Shaftesbury Inn was complex and excellent—although he remained a steak and potatoes man—and that there was more to gardening than he had hitherto known. Conversation consisted of enthusiastic references to turning the pile, newsletters from Rodale, and health benefits from fresh vegetables; dinner was cream of asparagus soup, followed by small browned fish, then a roast; and Thatcher, a look of spurious interest on his face, let his attention stray to the head table. What he saw there made him feel more grateful than ever for compost heaps.

Behind a floral setting sat two men—the mayor of Shaftesbury, no doubt, and a bigwig in the dog world. Both looked

50

like bookies to Thatcher. Between them, gracious and lovely, sat Olivia Austin. Flanking this focal point of interest, were rival armies. To the right, Brad Withers, Cynthia Kincaid, Bud Austin (who looked sullen) and Roger Kincaid (who looked dour). To the left, next to the dog man, Mrs. Lindsay smiled loftily at the assembly, while Gilbert Austin (looking dour) sat next to her with Elvira beside him and Donald Lindsay (who looked sullen) beyond her. This reshuffling did not keep eyes from the empty chair at the foot of the table.

"I do wonder where Miss Lindsay is," said Miss Finchley with sly bravado.

The Coopers—and Thatcher could only honor them for it—were firm believers in the *mens sana* as well as the *corpore sano;* they had no intention of discussing divorce. Both broke into loud descriptions of improved methods for turning compost heaps.

Thatcher seconded them with an inquiry about the scientific basis of organic farming, and in the succeeding half hour allowed himself only one or two glances toward the head table. If the smiles there were strained, he thought critically, they would at least pass muster. And Bradford Withers was injecting an easy note of naturalness; he was not smiling at all but talking with aggrieved intensity to Cynthia Kincaid.

The antlers, no doubt. Thatcher nodded to Dr. Cooper and wondered if his esteemed superior had hoped to ingratiate himself with the luscious Madame Dumont with forty pounds of stuffed animal head. It was not improbable—in itself a commentary on the thought processes of the rich.

". . . absolutely staggering results without one ounce of chemical fertilizers," said Dr. Cooper ferociously as the waiter poured coffee. Thatcher surreptitiously examined his watch; it was eight-thirty.

"Dr. Cooper, are there going to be speeches after dinner?" he asked, fearing the worst.

"I believe," Miss Finchley said with every evidence of anticipation, "that the mayor is going to say a few words."

"Old gas bag," the doctor grunted.

". . . then dear Mrs. Austin who has had so much to do with the Development Committee," Miss Finchley added piously, "then Mr. Bull who is in charge of the Housatonic Dog Show."

"I see," said Thatcher. The evening was going to be one of infinite tedium.

He was wrong.

As if on signal from him, Cynthia Kincaid, no doubt unnerved by the tensions around her, made an unwise if characteristic gesture that toppled a silver coffeepot, spreading brown liquid over the table, herself, and her immediate neighbors.

"Oh dear!"

Madame Dumont, who was sitting near the kitchen door keeping an eagle eye on developments, swiftly rose, and with a magically produced towel proceeded to deal with the mess.

"Do not disturb yourself . . . if you will move, just a bit, Mr. Withers . . . ah, thank you George . . . more towels perhaps." She cast a brilliant smile over the rest of the head table which was observing this little contretemps with lackluster eyes ". . . and now, I will get you more coffee. . . ."

Still talking, Madame Dumont moved to the closet near the kitchen doors, opened it and stepped in.

"Ah, Mr. Withers! Your antlers!"

"By George!" said Brad, pushing back his chair to join her.

He stepped to her side just as she screamed, and effectively secured the attention of the whole room (incidentally interrupting Dr. Cooper's disquisition on leaching).

"He's pinched her," Thatcher thought resignedly. But the rumble from Withers made him realize that it was something more serious.

"What is it . . . what . . ."

"Oh my God!"

"Look!"

Before anybody could stop him, Withers had pushed Giselle Dumont aside, and reached into the darkness of the closet, for the tip of one sharp antler. Pulling it forward, he looked at it.

"There," he said, sounding almost satisfied.

Wrapped around the mild-eyed head, either grasping it to her bosom or impaled upon its terrible great horns, was a dead body.

"It's Peggy!"

6 "... and responsible officials nearby."

THE NEXT TWENTY MINUTES WERE PANDEMO-
nium. Withers had to be forcibly restrained from trying to
disengage the antlers from the torn and bloody tweed jacket.
Mrs. Lindsay had hysterics in the grand manner. Gilbert
Austin, green and shaken, ineffectively tried to shield the
body from the trampling curiosity of the dinner guests. Roger
Kincaid dealt with Donald Lindsay's fit of shouting rage.
Cynthia Kincaid burst into tears on Thatcher's shoulder.
Giselle Dumont called the police.

It was just as well. Authority, in the person of Captain
Felix Parker of the Connecticut State Police and his staff,
swiftly imposed order and decorum upon the scene. The
dining room was cleared of spectators and the arrival of
medical examiners, fingerprint men and other technicians
mercifully reduced the murder of Peggy Lindsay from a
grotesque tragedy to an official problem with which bureau-
cracy was prepared and trained to cope.

Swiftly as Captain Parker acted, John Thatcher had been
even swifter. His first act after stemming Cynthia Kincaid's
sobs had been to thrust a glass of brandy down Bradford
Withers' throat. Now he had occasion to congratulate himself
on his foresight. No sooner had Captain Parker absorbed the
posture of Peggy Lindsay's body and the ownership of the
antlers than he was demanding Bradford Withers' presence
in the small parlor commandeered by the police as a working
office.

During Withers' interrogation Thatcher glanced around the
living room and examined his fellow inmates. The police had
been remarkably quick in separating the wheat from the

53

chaff. A few general questions, a ceremonial listing of names and addresses, and most of the unfortunate participants in the Development Committee Banquet had been dismissed. There remained, besides Withers and Thatcher, only the Austins, the Lindsays, the Kincaids and, of course, Madame Dumont. The luckless Elvira was upstairs ministering to Mrs. Lindsay. Gilbert and Olivia Austin, he noticed, had taken pains to sit as far from each other as possible. Olivia was staring unseeingly into space; Gilbert, badly shaken by the discovery of Peggy's body, sat with his head in his hands dully repeating to himself: "I brought this on her. It's all my fault. It never would have happened but for me."

In Thatcher's view this was a reasonable reaction from a man already feeling guilty before the tragedy. He could not bring himself to believe, however, that this was an opinion shared by the state policeman ensconced in a corner, stolidly taking notes.

Bradford Withers had been absent about fifteen minutes when one of Parker's subordinates appeared and requested Olivia to follow him. Everybody in the room, except her husband, watched her exit. Donald Lindsay softly muttered something to himself.

But Olivia returned quite shortly, accompanied by her brother. Withers had pulled himself together surprisingly well. Looking very tired and very middle-aged, but with the remnants of a stubborn dignity, he took his position behind Olivia's chair, one hand protectively on her shoulder. It took more than a resident policeman to quell his conversational instincts.

"That fellow Parker has found out about the divorce," he announced to Thatcher with dissatisfaction. Probably all of western Connecticut knew about it, thought Thatcher as his chief continued his complaints. "And he keeps asking me about those antlers!"

"What did you tell him?"

"What is there to tell?" protested Withers. "I went into Winsted to pick them up and got to the inn around five. There wasn't anybody there so I left them on the hall table. Then I went out and watched the parade." Like so many simple-minded men, Withers lived in a constant state of irritation with a world determined to complicate things.

"Did he say anything about how the girl was killed?" persisted Thatcher.

"He didn't tell me a thing, but I can recognize a broken neck when I see one," replied Withers with unconscious brutality.

Under his hand Olivia Austin shuddered.

Reminded of her presence, her brother went on to say that her story had been equally brief. She had been alone at home until leaving for town. Once arrived at the parade, she had felt herself to be a focal point for gossip and, accordingly, avoided joining any group, until she fell in with Thatcher and Cynthia Kincaid. She had told her story clearly and calmly, said her brother admiringly.

"Of course, I knew she would," he went on, "but all the same, I thought it best to insist on being present."

Thatcher, watching Cynthia Kincaid depart to join her husband in Captain Parker's office, realized that the police were finding it expedient to tread lightly with the inhabitants of Shaftesbury. He wondered how long this docility could last, and turned his thoughts to what must certainly be occupying the police—the question of timing. At some point between the moments when Withers deposited the antlers in the hall and Madame Dumont opened the closet in the dining room, the inn had been the scene of feverish activity on the part of a murderer. Unbidden came the recollection of the inn staff, emerging onto the green in obedience to Giselle's dictum regarding civic participation.

"Well, that wasn't so bad," said Cynthia Kincaid in subdued tones.

"You did fine," said Roger Kincaid comfortingly, his arm around her shoulder. "We told him about seeing Peggy this afternoon," he explained to Thatcher.

"He said it was important. Maybe Peggy was on her way to quarrel with somebody in town." But Cynthia was pale. She was not enjoying realization of one of the tragedies she had predicted so freely. "Oh, it's terrible that this could happen!"

Her husband tightened his arm about her. Captain Parker, it appeared, had been insistent on pinpointing the time of Cynthia's encounter with Peggy as accurately as possible. Cynthia had finally decided that it must have been close to four-thirty.

"I think that's right," said Roger. "And she passed me about ten minutes later. That means she must have got into town just before the parade started, if she walked all the way."

Cynthia seemed to be recovering. "We didn't pass her on the road so probably somebody gave her a lift." Her account of the rest of the Kincaid afternoon could not have helped the police substantially. Roger had dropped Fanny and her mother, then gone off to park. In carefully neutral tones, Cynthia had told Captain Parker about her encounter with Bud Austin who was seeking his mother. Clearly she was rather proud of not having included reference to Bud's towering rage.

Roger took up the tale. "I told Parker that I came back and advised Bud to wait until after the parade. But I had to tell him that Bud went off anyway." He came to a depressed halt. Then in an undertone to Thatcher, he said, "Isn't Parker keeping Gil in there for a helluva long time?"

Olivia Austin overheard the uneasy question. Thatcher saw her glance quickly and almost with fright at Roger Kincaid. It was true that Gilbert Austin had been closeted with Captain Parker longer than his predecessors. But then, no matter how delicate Parker's approach to crime in Shaftesbury, he must realize by now that Austin would be his most fruitful source of information about Peggy Lindsay's last days of life. And Austin, Thatcher was reasonably certain, would not be making a good impression. Exhausted wooden reserve would be his natural defense to any intrusion into his private life.

When Austin returned ten minutes later, he was accompanied by an officer requesting John Thatcher, and Thatcher himself felt the onset of a certain constraining reserve. Nevertheless he detailed for Captain Parker the events of his weekend with meticulous care. No, he had never met Peggy Lindsay before. His last visit to Shaftesbury had been six years ago. Yes, he had left Bradford Withers alone in his home early in the afternoon. There followed a painstaking review of his activities and encounters during the parade. He was more forthright than the Kincaids about Bud Austin.

"So you can't swear to the movements of any one of these people during the entire parade?" asked Parker in conclusion.

"No," said Thatcher apologetically, "I'm afraid not."

It was obvious that Parker's analysis of the timing of the murder had led him to the same conclusion as Thatcher.

When Thatcher left the official presence, to be succeeded

by Donald Lindsay, he was no wiser than going in. Captain Parker was not giving out any information in informal conversation. Thatcher rejoined the company in the living room, seating himself next to Giselle Dumont.

"I have been talking to poor Gilbert," she whispered. "He cannot stop reproaching himself for one moment. It is torture for him. And these police," she continued scornfully, "they do nothing but ask him if he has an alibi."

"Well, does he?"

Giselle widened her eyes. "But, no! How could he? He was in his room until the parade. Then he was with the crowd. In movement, you understand."

"I understand," said Thatcher grimly. In movement avoiding his son. A fat lot of good that did.

Suddenly there was a break in the ritualistic proceeding of the police. Bradford Withers was recalled. Thatcher had only a few minutes for his overactive imagination to conjure up the possible imbecilities perpetuated by his superior when the president of the Sloan was back. In a tantrum.

"Do you know what that poisonous little twerp has told Parker?" he demanded of the room at large. "He says he dropped his sister off at my place this afternoon. That she wanted to talk to me about the property settlement." As Withers wound himself up to do full justice to his subject, Thatcher cut in sharply: "What time?" he asked ferociously. "Four," replied Brad, surprised by the factual inquiry. "But, I tell you, she wasn't there!"

Thatcher firmly adjured his senior to sit down, keep quiet and let him think. Donald Lindsay's statement was explosive. Withers had been alone at home at four. It was his word against Lindsay's. But the Kincaids had already placed Peggy Lindsay on Ridge Road at four-thirty. Thatcher squared his shoulders. He had, after all, come to Shaftesbury to defend Bradford Withers' interests. And if those interests had expanded alarmingly in the course of his brief stay, he was not the man to shirk his responsibilities. A gimlet eye fixed unswervingly on his charge had the happy effect of closing Withers' jaw and returning him to his place by Olivia's chair. Any remaining desire for speech was nipped in the bud by the entry of Captain Parker.

"All right," the policeman said heavily. "I think we've finished our preliminary work here. Not that we've gotten much information from you." He examined the room resignedly. His tone implied that he had never been so foolishly optimistic as to expect much cooperation from its occupants. "You may as well know what you'll read in the papers tomorrow. Peggy Lindsay was killed by a blow on the temple hard enough to break her neck."

He paused dramatically but his audience was far too drained to respond with heroics. Donald Lindsay, who had returned with the Captain, sucked in his breath. Otherwise there was silence.

"We don't know what she was hit with. It could have been a fist or a soft weapon. We don't know what the hell she was doing with those antlers. We do know that it was sometime between four-thirty and six, medically speaking. The inn was empty between five and five-thirty when Mr. Lindsay here arrived looking for his sister. At least nobody admits being in the inn during that time. Miss Lindsay was last seen around four-thirty, give or take ten minutes, on Ridge Road. She arrived and started putting out place cards. The flowers she never got to. Presumably at some time during these two chores, she was murdered. At that time the parade was going on and you were all out front watching it. At least that's your story. None of you has got a good solid alibi."

The beginning of some no doubt inappropriate comment on Bradford Withers' lips died aborning. Parker waited courteously for a moment, then continued: "Needless to say, we'll do a lot more work. Maybe after we've talked to more of the townspeople some of you will have an alibi. But, by your own account, most of you were drifting around from place to place. I don't think we can accomplish anything more tonight. My man will take your phone numbers, and we can call it a day."

As one of the policemen started to circulate around the room with a notebook, Giselle drew Thatcher's attention once again to Gilbert Austin. He had contented himself with remaining in his corner, occasionally looking toward his wife with mute entreaty, apology and guilt.

"She is not behaving well, this Olivia Austin," announced Giselle censoriously. "Poor Gilbert, I feel for him. He is absolutely miserable, afraid to approach her. And will she say one word to him? She is cold and unfeeling, that one."

Thatcher disagreed. Olivia, he suspected, in spite of her reserve, was in profound shock. He told Giselle that he doubted if Olivia was even aware of Gil's glances.

"Then she ought to be. What right does she have to wrap herself up in this iciness, even if she is shocked? He needs her, that should be enough. So he has had this little *affaire*. What difference? It is the way of husbands. It should not be allowed to interfere with one's domestic comfort, *bien?*" Giselle obviously spoke with the authority of one experienced in conjugal infidelity. Thatcher allowed his mind to wander for a moment to the absent cellist who was Mr. Dumont. He might not be so negligible a factor as was generally believed. One thing, however, was certain. Giselle Dumont was not numbered among the admirers of Olivia Austin. Thatcher reminded himself that they were, as nearly as he could tell, the two most attractive women in Shaftesbury. And specialized in very different forms of attraction.

"Now," he said sheering off from a subject incongenial to him, "if someone is behaving badly, it's Donald Lindsay." The boy's earlier hysteria had been quite shocking.

"Donald?" Madame Dumont was surprised. "But he has suffered a great loss!"

Thatcher was irritated that Madame Dumont should accept as an excuse for young Lindsay what she would not accept for Olivia.

"You can't tell me he was that attached to his sister," he said skeptically. "That young man isn't fond of anybody but himself."

"But, precisely," agreed Giselle cordially. "And he has been living on Peggy for five years. And he expected to live on her at a much higher level once she was married to Gilbert. And now all that has come to nothing."

Giselle Dumont had not, after all, abandoned her own high standards of realism. Thatcher asked if she thought the same consideration was affecting Mrs. Lindsay.

"Of course," said Giselle simply. "You, all of you," she embraced the room with a comprehensive gesture, "have a very romantic conception of Peggy. It is because you view her in the light of all this tumult about Gilbert's divorce. You see her as 'the other woman.' To Mrs. Lindsay and to Donald, she was something much more fundamental. She was the breadwinner. Poor Peggy!" Giselle sighed. "It is not easy for a woman to carry that role gracefully. And she had not the slightest notion. She was not stupid, you understand. No woman is who makes that much money in business." Thatcher, who had already estimated Giselle's annual take from the Shaftesbury Inn at thirty thousand dollars, hastily agreed. "But she could not reconcile that with being the daughter of her mother's house. So she was gauche and awkward and didn't know how to refuse her mother or brother— but there, I think she may have been learning. So sad."

Happily, before Giselle could sigh herself into a fit of melancholia over poor Peggy Lindsay's inaptitude for the role of graceful breadwinner, Captain Parker demanded her attention.

"Things would be a lot simpler, Madame Dumont," he said reproachfully, "if you hadn't sent everybody out to watch that damned parade."

This had been a source of irritation to him since his first interview with her. At first inclined to view her action as heavily significant, he had been forced to moderate his suspicions when he learned that it was a habit of long standing and one duplicated in practically every household in Shaftesbury. Where, Giselle had inquired pointedly, were the servants of the Withers home and the Austin home? Given the afternoon off to watch the parade, of course.

"Bah," said Giselle Dumont. "When are these men going to be out so that we can clean up?"

"Madame Dumont, this is a murder investigation," Parker said sharply.

"That, I already know," she retorted.

Parker glared at her. "Would your staff have noticed anything unusual in the inn when they returned from the parade?"

"Naturally," said Madame Dumont. "They would notice anything big."

"The antlers," Parker began.

"For the fifth time," Madame Dumont declared, "it is impossible that anybody should overlook this huge object if it is in the front hall at six o'clock. Therefore—it was not."

Parker looked at her, then around the room. The prolonged session had depleted his own energy as well as that of his suspects. The roster of phone numbers was complete.

"All right," he said, loudly enough to interrupt the low conversation between Withers and Olivia. "We'll assume that the murderer did a good job of tidying things up . . ."

"Probably some tramp," Withers said.

". . . not that there was much beside the body and the

60

antlers," Parker continued. "I don't think that we'll get anything more done tonight. You can go home."

As they rose, he added expressionlessly, "But I expect that you'll be available for interrogation tomorrow."

Thatcher rose and stretched wearily. "Captain," he said to the passing policeman. "Do you require me?"

Parker looked at him. "Don't think so, Mr. Thatcher. You mean you want to go back to New York?"

Thatcher nodded.

Parker indicated that he felt that Thatcher's role in the proceedings had been that of unhappy bystander.

"Thanks," said Thatcher shortly. It was not so much that he wanted to get back to New York as that he wanted to leave Shaftesbury. But, he looked forward to the reaction of the Sloan's public relations staff upon being advised that the bank's president was being detained in Connecticut in connection with a murder.

It was not a problem with which they had had much experience.

7   "Convenient to New York, ..."

     BUT ON MONDAY MORNING, JOHN PUTNAM Thatcher was being forcibly reminded that some people consider enthusiasm an adequate substitute for experience.

A helicopter had transported him from the Shaftesbury Heliport to nearby Winsted where the Sloan plane waited, ready to remove him from Connecticut. By ten-thirty, he was at his desk. But the substitution of Wall Street's visible signs of power (glass-fronted buildings, terrazzo lobbies, Oriental shrubbery) for those of Shaftesbury (rolling acres, Colonial clapboarding, Black Anguses) had not materially altered his pressing concerns.

The topic under consideration was the murder of Peggy Lindsay.

"I look on it as a challenge, old boy," said Lincoln Hauser earnestly.

Thatcher surveyed the Sloan's director of publicity with mounting dismay.

"Do you?" he asked weakly.

"Certainly. It's all in the way you handle it." Hauser waxed enthusiastic. "Why, with the right treatment, we can present a picture of Withers as a man pilloried by the police because of his name and position. In fact, that's just the line to take. A vicious assault on the financial community! Isn't there some town in Connecticut with a socialist mayor?"

"I doubt if it's Shaftesbury," replied Thatcher drily.

"Never mind." The irrelevancy was waved aside. "We can work it in all the same. The thing you don't realize is that this is our big chance."

"Your big chance to do what?"

"To prove the importance of a flexible public relations program. You know," he said with a confiding smile, "we've had a lot of trouble getting the board to take a modern view of the role of publicity. They think a bank can operate back in the nineteenth century."

What he really meant, as Thatcher knew full well, was that he had been unable to persuade the board that the director of publicity was a position worth a vice-presidency.

"That must be very irksome."

"Well, well. These little differences have to be forgotten at a time like this. I've got to be getting back to my office. Things will be humming by this afternoon. A press conference around four, I think, and releases to get out. Pictures probably, and the boys may want an interview with you. We'll have to think about that and—"

Hauser paused in his catalog of delights as Thatcher coughed apologetically.

"What I really asked you to stop by for, Hauser, was to tell you that . . ."

"Call me Link," urged Hauser. "Everybody does."

Thatcher could readily believe it.

"To tell you that the board had a meeting this morning and decided on a minimum of publicity."

"A minimum!"

"That's right. No conferences," said Thatcher firmly, "no pictures, no interviews. You're to see to it that there's a minimum of coverage. They have, however, prepared a release which you may wish to examine before distributing to the papers."

His tone made it clear that the examination did not include any rights of revision.

Hauser gasped in genuine horror. "But look here, old man, this is sheer insanity. What you want to do is whip up public opinion in favor of Withers. You've got to make him look like a victim. Now that's not easy with a bank president," he conceded, "but with the . . ."

"With the right treatment. Yes, I know," interrupted Thatcher ruthlessly. "I think you may not understand the position in Shaftesbury. Withers is not on trial for first-degree murder. In company with about ten other people he has been asked to keep himself available for further questioning. He is being treated as if he were an important witness who was previously acquainted with the victim. That's all."

It was, agreed Hauser judiciously, a good story and one they should all stick with. But it had no appeal, it didn't get to the emotions. You couldn't sell it, if Thatcher saw what he meant.

In the end it took Thatcher another fifteen minutes to get rid of him, still protesting hotly and disclaiming any responsibility for the inevitable fate of a Brad Withers unprotected by a suitable publicity campaign.

"That man is a mental deficient," commented Thatcher bitterly.

Ken Nicolls, whose entrance had successfully levered Hauser out of the room, preserved the inscrutable expression appropriate for juniors receiving indiscreet confidences from their superiors.

He brandished the folder he was carrying. "You said you'd want to review the Austin holdings first thing on Monday morning, Mr. Thatcher. I was in here at nine but Miss Corsa said you were unavailable."

Subordinates have their own way of conveying reproach, and it is quite as effective as any devised by their seniors. Thatcher sighed heavily.

"There was an unexpected board meeting this morning. I should have had Miss Corsa warn you."

Mollified, Nicolls turned to the business at hand. "I think I've got everything you'll want. And the division shouldn't be much of a problem. They don't hold as much jointly as I thought. Except for the . . ."

"I can see that you worked very hard this weekend, Nicolls," said Thatcher gently.

Nicolls was puzzled by the interruption but prepared to be amiable. "Oh, that's all right, sir. I got it all done by Saturday afternoon. Now, if you'll just glance at this schedule." The folder was proffered invitingly.

"I'm afraid I have a blow for you."

"Sir?"

"There will be no immediate need for a property settlement. The 'other woman' was murdered yesterday." Thatcher did not waste time trying to cushion the blow.

Nicolls unfortunately uttered the first thought that occurred to him: "All of that work wasted!"

"Instead of feeling sorry for yourself, you might spare a little sympathy for the victim." Thatcher did not believe in letting occasions for a display of moral superiority slip by unused. They were too few and far between.

"Yes, of course, sir," said Kenneth hastily. "Are the Austins still going to get a divorce?"

"I have no idea. I doubt if they have given the matter any thought."

Nicolls brightened. "Well, I'll file it. You never can tell."

Thatcher was amused. "A very good principle to work on. Although a little callous in this instance, perhaps."

Nicolls, however, was not so hardened as to be devoid of all curiosity concerning the abrupt termination of Gilbert Austin's plans for the future. Thatcher gave him a suitably capsulated account of his weekend in Connecticut, and Ken's attention turned to the victim.

"What was she like?"

"Quiet, plain and unsophisticated. Not at all the kind of woman you expect to be a murder victim or, for that matter, to take a rich, handsome man of forty-five away from his wife."

"Rich is right," said Nicolls with emotion.

"Ah, the portfolio was impressive, was it?"

"Very. So is Mrs. Austin's. I didn't realize she was so well off in her own right."

"She is, after all, Bradford Withers' sister. And, while we're on the subject of Withers, please bear in mind that our official position is that he is not a murderer. With the sole exception, apparently, of the Sloan's public relations department." Thatcher frowned at the recollection.

"You mean there's some question of it?" Kenneth was astonished.

"No, I don't mean that. I do mean that between his antlers, which will undoubtedly capture the imagination of the tabloids, and his messing up the body in a momentary panic, there is going to be a good deal of notoriety for a few days. With luck it will all blow over."

But Kenneth, although he had already received a detailed description of the antlers, was curious about the scene with the body. Thus far he had been privileged to see Withers only at public events, where the Sloan's president managed to convey an aura of rocklike stability. Thatcher obliged.

"He was in shock, you know, and anyone would have been. Between discovering that he had been unintentionally dragging a carcass around and the sight of the body itself—one

arm was pretty badly mangled by the antlers, you know—
and having everything he did just entangle that mass of blood
and tweed and horns more firmly, he lost his head. Thank
heavens he seems to have regained control now. He was
doing fine this morning. Having to stand by his sister helps.
Both she and her husband are worried about the publicity."

"The Austins don't go in for that sort of thing?"

"Most emphatically not."

"Well," said Kenneth unsympathetically, "when you go in
for messy divorces, you have to be prepared to wash your
dirty linen in public. Marriage," he proclaimed, "entails a
good deal of responsibility."

Momentarily taken aback, Thatcher recalled the confidences of Miss Corsa and was amused. Of course the boy
was expecting his first child. No doubt the coming months
would see Nicolls' conversation become increasingly patriar-
chal.

"A commendable point of view," he agreed gravely. "But
in this case I wouldn't be surprised if they get the notoriety
without getting the divorce."

"Then in that case," said Kenneth reverting to his original
grievance, "I have done a lot of work for nothing."

"It won't be the last time that happens to you," replied his
superior. "And while we're on the subject of work . . ."

By the time a luncheon appointment with Tom Robichaux
moved Thatcher to release Kenneth from attendance, young
Nicolls had picked up a surprising number of assignments,
not least among them personal attendance with the Sloan's
proxies at what promised to be a very lively stockholders'
meeting of a large automobile company several of whose
executives had recently been discharged for taking payoffs
from suppliers.

"It never hurts to let them know we're keeping an eye on
things," Thatcher pontificated.

"But how should I vote the things?" persisted Kenneth.

"For management, of course. But do it at the last possible
moment. And look very, very grave."

While Kenneth went off to practice looking grave, Thatcher
departed for lunch with Tom Robichaux, an investment
banker known to him since college days. Tom, it developed,
was underwriting the expansion of an old-line drug house
that was going public. And doing it with some enthusiasm.

"We'll let the Sloan in on the ground floor," he said with

simple magnanimity when they were settled at their table at the Downtown Association. "There isn't going to be any trouble moving this issue. Everybody on the Street wants a piece."

Thatcher was skeptical.

"The last time you let the Sloan in on the ground floor was with Stevenson Can. It fell nine points and stayed there as if it had been frozen."

"Now, John, why bring that up?" asked Robichaux plaintively. "Stevenson was a mistake. We all admit that. But this drug house is different. Wait until you see their earnings history."

Financial statements were flourished. The next ten minutes were heavily technical. With the removal of the main course Thatcher had agreed to turn the Sloan's research staff loose on Robichaux's material. It was all that was expected, and conversation turned to general topics.

"By the way, I hear that girl who was breaking up Gil Austin's home got herself murdered," Robichaux commented unexpectedly as dessert was being served. He shook his head sedately. "Francis is·in a great taking about the whole thing. Says he'd offer to run up to Shaftesbury and stand by but he doesn't know to whom he should make the offer—Gil or Olivia."

"Francis? You mean Devane?" Francis Devane was the other partner at Robichaux and Devane. "What does he have to do with the Austins? I didn't even know that *you* knew them."

"Oh, sure. Gil and Francis are both from Philadelphia. They're bigwigs in the American Friends Service Committee. Always getting together to send relief to some place like the Congo. In fact I think that's how they met. Francis, you know, was a great little ambulance driver in his youth. Libya, China, all sorts of hellholes. Of course, he's given up that sort of thing now." Robichaux was mildly defensive of his partner's disreputable past. His own had been spent in a succession of impeccable night spots.

Thatcher tried to imagine a younger Gilbert Austin dedicated to relieving suffering humanity. It was surprisingly easy. He should have thought of it by himself.

"Do you know Olivia too?" he asked, looking at Robichaux with new interest.

"Known her for years," said Robichaux promptly. "Really

know her much better than Gil. She and Tessie used to pa-
troness at balls and charity do's together." Robichaux sighed
reminiscently. Tessie had been his third wife. "You remember,
Tessie was great for patronessing."

Thatcher remembered nothing of the sort. While presumably he had met Tessie during her brief tenure as Mrs.
Robichaux, she seemed to have slipped in and out of his life
without leaving a ripple. Indeed this was a characteristic of all
the Robichaux wives. No doubt for a very good reason.

"Terrible thing. Just terrible," continued Robichaux disapprovingly, "Gil breaking up his marriage. That's what I
told Francis when I heard about it."

"Did you?" murmured Thatcher appreciatively. "He must
have enjoyed that." Francis Devane was notorious in the
financial community for refusing to discuss his partner's
divorces. It was rumored that he had gone into seclusion
during Robichaux's alienation of affection suit.

"What's that got to do with it?" sputtered Robichaux
indignantly. "It's not the same thing at all. You see," he said
with engaging sincerity as he pushed his plate aside and
leaned forward, "it's all right for me. Things slide off my
back. But these Quakers take things so damned hard."

And, remembering Austin's haunted face as he had last
seen it, Thatcher was inclined to concede some merit to
Robichaux's position. Gil's deep-set eyes had been surrounded
by harsh shadows and the white bone ridges had shown
through the taut skin as he watched an exhausted Olivia go
home from the police interrogation on the arm of Bradford
Withers.

Robichaux watched the cream swirl into his coffee as he
plied his spoon. "After all," he said somewhat inarticulately,
"there's no point in all this if you don't enjoy it."

Thatcher nodded. Austin had certainly never evinced any
sign of the simple gusto which accompanied the Robichaux
marital changeovers. It was all very complex, but basically
Tom was right. A Quaker conscience is incompatible with
lighthearted appearances in the divorce court. Robichaux's
butterfly approach consisted of initial enthusiasm fading into
rapid disenchantment, followed by mechanical vilification
during the property settlement, and ending up in detached
and affectionate recollection. It probably made it much easier
on the participants, Thatcher reflected. It certainly made it
much easier on the bystanders. Nobody's heart had ever been

wrung by the death mask of misery Robichaux presented to the world.

"What about Olivia?" Thatcher suddenly asked, remembering that lady's high-minded reserve. "Is she an ex-ambulance driver too?"

"No, no," protested Robichaux. "She's a damned fine woman. Not my cup of tea, you understand," he explained. This explanation was unnecessary since no woman over thirty was. But apparently there were other objections. "She's not a woman you forget easily. Seems sensible and cheerful and all that. But still you've got the feeling there's more there than meets the eye. You know—she's thinking a lot she isn't saying, still waters run deep and all that sort of thing."

Thatcher listened with respectful attention. Tom, on the subject of woman, was worth a hearing. At least he had the sense to recognize his own limitations.

Meanwhile Robichaux brooded silently. Finally he shook his shoulders impatiently.

"They're a funny couple when you come to think of it. I don't know that I ever have before. Icebergs, both of them. Seven-tenths submerged. And the funny thing is, I don't really think they're a bit alike."

It was a remark which Thatcher was to have occasion to remember.

8   "... a magnificent estate"

KENNETH NICOLLS, A LEVEL-HEADED YOUNG man as well as a promising trust officer, was determined to perform his duties satisfactorily even though his interest was currently engrossed by Jane, his wife, and by a brownstone in Brooklyn Heights. The latter had just come unaccountably onto the market; it combined every desirable feature lacking in the current Nicolls living quarters with a price well beyond the current Nicolls means.

Nothing was more likely to put those upstairs bedrooms into the palm of his hand than brilliant execution of the directions given him by John Thatcher. Metaphorically speaking, Kenneth squared his shoulders, and reviewed them: after representing the Sloan Guaranty Trust at the annual meeting of Michigan Motors with suitable gravity, he was to proceed, on Tuesday morning, to Shaftesbury, Connecticut.

This he had done. He was, at the moment, sitting in the opulent living room of the Bradford Withers country place, most emphatically no weekend cottage. It is one thing, he reflected as he waited for Withers, to know a man is enormously rich; it is another thing to see it proclaimed by acres of expensive land and quantities of museum quality antiques.

He sighed, and recalled Thatcher's second instruction. He was to deliver to the president of the Sloan Guaranty Trust some documents for which he had suddenly discovered an urgent, if unconvincing, need. Furthermore, he was to explain to that leader of the financial community exactly why Lincoln Hauser, publicity director of the Sloan, had been unable to suppress all mention of the Peggy Lindsay murder.

"We don't have much influence at the *World-Telegram*," said Thatcher eyeing the story which Miss Corsa had showed him. "But, you may hope that the *World-Telegram* has not penetrated to Shaftesbury, and thank God for the *Times*."

In this discussion Thatcher had loftily ignored the existence of the tabloids. Miss Corsa would never dream of reading them and Kenneth would never dream of admitting that he did. In deference to so much youthful purity, Thatcher had jettisoned the early morning edition which had enlivened his cab ride from La Guardia Airport to the office that morning. Peggy Lindsay's murder had been seized on with avidity, but curiously enough Bradford Withers, apart from his feelings as a brother, would have found very little therein to offend him. The Sloan Guaranty Trust was not mentioned. A hardy tradition of journalism which believed in rigorously eschewing the institutional whenever the personal was available had protected whatever feelings as a banker Withers might be presumed to possess. Headlined "Blonde Beauty Slain in Connecticut—Café Society Triangle Unbared," the article dealt exclusively with the three principals. Peggy Lindsay emerged as a kind of fatal Lorelei luring Gilbert Austin onto the rocks of marital shipwreck; Austin as a sybaritic pursuer of obscure and sinister pleasures of the flesh; and Olivia Austin as protector of hearth and home (between excursions into café society). The photographs were all wildly inappropriate. Mrs. Austin in ball gown at the opening of some charity festival looked imperially grand; Gilbert Austin in a publicity still released by his firm some years ago looked impeccably businesslike. Poor Peggy Lindsay fared worst of all. The *femme fatale* was shown in a moment of dog ring triumph, only the top of her head and the tips of her sensible walking shoes visible as they sandwiched a truly heroic portrait of an Irish wolfhound smiling idiotically.

Unfortunately the evening papers were not so single-minded in their pursuit of the salacious as to ignore the quite remarkable degree of wealth in which the crime was embedded. References to Bradford Withers, John Putnam Thatcher and the Sloan Guaranty abounded. Unkindest cut of all, one edition continued the story on its financial page. On the credit side, however, a picture of Withers shielding Olivia from photographers showed the president of the Sloan at his most sympathetic.

In the *Times* the murder story was carried on the front page and further dramatized by a photograph. The picture featured an isolated pair of antlers and was captioned:

71

"Horns of the *Cervus elaphus*." The accompanying text, after baldly stating the known facts of the murder, developed into an enthusiastic analysis of the finer points distinguishing the Scotch stag, the American moose, and the common European elk. Gilbert Austin's conjugal irregularity served merely as an introduction to a discourse bristling with references to *Cervus canadensis* and *Alces americana*, sufficiently learned to discourage all but the most dedicated zoologist. There followed an interview with a curator from the Bronx Zoo who dwelt in loving detail on the vascular covering known as the velvet, the brow antler, the bay antler, the royal antler and the crown antler.

"In common parlance," he cautioned his readers, "the crown antler is often mistermed the sur-royal antler." The Shaftesbury antlers, it developed, were as nothing compared to those gracing the head of a moose temporarily resident in the Zoo's Africa-in-the-Bronx. These, the curator concluded, were among the finest in captivity anywhere in the world. Having satisfied itself that events in Connecticut promised no contribution to the full sum of man's physiological knowledge, the *Times* firmly washed its hands of the whole affair.

Kenneth Nicolls only wished that he could do the same.

In speeding him on his way, Thatcher had said sardonically that he was to make himself as useful as humanly possible to Bradford Withers.

Withers, Ken discovered within twenty minutes, was in urgent need of comfort and the feeling of being wanted.

". . . don't know when I'll get down to the bank," he remarked crossly, accepting the documents that Nicolls presented with every evidence of a man who had forgotten all about them. "Parker wants me around, and I feel I ought to stay. Mrs. Austin, my sister Olivia, you know, can't be abandoned . . ."

"Certainly . . ."

". . . and God knows what's going on at the Sloan. I'll probably find that things there are a mess too." There was a hint of hopefulness in his voice. Nicolls, who like everybody at the Sloan knew how meager was the Withers contribution to its efficient functioning, deemed it prudent to maintain respectful silence.

". . . and I particularly wanted to be there for the opening of the new employees' recreation room," Withers complained.

He leaned back in his chair, and looked around the superbly appointed living room, discontentedly.

Mindful of John Thatcher's instructions, Nicolls exerted himself. "Is there anything I can do?" he began when Withers hitched himself forward.

"Don't know how long I'll have to stay here in Shaftesbury," he said confidentially. "John is just going to have to get along for a little while. Apart from the personal element, I have a feeling of . . . almost loyalty, you might say. Frankly, I gather that the police are in the dark, and I think the thing to do is to be very cooperative. Won't do to show them up, eh?"

"Oh no," Ken said hastily.

"That's what I thought you'd say," Withers said without sarcasm. "The difficulty is that that girl"—and Peggy Lindsay had become *that girl* to Brad Withers the moment she turned up entangled in the antlers around which so many of his wishful dreams had clustered—"that girl was killed any time from four-thirty on. Parker was out here yesterday—told me the results of the medical stuff, you know. And they know she went into the village—so you see what that means. Somebody just left the parade and went inside, hit her on the temple—oh, John did tell you about the Founders Day Parade, didn't he?"

"Er . . . yes."

". . . well, there you are. There's a good deal of confusion about where people were—frankly, I think it's beyond the police—but one wants to put on a good show, under the circumstances. Although why anybody should want to kill that girl when she was clutching my antlers . . ."

"Clutching your antlers?" Ken echoed weakly.

"That's what they seem to think," said Withers with mournful satisfaction. "Either she was holding them—and I ask you, why should she?—or she was put on top of them. It's a shocking thing. You know, they tore her clothes . . ."

"Good heavens!"

"Yes, and there were some scratches on the body, too. Nothing dangerous—but grotesque, don't you know. Well, of course it makes you wonder . . ."

"It does."

". . . and they've impounded the antlers, as well," Withers added with an access of irascibility. "You know Nicolls, I wouldn't be a bit surprised if that fellow Parker hadn't ex-

73

ceeded his authority there. Hadn't thought of it before . . .
but, you know, I may call up Carruthers and ask him for his
opinion. It's one thing to be cooperative . . . but one can't
have them taking liberties."

"No, no."

". . . and I've told Olivia that she must answer any questions they ask. No need getting impatient when they keep
coming out—we simply have to be courteous. . . ."

These confidences continued. It is one thing to recognize
that the top executive of your organization is ineffectual—
who does not?—but Kenneth, never before exposed to Bradford Withers, was taken aback by his old-family-friend manner.

It had not occurred to him that Bradford Withers would
tend to treat everybody with whom he came in contact as an
intimate. It was the task of Miss Prettyman at the Sloan, and
Mrs. Withers, in all other areas, to insulate him from situa-
tions where this was inappropriate.

But Miss Prettyman was in New York and Mrs. Withers
in the Bahamas. Accordingly, the president of the Sloan
Guaranty Trust looked at one of his junior executives with
touching faith.

"It will probably blow over," said Ken, rising to the occasion.

Withers brightened slightly. "I hope you're right. Well, let's
get down to work. I was sorry to see that Hauser hadn't been
able to keep this thing out of the papers. . . ."

The hour he was privileged to spend with his chief, while
instructive in many ways, did not tax Ken's abilities unduly.
It was simply a question of maintaining an impeccably respectful manner, while providing agreement, cheer and explanation, as needed. The result was that Withers saw him to the
door with a warm glow of gratitude, clapped a friendly hand
on his shoulder, and murmured something that sounded sus-
piciously like, "Knew I could rely on you."

"You're staying at the inn?" he said, seeing Ken to the
waiting taxi. "Good, you'll like it. They'll make you comfortable—and you're a lucky chap, let me tell you."

What would happen if some tactless underling reciprocated
the Withers egalitarianism? Probably get sent to a branch,
thought Ken, doing both Miss Prettyman and Mrs. Withers
a considerable injustice.

Kenneth got into the car and recalled John Thatcher's

second directive. He was to inform Gilbert and Olivia Austin that the Sloan thought it prudent to shelve their current activities in relation to the property settlement.

"Just let both of them know," he had said. "Now is no time for us to be digging around in their financial records—and I think that both of them will realize it. I rather expect that there's no particular hurry about the divorce—and if they don't think so, I'm sure we can trust Carruthers to make it clear to them. And, Nicolls, there's no need for you to mention this point to Withers. Not only will it not have occurred to him, he will find it worthy of comment."

"Yes, sir," Ken had replied rather blankly, eliciting a sharp glance.

"I trust, Nicolls, that I do not have to add that I rely upon you to do your best to keep Mr. Withers' comments centered firmly on noncontroversial areas. Talk about balancing the budget, or Walter Reuther, if nothing else occurs to you."

The comment no longer seemed eccentric. "Will you stop over there?" he asked the driver as they approached the end of the long driveway. Across the road was Ridge Road Farm. How long would it be before he could give Jane something like that? The house, perched on the crest of a hill, commanded a view of rolling, rich countryside; its white paint was almost too brilliant in the midday sun; the lawn was perfection itself.

He decided to take an option on the brownstone.

At the door of Ridge Road Farm, a maid informed him that Mrs. Austin was doing errands, then; since he had a nice smile, unbent enough to suggest that he try at the Kincaid farm. Following these directions, the taxi drove up the road to the next house, at the corner of the side road, and Ridge Road. What good was a brownstone without a staff?

They drove into another impressive driveway, around the house to the barn, before signs of life appeared. In Shaftesbury even the hired hands were housed with great splendor.

Ken saw two men, one of them sandy-haired and fit-looking in work clothes, busy hosing out a pickup truck, the second, in chinos, lounging against the barn door. "I'll talk to them, driver," he said.

Roger turned off the hose, as Ken got out and introduced himself.

"Olivia was here a few minutes ago," he replied, "but she

said she was going into the village. Did you know where she was going, Bud? Oh, this is Bud Austin, Mr. Nicolls."

Nicolls shook hands with the younger man.

"How do you do?" Bud Austin said. "No, I don't have any idea about Mother these days. Or Father either, since you insist that I be impartial about everything, Roger." He sounded irritable.

Roger's air of quiet competence suggested that if Nicolls had not been present, this youthful and ill-advised remark would not have gone unanswered. As it was, Kincaid merely shook his head slightly before turning courteously to Nicolls. "Are you here about the property settlement?" he asked.

A large portion of the Austin affairs were already public knowledge, Ken saw, but he replied that he had been detailed to offer aid and assistance to Bradford Withers, and to the Austins. He was about to remove himself when Bud again spoke.

"We can thank God for that," he said in measured, pipe-smoking tones that led Ken immediately to the mistaken conclusion that he must be a medical student. "At least we're going to be spared this insane divorce. I didn't understand it—and I'll bet that damn few people did. The Lord knows what Father thought he was doing."

"Bud," said Kincaid rather drily. "Seeing that Peggy Lindsay has been murdered, that your mother and father—and the rest of us—have had the police in our hair ever since, don't you think you could refrain from adding coals to the fire?" He turned on the hose again.

"Well, it's so damn silly, at his age," Bud persisted. "And if you ask me, he wasn't very happy . . ."

"If you ask me," Kincaid broke in, "if young Roger ever takes to criticizing me the way you're carping at your mother and father, I'll knock his block off even if he is twenty years old!"

The tone was friendly, but it had its effect. Young Austin flushed slightly. "It's been a shock, Roger," he said, almost apologetically.

"I know," Kincaid said calmly.

"You see," Bud Austin said, "I've been kind of hoping . . . that is . . . now that Peggy isn't around . . . well, Mother and Father have always gotten along with each other."

Kincaid splashed water over the tires impatiently. "Better

76

change the subject, Bud. Did I tell you about the letter that young Roger sent us? He's going out for lacrosse."

Nicolls retreated to the taxi.

"Shaftesbury Inn," he directed the driver, leaning back as the ancient vehicle took a wide swing and accelerated noisily. The driver, however, was as silent as the automobile (a 1947 Chevy) was noisy, and Ken was left with his thoughts.

Tactful exchanges with Mr. and Mrs. Gilbert Austin still lay before him. He was beginning to feel curious about the principals, which was just as well, since John Thatcher had given him a third directive. "Keep your eyes open, Nicolls. There's a lot in that situation up there that's interesting."

Ken was soon to find out how right he was.

9 "...with pleasant neighbors"

AN HOUR LATER, THE LOG FIRE FLICKERED, A hot whiskey toddy produced its own glow, and Ken, sunk deep in an old wing chair with his legs outstretched on a braided rug, gave himself up to the comfort of that semi-comatose condition which overtakes the habitual city dweller suddenly exposed to an overdose of brisk October air in the foothills of the Berkshires.

The Shaftesbury Inn, justifiably proud of its reputation for combining old-fashioned hospitality with continental cuisine, had received him tenderly. He had been relieved of his luggage, provided with drink, and ushered to his present location. The cocktail hour had not yet begun and he was alone in the room, drowsily listening to the crackle of burning wood and the quiet voices of two women at the reception desk opposite the double doors of the lounge.

He had already met the woman behind the counter. Although the brief ceremony of registration had not been accompanied by an introduction, Madame Dumont's fame had spread before her and he had no difficulty in identifying the Giselle who figured so prominently in Withers' discussion of his ill-fated antlers. The low throaty voice and the intensely feminine quality with which she had managed to invest her welcome were unmistakable and slightly alarming. Why make such a business of it? And while Ken appreciated her statement—for it had not been an invitation—that he would enjoy a drink in front of the fire, there was really no need for Madame to be so heavily sympathetic. He was not an invalid.

The second woman was mercifully unforeign. Her plain

wool dress was topped by a short leather jacket and a colorful silk scarf knotted around her throat. Very trim, Ken noted approvingly. She was the kind of woman who looked well in simple clothes, he reflected, as her clear light voice carried across the room. His wife would have known better. She would have taken one look at the jacket's edging of braid trim which matched the material of the dress and told him how much his idea of a simple costume cost. Even Kenneth was vaguely suspicious. A year of marriage had left its mark.

In more ways than one. The slightly astringent note which had just entered Giselle Dumont's full-bodied tones immediately alerted him to the fact that the ladies were about to get nasty. In a perfectly well bred manner, of course. It was the kind of warfare guaranteed to induce orgies of embarrassment in every male within earshot.

"With such short notice," Madame Dumont was saying, "it will be difficult for me. Very difficult."

"I'm so sorry," replied Olivia Austin without any audible hint of regret. "But I don't see that there's any choice."

Madame Dumont allowed herself to be short. "Except to go on as we had planned."

"That's out of the question."

"It is not at all clear to me why that should be so. Everything has been arranged. The exhibitors, they are to stay here. But on the afternoon before the grand banquet, it was agreed that you would provide a cocktail party and kennel tour. Now you say no. But how then am I to prepare the *salle à manger?*" Madame's voice was distinctly accusatory.

Two entirely natural pink spots made their appearance on Olivia Austin's pale features. "I cannot possibly be expected to entertain sixty-five people at a time like this."

"It is the same time for all of us. My staff is greatly disturbed. But still I am preparing to receive thirty guests." Real feeling deepened Madame Dumont's voice still further. "And seventy dogs. It is not my habit to permit pets. For the sake of Shaftesbury I make an exception."

"At a price," retorted Olivia nastily.

Ken was sorry that Mrs. Austin had allowed herself the luxury of hitting below the belt. But Madame Dumont was unmoved by the charge of running a profit-making business.

"This is a public institution," she replied with dignity. "Naturally I charge for the use of its facilities."

"Oh, for heaven's sake, Giselle, stop pretending you don't

understand." Olivia's clear voice was now just a little bit too high. "First, I'm left by my husband, and now I've got a murder to cope with. I'll be damned if I'm going to play the gracious hostess on top of it all."

Giselle was not disposed to be sympathetic. "Now that it's useful, you bring your husband into it. But it's only since the poor Peggy's death that you are upset," she said coldly. "It's the vulgar publicity you dislike. When Gilbert left you, were you being upset then? No! You are too proud. It is all calmness and composure. Then you were perfectly willing to play the hostess! You insist on it. Everything must go on as usual. You have nothing to be ashamed of. Let the others back down, but not you." She paused to take an impressive breath which expanded her bosom alarmingly. "For a woman of heart, *then* was the time to be upset with poor Gilbert needing your help. You should have gone to him and . . ."

"You leave 'poor Gilbert' out of this!" Olivia lost all sign of color. Her face was taut and white, her long fingers clenched themselves into small workmanlike fists on the counter.

"You want to bring your husband in or leave him out, just as is convenient for you," Madame Dumont retorted. "If we are to talk about people being upset by Peggy's death, it is Gilbert who is upset. It is a breakdown one should fear for him. And he is my guest when you come suddenly asking me to give large cocktail parties."

"It's a public institution, remember?" was the instant riposte.

"For Gilbert, it is a home in his hour of need," declaimed Madame Dumont dramatically.

"He's not your guest, he's your client!"

Kenneth could not really bring himself to believe that Olivia Austin was entirely innocent of the suggestion which this unfortunate remark conveyed. As for Giselle, she was all too clearly alive to the full innuendo. A tide of crimson suffused her bust and neck.

"So," she hissed, "you insult me in my own inn!"

Why this should add to the magnitude of the offense, Kenneth did not understand. He did understand that armed neutrality was now over. War had been declared.

"I'll insult you anytime and anywhere you have the impertinence to lecture me on my marriage!"

Giselle's reply was lost forever to Kenneth. A hand fell on his shoulder.

"Say, do you know what's going on out there?"

The questioner was a tall young man whose other hand was occupied in the manipulation of a long and elegant cigarette holder which had figured at some length in John Thatcher's nutshell review of the personnel involved in Shaftesbury's tragedy. Kenneth inspected it with something approaching the awe worthy of an object inextricably associated in his mind with Marlene Dietrich and long-feathered boas.

"Well, it looks like the lady of the manor has come down off the pedestal," continued Donald Lindsay with ill concealed pleasure.

Kenneth announced that he was a stranger here himself.

"Then give thanks for small blessings," advised his companion, abandoning him and strolling, somewhat unsteadily, into the midst of the fray. The aroma he left in his wake confirmed Ken's suspicion that Peggy Lindsay's brother had been seeking consolation out of a bottle. So did his subsequent conduct.

"Good for you, Giselle," cheered the new recruit. "Pitch it on hot and heavy."

Madame Dumont was appalled at this unexpected support. Pausing midway in a comprehensive indictment of Olivia's failure to achieve true womanliness—a failure Kenneth would have been prepared to refute on the spot—she readjusted her vocal register to its normal volume and attempted to regain control of the situation.

"Donald," she said warningly, "be a good boy and go away. This is not for you. Mrs. Austin and I are discussing a cocktail party."

"A cocktail party, is it?" asked Donald Lindsay unpleasantly. He disposed his arms over the desk with an air of permanence. "That isn't the way it sounded from where I was standing. Why so shy, Giselle? Go on and give her hell. You were doing fine."

Olivia, without budging an inch, managed to assume a posture indicating complete dissociation with the other two occupants of the desk. Madame Dumont was not doing nearly so well. Mortification was visible in every feature as she addressed her unwelcome ally in surprisingly placatory tones.

"It is your imagination, Donald," she said, almost pleading.

"There is nothing at all. It is only that Mrs. Austin does not find it convenient to give a party during the dog show."

"Oh, Mrs. Austin doesn't find it convenient, does she?" he mimicked brutally. "And of course we all have to be very careful about what's convenient for Mrs. Austin."

Olivia's heavy-lidded eyes slid sideways in a contemptuously dismissive glance. "You've been drinking," she announced flatly.

"And what if I have?" Lindsay demanded. "Does no one have the right to grieve as long as the Austins keep a stiff upper lip?"

He sprawled along the counter, thrusting his jaw forward as if to compel some reaction—any reaction—by sheer force of suggestion. But Olivia only removed her hands from the desk. This fastidious little gesture stung Donald into a fresh outburst.

"Oh, it's easy enough for you," he roared. "What have you got to be sorry for? Everything's lovely in your garden now. Just a decent moment of silence and then we can all go on as if nothing ever happened. The perfect couple with the perfect family. Tell me," he asked, suddenly dropping his voice to a conversational pitch, "does it ever cross the still surface of that immobile mind of yours that my sister would be alive today if she hadn't gotten mixed up with your pretty little lot? Or are you so bloody thankful to have your problem neatly removed by the mortuary truck that you can't think of anything else?"

"Stop this at once. You do not realize what you're doing," moaned Madame Dumont in an agony of professional embarrassment. This was very definitely not the tone so artfully contrived for the Shaftesbury Inn.

"You! You're just as bad as she is," snarled Donald rounding on her. "You're not weeping in your beer for poor Peggy. Oh, no! You're too busy trying to fill her shoes. It's *cher Gilbert* this and poor little Gilbert that. Must have peace and quiet for good old Gil. Afraid to quarrel with his wife while you play the ministering angel to him in his troubles. What's so special about his troubles? What's he done to deserve all this sympathy? Hell, if he weren't Gil Austin it isn't sympathy he'd be getting. Plenty of guys have murdered in his place. All he's done is . . ."

"Donald!" rapped out Madame Dumont sharply.

"No, Giselle. Let him go on," said Olivia quietly, her eyes narrowed in speculation.

"That's right. Always the perfect lady willing to listen to the tenants. Well, let me tell you, you may be able to hush up everyone else but you damned well can't keep me quiet. What do I care about your precious reputation? Who the hell do you Austins think you are anyway? Gil comes romping down from Ridge Road to play around with Peggy. She was too good for him if you want the truth. He finally gets her in trouble and you don't see why that should make . . ."

"What!"

Olivia had abandoned all pretense of being above the battle. Her breath sucked in sharply through flaring white nostrils as she swung around to glare at Donald Lindsay. Madame Dumont shook her head mournfully.

"Are you trying to tell me that Gil got Peggy pregnant? That she was going to have his child? Answer me, you contemptible little worm!"

"Very good," applauded Donald Lindsay, "A fine performance of shocked realization. As if you didn't know all along." But his eyes shifted uneasily as Olivia advanced, stiff-legged, in his direction.

Her voice was menacingly hoarse as she swept aside his interruption.

"So! Peggy was pregnant and you were all playing it for everything you could get! Oh, how blind can one be! A chance to recoup the family fortunes. What a godsend for the likes of you."

Her tone shook Lindsay. "Now look here," he blustered, nervously retreating a step, "that's my sister you're talking about."

"You!" Olivia's voice cracked in an unpleasant laugh. "A picture of fraternal grief. Why, you've been living on Peggy since the day you put on long pants! You've never worked a day in your life. Look at yourself," she invited jeeringly, "drinking yourself into a stupor because you thought you were in a featherbed for life. Talk about sheer stupidity! This takes a prize of some sort. And what role in all this did the devoted brother play? Were you the go-between? I believe that's common practice in some circles."

A tide of crimson swept over Donald Lindsay's face.

"You can't say that to me," he snarled, stunned into complaint. Olivia's counterattack had taken him by surprise. He had not contemplated being on the receiving end of this slanging match.

"Twenty years of marriage down the drain because of a barnyard mistake. It's hilarious. How much you all must have enjoyed it. Gil Austin, passionate lover. . . ."

There came an interruption.

"What was that?" inquired a new voice hesitantly as its owner stood on the threshold.

Ken Nicolls, a spellbound spectator to Olivia's rising wrath, realized with a sinking heart that the entrant must surely have been attracted by the sound of his own name. And there couldn't possibly be more than one man walking around Shaftesbury with deep lines of strain carved over shadowed eyes.

"Er, did you want me?" continued Austin as his audience merely stared silently, generating an emotional climate ranging from horror to rage to sullenness.

"Join us by all means," purred Olivia with ominous calm. "We're just discussing your paternal feats. You didn't tell me you were expecting to become a father."

Austin winced. "Oh, lord."

His wife looked at him contemptuously.

"Olivia, if you'll just give me a chance to explain . . ."

"Don't you say one word to me!" Olivia's fists pounded on the desk as her voice rose into a shrill scream. "When I think what I've gone through for you! When I remember what I've done to try and keep my family together! And Peggy Lindsay tried to make me fight for you! For you! I could laugh now. You've made a fool of me and of yourself and of her." Exhausted Olivia leaned on the desk and fought for breath while the tip of her tongue swept along her dry lips.

"Olivia," Austin cried in agonized tones, "you've got to listen to me. You mustn't say these things . . ."

"I won't listen to you! I'll say anything I please. It's time somebody did. When I think how she looked—coming to me all fury—talking about the house, ranting about you, complaining about the three of us going to dinner together that night. What an idiot I was not to see the nose in front of my face. All the time you were . . ."

"I knew it," howled Donald Lindsay triumphantly. "I knew she wasn't going to see Withers that afternoon. But I thought she was trotting off to Gil somehow. But all the time it was you!"

"You shut up, Lindsay!" Austin said furiously. He turned to his wife and stretched out a hand. "I know it wasn't that way, Livvy. You're just upset . . ."

"Don't you dare touch me! You unspeakable . . . What do I care? Of course it's true. I should have known from the beginning. And it was all wasted, wasted. Leave me alone, all of you. I can't stand any more. If you try and stop me, I'll scream."

Rushing past her husband, with tears frankly streaming down her face and her gloved fists clenching and unclenching at her sides, Olivia Austin ran out of the inn leaving behind only the echo of her hysterical voice and of the slamming door.

10 "...and many interesting views."

AFTER THE WILDEST STORM, SAYS THE POET, the sun retouches the world with life-giving rays, proof incontestable that the violence of wind and rain is but nature's wondrous way of providing needful moisture for all growing things. The poet regularly ignores washed-out roads, flooded basements and leaking roofs.

After Olivia Austin's outburst, nobody in the Shaftesbury Inn was inclined to talk about clearing the air; the debris strewn about during the altercation was too insistently in evidence.

Kenneth Nicolls, a prey to emotions ranging from hideous embarrassment to irritation with his Uncle George, at whose advice he had entered banking, found that minutes after Mrs. Austin swept out of the inn he was still rooted to the spot behind the heavy wing chair from which he had witnessed the whole unedifying spectacle. With an effort, he pulled himself together and was about to remove himself unobtrusively. Donald Lindsay was already slinking out the door when Giselle Dumont spoke.

"Gilbert," she said with a calm that struck Kenneth as nearly inhuman. "Come sit down. You must not let this distress you more."

Like Nicolls, Gilbert Austin remained immobile. The emotion that gripped him, however, was more powerful than embarrassment. Kenneth, who had never before seen him, knew instinctively that this was the set still face of a man at the limit of his endurance.

The flinging open of the front door released him.

"What's going on here?" demanded Roger Kincaid striding into the reception hall. "I saw Olivia tearing out of here."

As his glance fell on the ashen-faced Austin and Donald Lindsay inching toward the door, his brows drew together in a deep scowl. "What is it?" he asked sharply. "By God, Donald, have you been creating more trouble?"

He took a step toward the young man that led him to shrink back.

"Nothing," said Gilbert Austin quickly. "There's no trouble, Roger. We've just had a misunderstanding."

"Misunderstanding!" Donald bleated sardonically.

This roused Madame Dumont. "Donald," she said positively, "get out. Now! I don't want you here. Out!"

Since it was clear that Roger Kincaid, if not Gilbert Austin, would be happy to lend force to Madame Dumont's injunction, Donald Lindsay had no alternative. With a crooked smile, he left the room.

"Good," said Madame Dumont. "It is good that you are here, Roger. You can join us in a drink, which we all need. And perhaps you too, Mr. . . . ?"

It took no more than this (although it was, in its way, remarkably communicative) to bring Kenneth Nicolls to his senses. Murmuring something incoherent, he fled in Donald Lindsay's wake, unnoticed by both Kincaid and Austin. But before he left, he heard Austin's reply to Kincaid's urgent question. "Olivia found out, Roger. Now, there's nothing I can do!"

Meanwhile, the eye of the hurricane was sweeping out Ridge Road. Olivia Austin, driving at a dangerous rate of speed, nearly frightened Dr. Cooper out of his wits by passing him at the corner of Chestnut Street with a wicked swerve. But characteristically, in a few moments she let the Jaguar drop to thirty miles an hour. By the time she pulled into the driveway in front of her home, she was driving carefully.

Her emotions underwent a similar change of form. She was still bitterly angry. But now it was a cold, contained rage. She wasted no time regretting the outburst into which her treacherous temper had betrayed her, but vowed only that there should be no recurrence. There was more to Olivia Austin, as Tom Robichaux had remarked, than met the eye.

She found, when she walked into her handsome living room, that her brother had decided to pay a call.

"Just made myself at home," he said from the Directoire sofa, referring presumably to the glass he held in his hand.

"Fine," replied Olivia, who wanted nothing more than to take two aspirins and retire upstairs with the headache that had begun pounding at her temples. "Ring for Althea . . . oh, Althea. Will you freshen up Mr. Withers' drink and bring me. . . let's see, oh, a sherry."

Olivia sat opposite Brad, and leaned back.

"You're looking a little tired, Liv," he said. "You've been wonderfully strong but Carrie says—she wrote today, by the way—that you want to keep up your strength."

"Yes," said Olivia tonelessly, briefly grateful that her sister-in-law was still in the Bahamas. Carrie Withers was even more prone than her husband to tell people they were looking tired. There was a moment of silence during which Althea brought a tray into the living room, set it beside Brad and withdrew.

Brad, a look of mild embarrassment on his face, waited until they were again alone, then cleared his throat. "Now Olivia," he began, "there are a few things that I want to talk to you about . . ."

"Maybe you'd better hear my news first," she said calmly. Her considerable affection for her brother in no way impaired her estimate of his abilities. She knew that the news of Peggy Lindsay's pregnancy would be best broken to him by her. Therefore, in a perfectly detached voice, she described her encounter with Donald Lindsay and its results.

For a moment, it appeared that the news had rendered Bradford Withers speechless. But after a revivifying gulp of neat bourbon, he found something to say.

"Who would have thought it of Gil?" he demanded. "Of all people! Carrie is never going to believe this . . ."

"Brad," said Olivia dangerously. He was oblivious.

"Can't help feeling sorry for him, once you understand," he continued thoughtfully. "Terrible thing . . ."

"I do not feel sorry for Gil," Olivia snapped.

"Still, it explains a lot," Withers continued as she tried to control herself. "Why he did it, I mean."

"Did what?"

The sharpness of her voice made him look up. Olivia gave him no chance to speak, but sprang to her feet. "God knows,

Gil is the greatest fool it has been my misfortune to encounter!" she raged, "but I can assure you of one thing—he didn't kill Peggy Lindsay!"

She looked down at him with blazing eyes. Then, with a short laugh that he liked not at all, she turned and stormed from the room.

Alone in the living room, Bradford Withers was suddenly deeply troubled.

Tuesday's storm had repercussions on Wednesday. Kenneth felt that it would be unfeeling to pursue the Austins after their shocking encounter at the inn. His suggestions along these lines, telephoned to his superior late Tuesday afternoon, resulted only in prolongation of his visit to Shaftesbury.

"Don't let yourself get shaken by a scene," advised Thatcher from the safety of New York. "Try to see them tomorrow. And Nicolls, keep me informed."

Accordingly, Ken spent a profitless evening in Shaftesbury, a community already gossiping avidly about the afternoon's events. After a solitary dinner at the inn (where there was no sign of Madame Dumont) he debated the economics of a call to Jane. Deciding against it, on the grounds that tuition charges are rising everywhere and it was none too soon to start saving for his son's education, he sought the Shaftesbury Playhouse. It was closed on weekdays. He retreated to the tavern room of the inn. There, he drank more beer than was good for him and listened to the locals animatedly discuss Peggy Lindsay's pregnancy, Peggy Lindsay's murder and the unpredictable Austins. "I always said that still waters run deep," said one red-faced man pontifically.

"Roger!" somebody else cried. "You're the boy who can tell us the latest."

Nicolls looked up as Roger Kincaid entered the bar. There was a quickly banished look of anger on the man's face when he replied, "No, I don't know a thing, Fred."

"About the pregnancy, I mean," Fred unwisely persisted.

"Let's just drop it," Kincaid snapped. He glanced away, and, catching sight of Nicolls, asked the younger man to join him, but Ken, refusing, drained his beer, and retreated to the cubbyhole on the second floor that was his bedroom, obscurely sorry for himself.

He awoke on Wednesday morning with a slight hangover and a grim determination to hasten his departure from

Shaftesbury by seeking the Austins. Never had Brooklyn Heights looked more inviting.

As he entered the dining room for breakfast, Bud Austin waved an invitation. There being no escape, Ken threaded his way to the table. Before he had given the waitress his order, he discovered that young Austin was virtually rigid with indignation.

"I have to talk to Dad," he said. "That's why I'm here but he's already gone out. Probably couldn't face me." He gave a knowing and bitter little smile. "God knows how I'm going to break this terrible news to Nancy."

"Nancy?"

"My wife," said Bud Austin importantly. "She's . . . that is, we're expecting our first child. I'm up at the Business School, you know."

Momentarily, Ken wondered if the entire student body felt it necessary to procreate before achieving the Master of Business Administration. With a sudden access of superiority, it occurred to him that he and Jane were also expecting a child, but that he was gainfully employed. This obviously put him into a very select category.

Bud Austin, speaking with a measure of dignity, was continuing, "I wouldn't say it to everybody, but I understand that you were here when Mom found out. About Peggy's pregnancy I mean." He blushed violently, then frowned. "Everybody in Shaftesbury is talking about it, you know. I don't know how Dad could do a thing like this to me." It was clear that getting Peggy Lindsay pregnant was in no way similar to the activity of himself and Nancy in producing a child.

"And Mom is heartbroken," said her son with palpable afterthought. "Disgusting." The voice hovered perilously close to a crack but Bud cleared his throat portentously and busied himself with his pipe. Then, with a puff of Balkan Sobranie that floated between Ken and his grapefruit, he brought his voice down a half-octave. "I'm going to do what I can to support Mom, of course."

As he listened to these confidences, Ken recalled Mrs. Austin. Heartbroken was not precisely the word he would have chosen.

Kenneth left the breakfast table only after exhaustive discussion with Bud Austin on a number of separate, if related subjects. First, he heard his companion's views on the responsibilities of parenthood: "I think that becoming a father is the most important thing that can happen to a man. It's a responsibility, if you see what I mean." Ken said that he did. This led to the problems of education of the young. "If it's a boy, we're going to send him up to Kent. I went there myself, and they turn out a really all-round boy. Roger's boy is up there now. A boy's education is pretty important, let me tell you." This led young Austin to the role of the Harvard Business School in modern American industry: "I mean, the seat-of-the-pants approach to business decisions is definitely out. We have a case method way of going about things that really lets you know what's going on."

After successfully escaping from the dining room, Ken stood for a moment by Shaftesbury Common indulging himself in an optimistic assessment of his long-term professional prospects. With enough Bud Austins in the world, it should be possible to become a John Thatcher. In fact, it should be a cinch.

He smiled, and looked at October sunlight dappling ancient elms with golden light. The Congregational Church, solid and reassuring, presided over the common, and two very small children and a large red setter frolicked in the leaves that had blown into a pile before the statue of Eleazer Pinckney, 1697-1782, "Age did not dim his love of liberty nor deter him from bearing arms against the tyrant. Erec. Shaftes. Com., MCMXLIII." (Pinckney had hit a British officer over the head with an empty bottle one convivial evening in the Shaftesbury Inn but the act had had nothing to do with the War for Independence and in fact predated it by some ten years.)

Someday, Ken promised himself, he would bring Jane and his son to see Shaftesbury. He straightened his shoulders slightly. It was a beautiful town.

But his immediate goal was an interview with Mrs. Austin. He rounded the corner of the inn, and encountered a prospect even more unattractive.

Donald Lindsay, his pasty face twitching nastily, had buttonholed a reluctant Roger Kincaid, who was backed against his Buick station wagon.

"I thought you might understand," Lindsay said almost peevishly.

"Look, Don," said Kincaid, "I'm sorry as hell about this

story about Peggy, but what good is it going to do you or your mother if you go around telling . . ."

"Story!" Lindsay screeched. "What do you mean, story? Ask the coroner! She was carrying his child. Your holier-than-thou Gil Austin . . ."

Distaste roughened Kincaid's voice. "All right," he said. "I believe you. We all do. The whole town believes you, Don, and we're sorry. But what good is it doing anybody to stir up all of this dirt?"

"I'll tell you," Lindsay said venomously. "It's going to cost someone plenty, that's what good it will do! Hell, Roger, I thought you might be more human than the Austins because you're as poor as we are, but I guess that just working for them makes you sure that they can get away with murder . . ."

"Shut up, Don," Kincaid said evenly. "You're upset . . . or maybe drunk."

Lindsay laughed affectedly. "Very funny, Roger! Very funny, especially from you . . . well, look who's here. Enjoying your stay in picturesque old Shaftesbury, are you, Mr. Nicolls? Sorry I can't stay to talk to you but I've got a lot of people to see. Bye Roger. Be seeing you."

They watched him swagger to his car. Then Kincaid, with a rueful smile at Nicolls, said: "You wouldn't believe it, but normally we get along very well in Shaftesbury. Quiet, and all that sort of thing . . ."

"I don't suppose you can blame people for being on edge," said Ken. "Murder changes things."

Kincaid shook his head. "I guess so. I would have sworn that you'd never see Shaftesbury seething with gossip the way it is—but I guess you're right. Murder changes things." He took a deep breath, then: "Bud around? His father's up at the farm, so I'm picking him up while I'm down here."

Ken watched him disappear into the inn and came to another decision. He would show Jane and the baby some other corner of New England perfection—not Shaftesbury.

Not long after his disgruntled subordinate scratched Shaftesbury, Connecticut, from the list of communities worthy of his unborn son and heir, John Putnam Thatcher found himself lunching at the Bankers Club with Tom Robichaux and Charlie Trinkam, the Sloan's most rakish senior trust officer.

Seven urgent telephone calls from Bradford Withers had reduced to negligible proportions the possibility that Thatcher might fail to keep himself abreast of developments in Connecticut. What other purpose these communications served only Miss Corsa, dutifully listening on the extension, could have testified.

"You've made a note of that, haven't you, Miss Corsa?" Thatcher asked after the last call.

"A note of what, Mr. Thatcher?" she asked cautiously.

"Of what Mr. Withers wanted."

Respect for authority and incurable veracity fought together briefly in Miss Corsa's soul—then truth triumphed.

"Mr. Withers did not want anything," she informed her superior. "He just wanted to talk."

"Oh," said Thatcher innocently.

Fortified by so assiduous an intelligence system, Thatcher and Trinkam were able to come to the luncheon table armed with almost as much information as Tom Robichaux.

"Francis has known for days," he told them. "Austin told him about the girl's pregnancy right after the murder."

The meeting, ostensibly called to canvass the profit possibilities of Bay Vitamins, a small firm which promised revolutionary weight losses by rigid adherence to its high-priced pills, reached roast beef and potatoes in a welter of speculation about Gilbert Austin's peccadillos.

"Helluva thing for a Quaker," said Robichaux with mournful satisfaction.

"That's the trouble." Charlie Trinkam, himself a noted non-Quaker, was crisp. "No experience."

The two men nodded their heads in sober deprecation.

It was an indictment, Thatcher reflected, that both could make from the superiority of positions equally impregnable if otherwise remarkably dissimilar. Robichaux, harrumphing his way through life amidst a series of deeply felt grievances directed toward taxation, high salaries and government supervision, cherished an ineradicable fondness for marriage with young women. Trinkam, on the other hand, avoided marriage with a dexterity and *brio* buttressed by continual increments to his experience with rich, ripe, seasoned sirens. He had even survived his brief engagement to a sweet young thing contracted in a moment's aberrant attraction toward the pleasures of domesticity.

"You don't understand his kind, Charlie," said Tom, "and

I can't say that I blame you. He just didn't know what was the right thing to do."

"You're joking."

"No," Robichaux assured him, "you don't know these good men."

Thatcher decided to expand the field of inquiry.

"What about good women?" he asked.

Charlie said he didn't know any, thank God. But Tom announced they had more sense than their male counterparts.

"I was thinking of Olivia Austin," admitted Thatcher.

There was no doubt about it, Robichaux said. She was a remarkable woman and you could count on her to display more balanced judgment than her husband.

"And her brother, your revered president, too."

"That," Charlie commented, "would not be difficult."

Thatcher informed them that his latest bulletins from the front indicated that balanced judgment was the last attribute Olivia Austin had displayed upon being informed of her husband's situation.

"The heat of the moment," said Robichaux, waving aside Olivia's outburst.

"Can you blame her?" demanded Charlie, coming to the lady's support. "All this mess because of a little slip-up. She probably doesn't like being made a fool of."

Robichaux shook his head sadly. "They never do."

But Thatcher was not entirely convinced. Was it, he wondered, really likely that the serene Olivia Austin should display the fishwife fury Kenneth Nicolls had reported on discovering her husband had anticipated some of his marital prerogatives? Absently he listened to Trinkam and Robichaux, now back on the subject of vitamins.

"Look, Charlie, you want to think of the future. There's this little drug firm in Mexico that's come up with something really new. They say they've got a pill that combines diet control and contraception."

Trinkam maintained a moment's impressive silence. "It will," he said authoritatively, "make a mint!"

Thatcher watched Robichaux signal for more coffee. Olivia Austin, he felt, was capable of anything.

Of course she could be acting. But if not, then she was in the grip of some truly overpowering emotion.

And in that case, thought John Putnam Thatcher, he would like to know what it was.

11 "An opportunity
for dog lovers..."

OLIVIA AUSTIN'S OVERPOWERING EMOTION
might have been concern for Bold Baron of Austindale, as
Kenneth Nicolls could have informed Thatcher.

Kenneth had resolutely presented himself at Ridge Road
Farm at ten-thirty, in accordance with a telephoned appointment. Just as he was steeling himself to urge prudent financial
behavior upon a Gracious Hostess and Well Known Club-
woman, the door opened to his ring.

"Mrs. Austin isn't home and she doesn't have any statements to make anyway," said Althea sternly.

"I'm not a reporter," Ken cried as she shut the door. "And
I have an appointment with Mrs. Austin. My name is
Nicolls."

Althea peeked out at him. "There have been so many
people pestering us," she confided. Once again, his smile did
it. "Mrs. Austin is over at the kennel, Mr. Nicolls."

Thus, ever devoted to duty, Kenneth found himself following the path that led to the Austindale Kennels. It was lined
with Black Anguses. Unlike John Thatcher, Kenneth Nicolls
retained an inapposite moral objection to vast expenditures
on cattle and canines for the purpose of establishing a tax
loss. Especially when it entailed cross-country hikes on his
part.

Olivia Austin, trim in slacks, emerged from the kennel
office as Ken approached. "Mr. Nicolls," she called apologetically, "I thought that I would get back to the house
in time."

Roger Kincaid appeared at the door behind her. "Hello,
95

Nicolls," he said. "Listen, Olivia, don't worry. Whatever it is, we'll get it cleared up before the show."

"I hope so," said Olivia Austin very seriously. "It's Bold Baron," she explained to Nicolls. "He's been sick." Kenneth had been uneasily aware of the Doberman Pinschers eyeing him through the kennel fence when from behind Roger Kincaid another of these beasts emerged and joined Mrs. Austin on the path.

"Faust," said Mrs. Austin.

Faust looked hungry to Kenneth.

Roger Kincaid waved a farewell and disappeared into the office while Kenneth fell into step beside Mrs. Austin, taking care not to crowd Faust. Olivia maintained a flow of noncommittal remarks about the problems raised by owning kennels, the problems raised by the forthcoming Housatonic Dog Show, the problems raised by the postponement of the Austindale cocktail party. The town of Shaftesbury rang with gossip about the murder of Peggy Lindsay. The Heberts and the Wrenns were gossiping about Gilbert Austin's affair with the dead girl. Yet here was Mrs. Austin, self-possessed as ever, giving a convincing performance of a woman whose most serious problems centered on Doberman Pinschers. Kenneth was suitably impressed.

". . . Roger is a pillar of strength," she was saying, stooping to pull a long weed from the edge of the path, "but I know that he's worried. And if anything happens to Bold Baron we'll really be in the soup. Shall we go inside? . . . oh, for heaven's sake!"

Lounging at the gate that led from the pasture to the house grounds was Donald Lindsay. The brilliant sunshine was not kind to him.

"I want to talk to you," he said aggressively as Olivia Austin, after an initial check, continued her progress.

"Donald," Olivia Austin said flatly, "I have nothing to say to you." She took a firm grip on the collar of the Doberman. Unfortunately Donald Lindsay missed the gesture. Kenneth wondered uneasily if he would be required to knock the man down.

"You may have nothing to say to me," Lindsay said, "but I have something to say to you."

"Don't be a fool, Donald," Olivia said, advancing slightly. "I'm sorry about Peggy—truly I am. But I'm not going to put up with you."

Lindsay was working himself up to another one of his displays of unparalleled nastiness when a low rumble from Faust arrested his attention. For the first time he noticed the dog. Kenneth sympathized with the emotion he saw on his face.

"Will you get that dog . . ."

"Donald," Olivia said, "in two minutes I'll let Faust go. I want you to get out of here."

Lindsay wavered. Then with a look both furtive and menacing, he turned on his heel and retreated to his car.

They stood beside the cross-barred fence, and watched him drive away. Ken covertly glanced at Mrs. Austin. Her hooded eyes were enigmatic, but she seemed unconcerned. It occurred to him that Olivia Austin was a little inhuman.

"How exceptionally disagreeable," was all she said. She also released Faust, Ken noticed.

"Yes," he said.

They had circled the house and were about to go indoors when a distant halloo halted them. Bradford Withers, attired in jodhpurs, was striding down the driveway from his house, waving a crop vigorously. "Liv! Liv! Want to talk to you a minute!"

Olivia Austin obediently waited for her brother to cross the road. "Oh dear," she said, almost, but not quite, to herself.

"Hello there, Nicolls!" said the Sloan president heartily. "And Faust!" He then rose immeasurably in Nicoll's estimation by the casual yet decisive fashion with which he roughed Faust's noble head. Bradford Withers, as Thatcher could have told Kenneth, was always at his best with dumb animals.

"We're having a business conference, Brad," said Olivia with pleasant impatience. "What is it you wanted?"

Withers' hand with human beings was not so sure. "Just wanted to warn you about that damned sod, Donald Lindsay!"

"Yes, we've . . ."

"Pushed his way into my place just now! Muttering a lot of things—didn't understand a word he was ranting, Liv—but he sounded ugly. I threw him out, but I want to warn you not to talk to him. Roger says he's spreading a lot of talk around town, you know."

"Yes, Brad," said Olivia Austin.

"The man's likely to be a nuisance," he continued. "You

say that you two are talking business? I think that I may join you for coffee."

Ken sympathized with his hostess.

"Mrs. Austin," said Althea from the doorway. "There's a telephone call for you."

"Coming," she called. Without answering her brother's inquiry, she turned up the path. "Come along," she said over her shoulder. Apparently, that was invitation enough for Bradford Withers.

Withers and Nicolls were settled in the library with coffee, pecan rolls and Faust when their hostess rejoined them. In the interval, Withers had fluently explained to Nicolls his duty to protect Olivia from the Donald Lindsays of the world.

"Yes, sir," said Kenneth, reaching for a roll as Mrs. Austin reappeared.

He got up, so that he had a good view of her face.

"The police," she said quietly. "Captain Parker is on his way up here. It was courteous of him to call, don't you think?"

"Not again!" exclaimed Bradford Withers indignantly. "They've been in and out of here for days. Well, Liv, we'll stand by."

"I'd rather . . ." Mrs. Austin began, when the sound of a car crunching on the drive outside stopped her.

Captain Parker's courtesy call had been timed to leave no room for further maneuver.

Althea ushered him into the library a minute later. "Do sit down," said Olivia, with iron-plated graciousness. "Althea, will you get another cup of coffee?"

"Don't bother," said Parker quietly. Olivia raised her head at the tone.

"Now see here, Parker," Withers began.

Parker ignored him. "Mrs. Austin, I hear you had a fight with Donald Lindsay at the inn yesterday. He told me that you admitted seeing Peggy Lindsay last Sunday. Why didn't you tell us that?"

"I don't like your tone, Captain," she said while Withers expelled a mouthful of coffee in a convulsion of surprise. Kenneth wedged into a corner, saw Faust raise his head and favor the policeman with an appraising look.

"Mrs. Austin, Peggy Lindsay was murdered," Parker said flatly. "My tone doesn't matter. Did you or did you not fight with her?"

98

"I suppose that there's no use denying it since everybody in Shaftesbury knows that I did."

Withers recovered from a paroxysm of coughing. "Don't admit anything," he sputtered, wiping coffee from his vest. "Not a word until we get hold of Carruthers."

Olivia ignored him. "Peggy Lindsay and I had an exchange of words," she admitted.

"What about?" Parker pounced.

Olivia Austin frowned again—at his tone, presumably.

"We argued about Ridge Road Farm, if you must know," she said haughtily. "Not content with stealing my husband, she was accusing me of all sorts of things simply because she wanted my home. It was extremely vulgar—I lost my temper —and that's all."

"Not about the pregnancy?" Parker asked stolidly. "They're saying in town that you learned about the baby—and lost your temper."

"Not about the pregnancy," Olivia declared stonily. "She wanted the farm—and I wanted it. That's all." Remembered distaste curled her lips.

"What time was this?" Parker asked.

"About four o'clock. She stormed in, blew up with accusations, then stormed out, really before I had a chance to say anything," Olivia said.

Parker looked at her with undisguised interest. "You mean that's the way you learned that your husband . . ."

"I had not learned about Peggy Lindsay's pregnancy until that wretched Donald Lindsay . . ."

"Olivia!" shouted Withers.

It brought Parker to a decision. "Mrs. Austin, I would like to talk to you in private."

"Certainly," she said coldly. "Brad, Mr. Nicolls, will you excuse us?"

Faust remained.

"She said what?" John Thatcher's vigorous incredulity was undiminished by the telephonic communications. Ken, in refuge at the inn, shifted uncomfortably in the public telephone.

"That's what she said, Mr. Thatcher."

"Good Lord, Nicolls, couldn't you or Withers stop her?" Thatcher retorted. "That farm is a drop in the bucket in their estate and Parker knows it. Why should she and Peggy fight about that, when she gets into murderous rages just hearing about the pregnancy . . . ?"

Boldly, Kenneth Nicolls interrupted him. "I really don't know, sir," he said. "I just wanted to tell you about this. And ask if I should stay."

"Obviously," said Thatcher brutally.

Ken repressed a sigh. "And to tell you that you will no doubt be hearing from Withers."

"If you're being sarcastic," Thatcher said irritably, "stop it. Were they going to arrest Mrs. Austin?"

"I don't think so, sir," said Kenneth carefully. "But the police were certainly not very friendly."

"Fine," said Thatcher ringing off. He glared at the telephone for a moment, as if daring it to ring again. It did.

"Mr. Withers," said Miss Corsa.

"John!" came the financier's harried tones. "John, things are terrible up here. The police are after Olivia . . ."

"Now Brad . . ."

"She admits having a fight with Peggy Lindsay. It's all over town anyway. Says that the girl marched in at about four o'clock, started abusing her, then just raced off in the middle of things . . ."

"Nicolls told me . . ."

". . . of course Peggy was alive after that," Withers said, seeking comfort in this rather grim fact, "but it doesn't look good, does it?"

Thatcher's instincts were as kind as the next man's but he had to admit that it didn't look good.

"John, do you suppose that you could come up . . . ?"

Kenneth Nicolls was revenged.

12 "... and gentlemen farmers."

THAT HE SHOULD BE CALLED FROM THE SIXTH floor of the Sloan to Shaftesbury, Connecticut, to render aid and support to Bradford Withers, Thatcher accepted philosophically. Every occupation, after all, has its peculiar hazards. But it seemed excessive that standing by Withers should entail attending the funeral of Peggy Lindsay.

"It would mean a lot to Olivia," Withers said at the breakfast table as Thatcher and the family lawyer retired for a five-minute conference in the library.

"It could be worse," Carruthers said when Thatcher taxed him about Olivia Austin's interview with the police. "Your young man, Nicolls, can tell you about it. The quarrel with the Lindsay girl doesn't look good, but at least she was seen on her way back to the village after she left Mrs. Austin. With all this"—the lawyer waved vaguely toward a shelf of rare first editions—"the police have to be careful, you know. So long as there's no evidence of a fight down at the inn, Mrs. Austin should be all right. Of course, that's just my opinion. I'm not a criminal attorney, you know. I just handle the estate," he concluded with due legal caution.

Thatcher nodded abstractedly. He knew, as Curruthers knew—and Bradford Withers did not know—that the chief function of Withers' legal adviser at the moment was to remind the police of "all this." No one had more experience than Stanton Carruthers in conveying such information with a maximum of delicacy and a minimum of ambiguity.

But Carruthers' departure left Thatcher helpless against the demands of funeral attendance. Not much later, he found himself standing by an open grave under a brilliantly blue

October sky while the breeze stirred the golden leaves of an immense oak tree arching overhead. The solemn church service had been attended by the entire community including collaterals and offshoots hastily summoned to Shaftesbury from desks in Boston, New York and Washington to pay last respects to a girl who had grown up in their midst, flowered into brief notoriety and come to an untimely end. It was an echo from an older society, moving at a pace leisurely enough to let everyone take time to mourn those who died young. An older society, Thatcher noted, that had still not lost its prerogatives. Whatever their suspicions, the police had firmly prevented intrusion by reporters and curiosity seekers. The ceremony at the church was brief, the Reverend Mr. Baines wisely confining himself to the youth of the departed and leaving untouched her manner of going. The procession was even shorter for Shaftesbury's graveyards still nestle within the grounds of its churches and there was no motorized cavalcade to some distant commercial establishment.

Mrs. Lindsay had emerged from her retirement to lead the mourners. Supported on one side by her son and on the other by the minister, she watched dry-eyed as the coffin was lowered. Behind her a nurse was carefully watchful. Heavily draped in flowing black, Mrs. Lindsay moved slowly and seemed unaware of her companions.

Not so her son. Donald Lindsay, strangely subdued in a dark business suit, shot nervous glances around the gathering. His pale lips drew into a muted snarl when he caught sight of the party from Ridge Road Farm at the rear of the crowd. His face was white and he shivered occasionally in the wind.

"That boy looks sick," Withers said softly after intercepting one of Donald's glares.

"Probably a hangover," said Thatcher testily.

Olivia Austin paid no attention to this exchange. She had dispensed with her brother's arm gently but firmly and now stood very tall and straight, quite unsupported. Her lovely face was composed into an expression of serious attention as she quietly listened to the service, oblivious to the speculative looks she was attracting.

Gilbert Austin was drawing even more covert attention than his wife. However well bred, Shaftesburyites could not resist glancing at him from time to time with interest, with compassion, or with open inquiry. He stood separated from both the Lindsay family and his wife. At his side, unquenchably exotic, was Madame Dumont who somehow escaped the funeral pall which settled over all the other attendants. Possibly it was because she so often affected a black crepe that it did not suggest obsequies. She had abandoned the effort to engage her companion in a series of whispered remarks. Gilbert Austin looked as if his thoughts were very far away.

"If you want to be sorry for someone, what about him?" said Thatcher directing Withers' attention to his brother-in-law. "If you ask me, he's near his breaking point."

"Oh, Gil's tougher than he looks," replied Withers unsympathetically. "Only natural that he's upset."

Olivia Austin shifted her position slightly, turning away from them.

As the first shovelful of earth fell on the coffin, Mrs. Lindsay's composure gave way. Her heavy body suddenly became wracked with noisy sobs and she put up both hands to cover her face. The Reverend Mr. Baines paused uncertainly and there was a moment of nervous silence broken only by the sounds of weeping. Finally the nurse hurried forward and put an arm around her patient. Nodding to Donald Lindsay she disengaged his mother and led her off to the waiting car under cover of a flow of soothing remarks. Lindsay hesitated for a moment, then with a defiant look he settled himself more firmly, apparently determined to see the funeral through, and Mr. Baines proceeded.

Cynthia Kincaid, looking very odd under a black hat she had resurrected from some long disused trunk, nodded with satisfaction. The long string of melancholy forecasts which had fallen from her lips during the last hour—concerning the prostration, collapse or arrest of everyone present—was finally bearing fruit.

"There'll be trouble with Donald before we get away. You mark my words," she predicted confidently. "He's building up to something."

Her two companions were unresponsive. The proceedings had impaired her husband's ordinary fund of sturdy cheerfulness. He was looking almost morose and Kenneth Nicolls remembered that Roger Kincaid had been fond of Peggy Lindsay. As for Kenneth himself, he had adapted his chief's advice concerning stockholder meetings and was looking very, very grave.

Bud Austin, present under protest, had disassociated himself from his nearest and dearest. Somehow inserting himself into the midst of the Shaftesbury Development Committee, which had turned out en masse, he looked very young standing next to Dr. Cooper and remarkably uncomfortable whenever his glance lighted on one of the Lindsays. His attention had been so preoccupied with the culpability of his father in particular and parents in general that even a police interrogation of his mother had failed to undermine his conviction that divorce was the subject in issue. It had taken the coffin itself to bring home to him the fact of Peggy Lindsay's murder. Now he was ill at ease. Soon he would be aggrieved.

The last words were spoken; the final disposition of floral offerings on newly turned soil was made; and with a sigh of relief the participants turned away to take up their daily rounds. Conversations started, at first hushed, then swelling to a normal volume. Invitations were issued as groups broke up to proceed at a decorous pace toward the parking lot. Unfortunately the ensuing bustle was not quite loud enough to cover the tail end of Bud Austin's remarks to his mother as he hurried to her side.

"Well, dammit, Mother, if you won't ask Dad to come up and have lunch-with us, I will! Now that this is all over, there's no reason why we shouldn't all behave like adults."

The urgent young voice carried clearly over the churchyard, provoking mingled emotions in many who heard it. Gilbert Austin, his back mercifully turned to his wife at the operative moment, became heavily absorbed in conversation with Giselle Dumont while the nape of his neck turned brick-red. Olivia Austin stared at her son with a darkling gleam in her eye, biting angrily down on her lower lip. Bradford Withers' look of mild anxiety was replaced by a thunderous scowl as he opened his mouth and then shut it with a decisive snap. Thirty years of experience left him, for once, out of sympathy with his nephew. Thatcher, geographically a member of the afflicted group, allowed his gaze to fix itself firmly on the horizon and mentally reviewed the timetable of trains to New York. Roger Kincaid, a short distance away, cursed quietly but intensely.

It was Donald Lindsay who allowed himself the luxury of a wholehearted response to this piece of adolescent tactlessness. Shaking off the restraining hands of family friends, he advanced on Bud Austin instantly.

"So, it's all over with, is it? We've buried the dead and

now we can all go home and have lunch together. Why don't you invite my mother too just to show there's no hard feeling? You imbecile! Do you realize that my sister's been murdered? That she'd be alive right now if it weren't for your family?"

He paused for breath while Bud stood rooted to the spot, prey to the mixed emotions he had so recently evoked in others. Embarrassment, fury and shock struggled for supremacy. Most of all, he simply did not know what to do. Torn between a feeling that manly indulgence should be exercised toward the recently bereaved and outrage that any languid little aesthete dared speak to him in such a tone of voice, he groped automatically for his pipe. Sheer stage fright betrayed him.

"Now I'm sure we all want to be reasonable . . ." was his unfortunate opening.

"Reasonable!" shouted Donald, in no mood for stately enunciations modeled after the style of a popular professor at the Harvard Business School, since called to Washington. "Who the hell wants to be reasonable?" He looked around the little family group as if calling for volunteers. None stepped forward. Then he lowered his voice to the pellucid clarity appropriate for converse with the mentally retarded.

"Your mother would be in jail right now if it weren't for her money," he said softly, hitting each word with a separate little hammer blow. "What alibis do you think the police are checking? You'd be in the middle of this up to your neck if everyone didn't realize you're too stupid to know what's going on. Oh, don't worry. The Austin money will clear things up. That's been the trouble all along. The Austin money and everyone wanting a piece of the pie. And why not? Do you think you've got a right . . ." Donald's voice was rising shrilly when he was interrupted.

"That will do!" Bradford Withers said with a surprising show of authority. "You're overwrought and you don't know what you're saying." He continued in a kindlier but still forceful tone. "Roger, take him home and see that he gets a sedative and some sleep. Olivia, Bud, come with me. We're going home." Snatching up a reluctant relative on each arm, Withers turned his back on the gaping multitude and marched out of the graveyard. It was, Thatcher was forced to admit, the most effective moment of his life.

There is no cloud without its silver lining. Bradford Withers, continuing his masterly performance at the church, announced immediately upon his arrival home that he wished, if John Thatcher would excuse them, to be private with his family. It was time, he said without a flicker of humor, that somebody talked to Bud like a Dutch uncle. Olivia also must be brought to realize that her preposterous concern with her marital problems was subjecting the family to hysterical attack every time they ventured out of seclusion. Radiating a strong sense of purpose he herded his sister and nephew off to the library, leaving Thatcher free to disengage himself from the immediate problems of the Withers-Austin ménage. Somebody, he recalled, once said that we are all good at the things that really matter to us. Presumably the public respectability of his family was a good deal more important to Withers than the profit reports of the Sloan Guaranty Trust. "I understand, Brad," he said gravely watching the family settle itself for the conclave. "I think I'll take a walk."

Not only did he applaud Withers' sudden emergence as a man of action, he was delighted with the opportunity to escape.

Ten minutes later, he was approaching the Kincaid farm. Mrs. Kincaid, busy with her daughter in the garage, waved a friendly greeting. "Wasn't it just awful?" she cried. "Roger's in the field up the road, if you're looking for him." Thatcher was not, but he equably followed her directions and soon sighted Kincaid happily involved in the intricacies of replacing a strand of barbed wire in one of the fences. The sun was beginning to lower in the sky, and its angled beams brought new color to the glowing hillside. Thatcher availed himself of Kincaid's invitation to perch on the tailboard of the pickup truck, carefully arranging himself so as not to conflict with the coils of wire, and watched the work.

After a silence, he said, "Does me good to see somebody doing something with his hands."

Kincaid replied to the spirit, if not the letter of the comment. "I wanted to get outside," he said quietly. "That scene at the grave just about turned my stomach. Donald isn't usually that objectionable, you know. By the time I got him home, he had calmed down."

Thatcher agreed that the Lindsay family must be under considerable strain. Kincaid tried to think of another good word for Donald Lindsay, failed, and abandoned the subject.

"Got a lot of work to catch up on," he said, bending to his task. "Hasn't been easy, around here. Work has to be done, and if the police aren't around all day taking up time with questions, we're off to the funeral. Lot of things have piled up." He sank back on his haunches, wiped his face, and inspected his handiwork.

The sun was casting long golden beams over the scene.

"Beautiful country," Thatcher said idly.

"Beautiful to look at," Roger corrected him. "Farming it is another thing."

Thatcher smiled. "Connecticut isn't exactly the bread-basket of America, is it?"

"Rock," said Roger with feeling. "Rock and clay. Hell of a place to try and raise beef."

Thatcher was entertained by this insight into the difficulties raised by a persistent attempt to take your tax losses in the form of a revolution against nature.

"I suppose the fencing gives you a good deal of trouble too," he said, nodding toward Kincaid's task.

"It does. The country's too small for this kind of farming. And if you let your cattle stray, you wind up with a lawsuit. Everyone here has a lawyer on a full-time basis." He sighed darkly at this aspect of dealing with the rich.

"I'm surprised you still use barbed wire. I noticed that Brad has electrified fencing."

"So do we. We're just bringing this field into condition. Takes a lot of work. We'll get around to doing over the fences here in another year or two."

Thatcher noted that of all the participants, Roger Kincaid alone seemed capable of taking the long view. He could speak of another year or two quite calmly. Everyone else was absorbed in the problem of surviving the next few weeks. It was the long view of the farmer. And the banker. Thatcher knew as well as Kincaid that Ridge Road Farm and its inhabitants would continue to occupy a place in the community of Shaftesbury and on the books of their banks long after the furore caused by the death of Peggy Lindsay had died away into nothingness.

It was a view that left Thatcher feeling more at peace with himself and his surroundings when he accepted Roger Kincaid's invitation to return home for a drink and they drove toward the farm through a twilit purple countryside.

13   "Easy commuting . . ."

THE EVENING TRAIN TO NEW YORK WHICH HAD
played so prominent a role in John Thatcher's thoughts during Peggy Lindsay's funeral gave way to the morning train
in the face of Bradford Withers' importunities.

"You can have the bank send up the plane," Withers
pointed out.

"Apparently," Thatcher said acidly, "apparently you have
put it at the disposal of those Indian promoters."

"Oh yes, I'd forgotten. Well, John, you can always take
the train tomorrow night."

At this point, Thatcher became adamant. Some attendance
at the bank was necessary, he said, promising an early return
to Shaftesbury if conditions warranted. Kenneth Nicolls, who
was present after dinner to help his chiefs review some pressing business, repressed the statement that a little attendance
on his expectant wife would also be appropriate. "You said
you wanted to see the International Oil financials, Mr.
Withers."

They succeeded in turning Bradford Withers' attention to
the affairs of the Sloan Guaranty Trust for a full fifteen
minutes when chimes announced a caller, and Gilbert Austin
was ushered into the room. Since he was virtually barricaded
into cloistered seclusion at the inn—and forbidden by the
police to return to his work in New York—Thatcher and
Nicolls wondered what could have drawn him forth.

. Ostensibly, it was the Dog Show. For almost half an
hour, Austin grimly discussed his success in inducing three
major dog-food producers to display their wares at the
Housatonic Dog Show. Withers, it appeared, would distribute
the temporary feeding pans made available by this commercial largesse. Watching him make notes of Austin's directions,

108

Nicolls was shocked at the juggernaut aspects of the forth-coming exhibit which could command the devotion of its participants in the wake of murder, mayhem and marital disruption.

John Thatcher, on the other hand, was reassured to find Gilbert Austin fulfilling his civic commitments. Not only did this imply that Quaker training left its mark, it suggested that Austin had reserves of nervous strength still untapped. A good thing, Thatcher suspected.

Austin came to the end of his instructions concerning feeding pans. "To tell you the truth," he said gloomily, "I came up to get away from the telephone. Bud's been calling me. And Don Lindsay."

Bud, of course, was still bent on reproach. Donald Lindsay's motives were more mystifying.

"Said he wanted to see me," Austin replied when Thatcher questioned him rather sharply on the subject. "Something about money and Ridge Road Farm."

"No!" Withers exploded. "That little runt hasn't given up yet. He still thinks he's going to make his fortune out of you."

Austin flushed with annoyance. "All right, all right, Brad. I know the boy's a parasite. But I don't think he's trying to capitalize on the fact that he almost became my brother-in-law. Anyway it sounded different this time. He said he had some information I might be interested in."

Thatcher stirred uneasily. Blackmail by any other name would smell as noxious. And bankers have highly developed olfactory senses.

"What did you say to that?" he asked quickly.

"Told him I was too busy to speak with him tonight," replied Austin promptly. "Considering the way he blew up at Bud this afternoon, I could scarcely sit down with him at the inn for a cosy chat."

"I should think not." Withers was indignant. "Anyway, Donald's been behaving like a madman all this week from what I hear."

"Well, you've got to admit that Bud's pretty infuriating himself," said his father with some heat, "and the Lindsays are upset. You saw Mrs. Lindsay this afternoon. She was on the brink of a complete collapse."

"She may have been collapsing this afternoon, but she was well enough this morning to see Peggy's insurance agent!"

Thatcher and Austin both stared as Withers produced this tidbit.

"Where did you hear about that?" Thatcher demanded.

"Er . . . as a matter of fact, Giselle happened to mention it this afternoon. Just dropped down to see her after Olivia and Bud left."

Under the accusing stares which were leveled at him, Withers' voice became mildly defiant. "Not what you think at all. Just wanted to straighten out this business about the antlers, that's all."

"What business about the antlers?" asked Thatcher in rising exasperation.

"Some damn nonsense the police have dreamed up. They want to keep the antlers. I just wanted to assure Giselle . . . Madame Dumont . . . that I would leave no stone unturned . . . that is. . . ."

Faced with Withers' rapid degeneration into complete incoherence, Thatcher abandoned the antlers and returned to a subject which interested him more.

"About this insurance on Peggy. What was her coverage?"

"Giselle didn't know," Withers replied simply.

"You surprise me," murmured Thatcher.

But he was still thinking of this insurance the next morning as he unsuccessfully tried to get comfortable in a train bent on servicing every station in western Connecticut. As they resumed their intermittent progress southward he unburdened himself to Kenneth Nicolls.

"It's surprising nobody's mentioned this insurance before. Of course its value could be nominal in view of Peggy Lindsay's expectations."

"Oh, a girl like that wouldn't be apt to carry much," said Ken sleepily. Their train had left Shaftesbury at six-thirty.

"That girl was making twenty thousand dollars a year," said Thatcher tartly.

"From dogs?" expostulated Ken indignantly. Neither he nor Thatcher expected Kenneth to make twenty thousand dollars a year for some time.

"Apparently. I know it seems odd, but she was one of the best known handlers in New England."

"But, good Lord, sir, if she'd been a man making a salary like that with a wife and children . . ." Ken had trebled his own insurance the day he learned of his wife's pregnancy.

"Exactly. A coverage of two hundred thousand dollars

would not be unusual. But in her position would she be likely to go in for that much?"

"That mother of hers would have seen to it," said Ken darkly.

"I was thinking the same thing," admitted Thatcher.

"If she was making that much money, why do the Lindsays run around Shaftesbury acting as if they were sharecroppers? Donald made some remark the other day about the Lindsays and the Kincaids being poor."

"Because," explained Thatcher kindly, "in Shaftesbury people don't think much in terms of earned income. It's capital they think about there. You don't run around raising beef cattle at a spectacular loss if you're operating on a salary. It's a different kind of money altogether. And not one you see much of these days outside of communities like Shaftesbury. But, I might remind you," he added on a tarter note, "one of the other places you see it is at the Sloan Guaranty Trust."

Kenneth sank into an abashed silence which Thatcher did not disturb until they were leaving Waterbury. Then he said:

"It's not hard to see how Olivia Austin and Peggy Lindsay wouldn't see eye to eye on Ridge Road Farm, but it's not much of a story to explain their last quarrel. How exactly did Mrs. Austin put it?"

"Well," said Nicolls, "she was pretty crisp with Parker about the whole thing. Just said Peggy Lindsay had come up and made a vulgar attempt to steal the house. But after Parker left, Mr. Withers insisted on going over the whole thing again."

"Naturally. Did she divulge any additional detail on the second round?"

"In a way. She said Peggy started the whole thing off on the wrong foot by sticking her chin out and saying it was time they settled the thing like rational adults. She—Peggy, that is—wasn't going to have Gil taken advantage of."

Thatcher could almost visualize the scene. Peggy Lindsay had no doubt nerved herself for the interview with Olivia and then, before her courage could fail her, had hurled herself into the subject with an abruptness and tactlessness guaranteed to render the entire interview fruitless. How the notable Mrs. Gilbert Austin must have felt—having mature rationality urged upon her by the chit who was stealing her husband and flaunting her proprietary rights!

"It would be enough to make anyone lose his temper," he commented.

"Mrs. Austin admits she lost hers, all right. Told Peggy what she thought of her behavior in no uncertain terms. Upstart, gold digger, all that sort of thing. Said she'd never let Peggy Lindsay queen it on Ridge Road. If she wanted to play lady of the manor she could have the decency to do it someplace else."

"What then?"

"Then Peggy lost *her* temper. Called Mrs. Austin a thief. Said she was making hay out of Mr. Austin's easygoingness. According to Mrs. Austin she was just blazing with fury. But the thing that maddened Mrs. Austin the most was that after Peggy finished ripping her to shreds, saying every unforgivable thing in the book, she just came to a dead halt and slammed out of the house without waiting to hear the reply. Mrs. Austin said she had a pretty fiery denunciation all ready to be delivered."

"And all of this quarrel revolved around the farm?" asked Thatcher skeptically.

"That's what Mrs. Austin told us," said Ken firmly. "She went on to say that she was so upset, both from the quarrel and the frustration of being left in midstream, that it took her some time to get down to the parade. Once she was there she avoided people because she was still trying to calm herself down. She'd forgotten all about meeting her son."

"The inference that everybody will draw, of course, is that she met Peggy again while she was still in a rage. Hmmm. Not a word about the pregnancy, I gather."

"Not a word. Mrs. Austin insists she didn't know about that until Donald blew the lid off the whole thing."

"It seems like a very one-track quarrel," mused Thatcher. "If Peggy were that mad, you'd think she would have hurled her pregnancy into Olivia's teeth."

"Mrs. Austin's fights do tend to cover a lot of ground," Kenneth agreed apologetically, recalling the free-for-all at the inn.

"She is reputed to be a lady of very equable temperament." The statement was advanced dispassionately.

"That may be her reputation," replied Kenneth stubbornly, "but in my book she seems fully capable of a murderous rage."

"Well, you've been a witness to one. How long do you think it would last?"

"How long?"

"Yes," repeated Thatcher, "how long after the fight's over? Do you think she would still have been homicidal if she'd met Donald Lindsay an hour after their encounter the other day?"

"Oh, I see what you mean. I just don't know."

"After all, the important time is during the parade when everybody was milling around. You have no idea of the confusion that one parade generated. People parking cars, refractory children being rounded up, bands playing, the entire staff of the inn out front. And practically everybody who might have murdered Peggy Lindsay wandering about alone."

Ken tried to conjure up the scene. "Didn't anybody see Peggy?"

"Nobody who'll admit to it. As a matter of fact, I'm almost sure Gilbert Austin met at least one of the Lindsays. I saw him that morning with Peggy and he was very pleased with himself. Oh, a little nervous about the dinner that night, but nothing more than social embarrassment. But when I met him later at the parade, he was fed up with the Lindsays. I wouldn't be surprised if he'd had a run-in with Donald Lindsay which he's keeping quiet. That's one of the reasons I'm worried about the boy's trying to get in touch with him now. If additional suspicion can be aimed at any Austin, Donald Lindsay will take real pleasure in doing it."

Ken had no difficulty in agreeing with this assessment.

"We've only got his story about dropping Peggy at Mrs. Austin's that afternoon. He might have put her up to the whole thing and been waiting for her someplace where the Kincaids didn't see him. After all, Mrs. Kincaid said Peggy looked on her way to bawl somebody out. Maybe Donald let her in for more than she was prepared to take on."

But Thatcher was unprepared to believe that anybody in his right mind could have been persuaded into action by Donald Lindsay. There was no reason to suppose that Peggy had been mentally incompetent.

"There's just one other thing," offered Ken a little nervously, "while Mrs. Austin was telling us about her fight with Peggy, I got the impression maybe Mr. Withers might be holding something back. It was just an impression . . ." he went on hastily before Thatcher interrupted.

"Of course he's holding something back," he said impatiently. "Anybody can see that. It's probably nothing more than some piece of nonsense with Madame Dumont that he doesn't want Carrie to find out about."

"Carrie?"

"Mrs. Withers." Thatcher paused significantly before compromising on a neutral statement. "Caroline Withers is a very forceful woman. When she gets home from the Bahamas, she'll find out what Withers was up to before the day's out. I wouldn't waste time worrying about it. What I'd really like to know is what's going on between Gilbert and Olivia Austin."

"How do you mean, sir?"

"They've both been behaving very strangely. Oh, I don't mean all this turmoil about Peggy's pregnancy. I mean their general aloofness toward each other. After all, they've been married for almost twenty-five years and Austin isn't a man to take his responsibilities lightly. But you don't find him rallying round in support. Of course, he may have tried and Olivia made it clear that his presence would be unwelcome. But still, it's very odd."

Ken was impatient with the internal workings of marriage in Shaftesbury. What possible relationship could it have with the murder?

"It could mean that they suspect each other," replied Thatcher with asperity. "In fact, I wouldn't put it past either one of them to maintain a reticent silence in spite of being an eyewitness to the murder."

But here Nicolls felt his superior was indulging himself in a deep-rooted tendency to assume the worst of everyone— and particularly of everyone taking his business to the Sloan Guaranty Trust.

At New Haven, they switched over to a through train from Boston, and became passengers to be pampered rather than tiresome adjuncts to the movement of agricultural produce. A dining car was available and they made full use of it during the remainder of their journey.

Mellowed by a large if belated breakfast and a leisurely perusal of *The New York Times,* Thatcher congratulated Nicolls on the performance of his duties in Shaftesbury. They parted at the Sloan elevator, Kenneth to call his wife and hurl himself with renewed zeal into the study of various portfolios, Thatcher to brighten his secretary's day with his return to duty.

"Well, Miss Corsa, I imagine there's a backlog piled up. If you'll bring your book in right away, we can clean up the urgent correspondence now. Then I'll want to see quite a few people."

Miss Corsa controlled her enthusiasm. In a voice even more devoid of expression than usual, she remarked that Mr. Withers had been on the phone.

"Already?" Thatcher was unpleasantly surprised. He expected hourly communications from Shaftesbury for the duration of the crisis; he had hoped that his chief might allow him enough time to settle in.

Miss Corsa rummaged through her desk for the memo.

"Mr. Withers would like you to return his call immediately," she read precisely. "And asked me to tell you that a Mr. Donald Lindsay—yes, that's the name, Lindsay—was murdered last night. His head was bashed in. . . ."

Thatcher sank into a chair and eyed her speechlessly.

"I'm not sure about this," Miss Corsa continued, frowning worriedly. If murder was powerless to stir her, inaccuracy was not. "Tell Mr. Thatcher that the body was found this morning by one of the farm hands in the Number Three field."

"Good God!" Thatcher exclaimed, appalled. "Does that mean that the body was found on the Withers' place?"

Miss Corsa looked up. "Yes, Mr. Thatcher."

Thatcher sank back, and closed his eyes as a remarkably detailed preview of the next few days flashed across his mind. Then, with an effort, he roused himself and prepared to enter his office.

"We'll have to face things as they come," he muttered. "Might as well get Gabler in here." He broke off as another thought struck him. "I suppose," he said sourly, "that we should thank God that the Black Angus is shorthorned."

"Tsk," said Miss Corsa. She did not approve of profanity.

14   "...to downtown financial district"

NOBODY CAN DENY THAT MURDER IS SERIOUS. And nobody in the village of Shaftesbury felt the slightest temptation to venture upon such a denial after the discovery of Donald Lindsay's body. Two murders, one following hard upon the heels of the other, generated an aura of cataclysm unmatched since the defeat of Governor Dewey in 1948. Little bands of householders marched through their extensive residences, securing doors and French windows traditionally unlocked. It was rumored that the Hebert estate had produced twenty-eight means of ingress. And while Miss Finchley remained alone in her determination not to sally forth onto the streets of the village proper, her precaution in providing her desk at the library with a lethal volume of the Britannica kept close to hand was reflected on a more warlike basis in the surrounding countryside. There, demands for police protection to blanket sprawling acres were coupled with rapid inventories of domestic arsenals by the more martial element of the community. The Reverend Mister Baines, capitalizing on the situation, was drafting a powerful sermon on the ephemerality of mortal life, and more than one person was heard to refer to the Lindsay family in terms generally associated with Greek tragedy.

But, if murder is a very serious matter, so is business.

At the Sloan Guaranty Trust the forces that produce satisfactory annual profit statements have a vitality that renders them independent of human frailty. If, by some ghastly mischance, the personnel of the Sloan found itself under enemy fire, decimated by guerrilla attack, debilitated by grueling hardships, *Research Report A16* (Prov.) (For Distribution to Trust Officers, Senior) would appear on the first Thursday of each month so long as one member of Walter Bowman's gallant band of researchers had the strength to dictate. The *Weekly Clearing Statement* would emanate from the fourth floor if only one lowly clerk survived. And the *Daily Reserve Position Report* (with Estimated Federal Reserve Bank Clearances) would no doubt reach those desks worthy of it even if the entire Inter-Bank Exchange Division were wiped out.

These are things that make a bank great.

Nevertheless, no sooner than John Putnam Thatcher had assimilated the fact that somebody in Shaftesbury, Connecticut had cracked Donald Lindsay's skull, than he was made aware of yet another fact; the Trust Division, the Investment Division and the Executive Offices of the Sloan Guaranty Trust were being seriously inconvenienced by the prolonged absence of Bradford Withers and his own truancies. Since no one at the Sloan had known Donald Lindsay (nor for that matter, would anyone at the Sloan have mourned him had they known him) there was no doubt which of these two facts was locally regarded as the more important.

"This can't go on, John," said Everett Gabler when Miss Corsa ushered him into Thatcher's imposing suite of offices. He was a senior trust officer, Thatcher's oldest subordinate, a conscientious employee and a born fusser. "I had to send the Strauss account off yesterday without your signature, and you know what that means!"

Thatcher did, but Gabler, settling himself foursquare in the chair across from him, did not spare him a number of horrible possible difficulties, based on the assumption that Mrs. Strauss (ninety-seven years old and a client of the Sloan for seventy of them) might suddenly have developed a litigious streak. Like Cynthia Kincaid, Everett Gabler tended to think the worst.

"I know there have been difficulties," Thatcher interrupted his jeremiad to say, "but with Brad up in Shaftesbury . . ."

Gabler pounced. "That's another thing! Withers was supposed to be available for the Flinders contract. God knows why, but it's a good thing to have the president around when the bank undertakes large commitments . . . and Withers always enjoys it."

Gabler was genuinely upset. Thatcher diplomatically suppressed a smile and listened to his uncharacteristic abuse of Bradford Withers. Normally Everett was the old-fashioned sort of employee who denied himself this luxury. He looked old-fashioned too, and rather out of place in the chrome and crystal New Sloan. It was the pinstripes.

"They've found another body. And it's on Withers' estate," Thatcher cut in, when Gabler gave no sign of abating.

Gabler halted in mid-sentence. "A body?"

"Another murder," Thatcher said grimly. Miss Corsa might be unimpressed with wholesale slaughter, but Gabler was outraged. He opened his mouth, shut it, took off his rimless glasses, gave them a savage swipe, then, with some waspishness, resumed his discourse.

"I have not complained," he said untruthfully, "about the serious inconveniences caused to the Trust Department by Withers' frequent and unscheduled absences—whether for tuna fishing, grouse shooting or stalking whatever it is that he stalks . . ."

"Now Everett," Thatcher began soothingly, but to no avail.

"We've adjusted to Withers," his subordinate said ringingly, "but John, when he starts dragging you off for these—these entertainments—then I frankly find it difficult to see how we will be able to get any work done."

Thatcher was spared the necessity of replying when Miss Corsa buzzed: "Mr. Withers, Mr. Thatcher."

"Put him through," Thatcher commanded, swiveling away from Everett Gabler's martially accusing eye. Gabler clearly regarded murder as some sort of sporting activity.

Withers, sounding remote and dimly hopeful, had rung up, he said, because he wanted to be sure that John had all the facts.

"I got your message," said Thatcher carefully. "How bad are things?" He avoided asking if there were anything he could do.

"Terrible," said the president, his voice eloquent of hopes dashed. "They found Donald Lindsay's body in my pasture. Everybody up here is in a pretty bad state, too. There was some sort of protest meeting at the Grange this morning. Anyway, I want you to say a word to Hauser about the publicity."

The protest meeting rather intrigued Thatcher. Had the burghers of Shaftesbury boldly come out against murder? "I don't know how we're going to soft-pedal publicity," he said aloud, "when there are two murders to cope with. At least you're spared reporters swarming around."

"Well, I should hope so," said Withers heatedly. "I'd like to know what we pay taxes for if we can't get cooperation from village authorities."

Thatcher wondered, not for the first time, if great wealth is necessarily a deterrent to rational thought. "What are the police doing?" he asked.

Diverted from taxes, Withers was momentarily confused while Everett Gabler, frankly listening, shook his head. "The police? Well, they're all over the place of course. Asking the damnedest things about what we were doing when Lindsay got himself killed."

Against his will, Thatcher asked, "When was he killed?"

Gabler glared at him.

"In the middle of the night," replied Withers, encouraged by this interest. "Everybody was in bed—or at least everybody says he was in bed. Dammit, John, you were here. Gil was back at the inn. Olivia stayed home, Roger was in and out of the kennel with Bold Baron—and let me tell you, we've all had to put up with a good deal of impertinence from that man Parker. I'm beginning to get incensed about his attitude. They're nagging at Olivia . . ."

"I don't suppose you're going to be able to get down to the bank then," Thatcher said hastily. "We need you here."

This patent falsehood consoled Withers. "Don't see that I can leave," he said importantly. "I know that Gil wants to get back too, but they're keeping us here."

He sounded so indignant that Thatcher yielded to temptation. "And how is Mrs. Lindsay?" he asked.

"Pretty hysterical," Withers said unsympathetically.

"You might find out if Donald Lindsay carried a lot of insurance," Thatcher said bracingly. "Well, I'll keep in touch. Goodbye." He hung up without giving Withers a chance to reply. "And that, Everett, is that."

He was wrong. Scarcely had Gabler taken a grumbling departure, when Walter Bowman, head of the Sloan's Research Division, rang through.

"You're back?" he bellowed joyfully. "Good! Now, John, you have to take a look at this trucking stock situation. I'll send the figures up. The market's picking them up—I've cleared this with Charlie—and I want us to move fast. So, if you . . ."

Thatcher moved the receiver an inch from his ear. "Hold it a minute, Walter. Yes, Miss Corsa?"

Miss Corsa looked at her harassed chief from the doorway. "Miss Prettyman," she said referring to her arch-foe, the president's secretary. "Miss Prettyman says that three Indian businessmen have an appointment with Mr. Withers at four this afternoon, because Mr. Withers told her he would be back today."

Thatcher scowled at her but she stood her ground. "And should she cancel the appointment or do you want to see them?"

"I do not want to see them," Thatcher said bluntly; Miss Corsa, correctly interpreting this as irrelevant, waited for his considered opinion. The weighty business of the Indian loan had already been hammered out by efficient underlings, but some sort of ceremonial reception was necessary. Indian sensitivities being what they are, canceling the meeting was out of the question.

"Why don't we do business with the Swiss?" Thatcher asked savagely but Miss Corsa had no answer. "All right. I'll take them. Four o'clock? You'd better tell Gabler that I won't be at his meeting. Walter—still there? You're going to have to go ahead."

The afternoon proceeded along these unsatisfactory lines. Even as he exchanged stately and meaningless courtesies with the Asian delegation (in Bradford Withers' opulent office) Thatcher found himself ruminating on the amount of simple chaos caused by the removal of even so insignificant a cog as the president of the Sloan Guaranty Trust.

"It isn't Withers," Charlie Trinkam told him as they returned to the sixth floor after smiling the Indians off in the direction of celebrated fleshpots. "Although it turns out that we need his signature on a hell of a lot of things, doesn't it? It's you, John."

"From here on in," Thatcher declared, striding down the corridor to his office, "Shaftesbury buries its own dead."

Trinkam kept pace with him. "And what are you going to do when our revered chief yells for help . . . ?"

"Mr. Withers on the line," Miss Corsa greeted them.

"Hell," said Thatcher. "I'll take it inside. Come on in, Charlie. This is going to be short . . . Hello, Brad? Yes, we're getting things under control. Yes . . . Now, Brad, I'm sure you're looking on the dark side of things. What does Carruthers say? Oh? Yes . . . Well, I'll keep in touch."

With some vehemence he put down the receiver and glared at Trinkam, who raised an eyebrow.

"We'd better come in tomorrow to try to clear up the Handasyde report, John," he said. Tomorrow was Saturday and Charlie was no lover of weekends in the office.

"Yes," Thatcher said absently.

Trinkam's next comments were not about business. "Has it ever occurred to you that Brad Withers must be having a hell of a time believing that his own sister is a serious suspect?"

Thatcher looked up at him.

"She's in the papers," Charlie said, rising to go.

A serious suspect? Inescapably, the death of Peggy Lindsay and now of Donald Lindsay was bound up with the divorce of Gilbert and Olivia Austin. But was Olivia the kind of woman . . .?

Thatcher firmly shook his head, and reached for the folder that Trinkam had deposited on his desk. His attention was going to be riveted on matters germane to investment banking.

Trinkam however had not quite finished. "Specially hard on the Witherses," he said reflectively. "They've lived like aristocracy—if aristocracy lives well these days. Insulated from most normal human experiences." He shook his head; Charlie Trinkam was a great booster of normal human experiences. "Hell of a way to take the plunge, isn't it? With murder. Well, I'd appreciate it if you'd read that summary, John."

When the door closed behind him, Thatcher stared idly at the papers before him. Trinkam, essentially amoral and nondomestic, had put his finger on it. The murders in Shaftesbury were more than a tragedy; they were a revelation.

He brought himself up short. Possibly the experience might be a revelation for the Austins. Bradford Withers would escape unscathed; he had his own defenses.

Thatcher drummed irritably on his desk. Assiduous efforts on Saturday and Sunday should bring the situation under control. Before departing for the day, he indicated to Miss Corsa that he would need her Saturday morning. Miss Corsa, as ever, was unmoved. The same message left Kenneth

Nicolls, on the other hand, excessively polite. "Yes, sir," he said. And no more. It was enough.

Thatcher's last visitor of the day was a broken man. It was not immediately obvious. Although it was after six o'clock, Lincoln Hauser was still smiling. He advanced into Thatcher's office on the balls of his feet, an incongruously boyish air about him.

But he was no longer thinking positively.

"I expected the worst," he said after a hearty exchange of salutations. There was a measure of satisfaction in his voice.

"You did?" Thatcher asked cautiously.

"A minimum of publicity," Hauser quoted, bitterness entering his voice. "Now look where we are! This thing is completely out of hand."

"Yes," Thatcher said shortly. "Well, Hauser, I suppose you know about this second murder . . ."

"Certainly I do," Hauser said alertly.

"The body was found on Withers' place . . ."

"So the *Journal-American* says," Hauser retorted. "I've already talked to Mr. Withers about it. He wants it all kept out of the papers." He sounded dispirited.

"I know you can't do that," Thatcher said. "But if you can . . ."

But the artist had been pushed too far. He now gave a cry from the heart. "If only I had had a free hand, Thatcher! I can assure you that they could have gone on uncovering bodies in Shaftesbury ad infinitum. I would have had the whole thing under control, if you see what I mean. But—a minimum of publicity! I ask you! What can you do with that?"

Thatcher admitted that Hauser had been restricted.

"Restricted!" Hauser said bitterly. "Why, it's like giving Michelangelo some whipped cream and asking him to carve a statue! Oh, I'll do what I can, but frankly, Thatcher, I tell you I'm getting no pleasure out of this job. There's no challenge to creative thinking! It's plodding, unimaginative."

Thatcher let his gaze stray to the *Journal-American*, folded on his desk by Miss Corsa. "Sloan Prexy Detained in Second Murder."

"There seems to be a good deal for you to get your teeth into," he remarked caustically.

Hauser cast him a look of dislike. "Oh, I'll do my best to calm things down. But—what I could have done! You know,

I'm beginning to wonder if the Sloan Guaranty Trust offers enough scope for a man of more than routine abilities."

The Sloan Guaranty Trust would offer Hauser a vice-presidency over Thatcher's dead body, he decided, controlling the retort that sprang to his lips. He wrung from Hauser the further assurance that while the task was beneath their undoubted ability, he and his staff would leave no stone unturned to keep the press from pillorying Bradford Withers, his family and the Sloan.

"Not," said Hauser in parting, "that there's much we can do now! Two murders—and a minimum of publicity!"

Over the weekend, Thatcher was forced to the conclusion that, fool he was in every way, Hauser was in this respect correct. By the time two murders had taken place, it was too late to consider unfavorable publicity. Grimly determined, he read what came his way.

BLONDE BEAUTY'S BROTHER
SECOND VICTIM IN CONNECTICUT

October 19, Shaftesbury, Conn.: The body of Donald P. Lindsay, brother of Margaret Lindsay, who was murdered here last Sunday, was discovered this morning in the grounds of the estate belonging to Bradford S. Withers. The victim had been beaten to death by blows from a wooden club found lying near the body. Captain Felix T. Parker, State Police Officer in charge of the investigation, reports that Mr. Lindsay was killed between the hours of two o'clock and five o'clock this morning. The discovery was made by Daniel O'Connell, an employee of Mr. Withers, when he entered the field this morning to move the cattle.

Bradford Withers is president of the Sloan Guaranty Trust in New York and brother of Mrs. Gilbert Austin. Margaret Lindsay and Gilbert Austin were planning to be married after legal termination of the marriage between Mr. Austin and his present wife. Both Mr. and Mrs. Austin have released statements that their contemplated divorce had no bearing on the death of Margaret Lindsay.

The exclusive interview with Daniel O'Connell, field man, dealt heavily with the resentment displayed by the Black

Angus at the invasion of their domain by human passions. There was much speculation as to what the Angus had seen and what they could say if only they had tongues to speak. Personally Thatcher suspected that they had slept throughout the entire incident.

MURDER VICTIM WELL KNOWN
IN NEW YORK THEATRICAL CIRCLE

October 20, New York, N.Y.: Donald P. Lindsay, second victim of the crime wave sweeping Shaftesbury, Connecticut, was a familiar figure in the off-Broadway dramatic world. Shortly after graduation from the Yale School of Drama he joined the Little Theatre as assistant stage manager. The Little Theatre in New York's Greenwich Village was a repertory theatre engaged in revivals of the classics, remembered primarily for its presentation of *Oedipus Rex* in modern dress. More recently Mr. Lindsay was associated with the production of Arkansas Richards' *Winter of the Pelican* at the Christopher Street Theatre last winter.

Mr. Richards, interviewed in his New York City apartment this morning, said he spoke for the entire dramatic community in expressing grief and sorrow at the tragedy. Although still young, Donald Lindsay had shown great promise as assistant set designer, and would be mourned by those who had the pleasure of working with him.

A memorial service will be held at the Little Church Around the Corner on next Tuesday.

Withers, of course, could not be expected to display the same fortitude—at least, not in silence. On Saturday morning, he interrupted the morning's work to report, with barely concealed frenzy, that the police were making a dead set against Olivia Austin. "And why couldn't Hauser keep references to Olivia out of the *Times*, John? God knows, we advertise enough . . ."

"He's doing his best," said Thatcher, again thankful that Withers was spared the tabloids.

"He's a fool," said Withers. And when Withers called a man a fool, Thatcher reflected, that meant something. He waved Nicolls to a chair and gestured him to wait, when Withers was reminded of another grievance.

"And those damned police impounded my antlers and won't release them, John."

"Call the Governor," said Thatcher acidly. "I'm going to have to ring off, Brad."

The next two hours were notable for the amount of work that was cleared from his desk, and a telephone call from Stanton Carruthers who said, in suitably guarded tones, that somebody, unspecified, should try to shut Bradford Withers up. "He's making things . . . ah, worse," said the wily legalist.

"I take it you've been up there?" said Thatcher shortly.

"Just got back."

"How bad is it?"

Stanton Carruthers' reply, inaudible to Kenneth Nicolls and Walter Bowman who were waiting until Thatcher's attention could be recaptured by the documents they were bearing, was clearly not optimistic.

Despite a lowering frown, Thatcher said nothing. "Let's try to get that Wheeler portfolio cleared up, Nicolls," he said sharply.

The next interruption was from Miss Corsa.

"Mr. Thatcher," she said with considerable bravery, "there's a call for you from the Governor's office. It's about some antlers."

John Putnam Thatcher gave vent to a long-suppressed explosion of wrath.

When he finished, he found his Miss Corsa still waiting.

"I apologize for the language, Miss Corsa." he said.

"Certainly, Mr. Thatcher," she said frigidly. "About the antlers?"

"Tell him I'll call back."

On Sunday, Thatcher received four telephone calls from Bradford Withers, one from Stanton Carruthers, and one from George C. Lancer, Chairman of the Board of Directors of the Sloan Guaranty Trust.

On Monday morning, he arrived at his office to find that Miss Corsa was already at work, with two messages awaiting him.

"You're to call Mr. Withers," she said averting her eyes, "and Mr. Cooke says he has to have Mr. Withers' signature on the Rampollion closing."

Thatcher bowed to the inevitable. "Line up the Sloan plane, Miss Corsa," he said resignedly, half angry and half relieved. "Presumably now that the Indians are gone we can use it. And tell Gabler to get his files together—he wants Withers' signature too—and Trinkam, for that matter. They're going with me. This bank is going to function if Mr. Withers goes to the penitentiary."

Miss Corsa, who was practical-minded, did not respond to this pleasantry. "And Mr. Nicolls?" she said.

Thatcher was at the door of his office. "Nicolls? No, I don't think we'll need him . . ."

"Mr. Thatcher," said the realist, "if you and Mr. Trinkam and Mr. Gabler and Mr. Withers are in Shaftesbury . . ."

"Yes," said Thatcher impatiently.

". . . and your secretaries are here in New York . . ."

"Yes?"

". . . who is going to run errands for you?"

Thatcher grinned suddenly at this uncompromising view of the junior professional staff. "Right as usual, Miss Corsa," he said. "And Mr. Nicolls."

15 "... from this spacious dwelling"

BY NO STRETCH OF THE IMAGINATION COULD the delegation from the Sloan Guaranty Trust that ventured into the wilds of western Connecticut be described as joyful.

In the first place, a sudden localized fog rendered flight to Winsted impracticable.

"There's no visibility at all in Shaftesbury, Mr. Thatcher," reported Miss Corsa not long after his decision to remove to the country had been made.

"That," he growled, "is truer than you know. See if you can get us on that damned milk train again."

Accordingly, at eight o'clock on Monday evening (when the latest edition of the *Hartford Courant* was asking, "Is There a Homicidal Maniac in Shaftesbury?"), the local station welcomed two package-laden women returning from a shopping trip to Bergdorf's, and a tired quartet of financial specialists, each of whom looked with unconcealed distaste around the picturesque village, charmingly illuminated by historically accurate lantern-like street lights.

"It looks clear as a bell to me," said Charlie Trinkam sourly, depositing his attaché case at his feet and examining the sky. "Just another one of Mother Nature's little jokes. Shaftesbury seems full of them." A confirmed New Yorker, Charlie became uneasy when forced into areas in which the basic living unit is the family. He winced as a station wagon, with an inordinate number of toddlers hanging from its various windows, drove up to collect the Bergdorf contingent.

Everett Gabler, looking unaccountably dusty in the clean,

127

clear air of the Berkshires, compressed his lips. His passions in life were business—most particularly Rails and Industrials —and health food. Almost everything else was so much wormwood to him. Five hours on the New Haven Railroad had shaken him, as a man and as a specialist. "Well," he said resolutely, "if I can get Withers' signature tonight, I could Special Delivery the contract to Philadelphia. . . ."

As Miss Corsa had predicted, Kenneth Nicolls was doing the errands. He gestured for the ancient taxi that only last Tuesday had borne him on his appointed rounds. He was almost, but not quite, resigned to this further separation from Brooklyn Heights and all that was most dear to him.

"Why," he had passionately asked heaven (and incidentally his wife Jane) "why do I have to spend my life junketing around the country? I'm not a doctor! I'm not a space explorer! I'm not a politician! Just a banker trying to make a buck . . ."

"Exactly," said Jane with sinister emphasis. "I'll pack some extra shirts, just in case. . . ."

John Putnam Thatcher entered the taxi fully aware of the emotions gripping his little band. He made no ill-timed efforts to dispel the gloom. "Shaftesbury Inn," he directed the driver. "And Everett, resign yourself to the fact that nothing in Shaftesbury is going to be simple. We've moved here only to try to equalize the Sloan's chances."

The driver then entered the conversation. "Heard about our murders?" he asked with relish.

"Yes," said Kenneth Nicolls when his superiors showed no inclination to reply.

"Wouldn't advise going out in Shaftesbury after dark," said the driver, pulling up at the inn.

"An obvious attempt to drum up business," Gabler whispered to Thatcher. Thatcher's attention, however, was diverted by new perils. In the parking lot of the inn he saw many station wagons, each loaded with crates. No sooner had the Sloan contingent entered the inn than he realized he had never fully come to grips with the fact that, murders notwithstanding, Shaftesbury was host to the Housatonic Dog Show.

Directly before the registration desk was a pile of crates from which hideous yapping noises emanated. These noises were being ignored by an animated group of dog fanciers in professional discussion.

"I tell you, the minute we went into the ring at Hartford, Griselda sat down!" said a plump lady. "I was mortified."

"Overtired, probably. Now let me tell you . . ."

"I beg your pardon," said Kenneth automatically as he moved a step. He discovered that he had backed into a Saint Bernard who looked reproachful.

"Are you the Weimaraners?" a bald man darted up to ask.

Hastily, Charlie Trinkam denied it.

"Dammit," said the bald man, consulting a list. "They said they would get here before eight." He moved, still muttering, toward the sitting room which rang with a subdued hum, punctuated by canine comments.

There was, Thatcher noticed, a decidedly yellowing spot on the pleasant old carpet.

"Might as well try to register," he said, just as two things happened.

Madame Dumont, looking a trifle more tired than she had at last encounter, issued from the sitting room.

"Ah, Mr. Thatcher, and Mr. Nicolls," she cried, as if hailing a rescue party. She made her way through the crush to them. Charlie Trinkam, assimilating the lady's undeniable charms, brightened immediately.

And, a plucky little Scotty, eluding his master's slack grasp, did some clever broken field running from the sitting room, across the hallway, around legs and crates, and reached his goal. There without pausing a moment, he sank his firm little teeth into Everett Gabler's meager calf.

After a surprising amount of vituperation during which a number of bystanders claimed that Everett Gabler had provoked Ch. Brian Boru, the Sloan contingent was escorted from the scene of battle under a truce flag borne by Madame Dumont who also took charge of ministering to the wounded.

"That dog should be quarantined," said Gabler irritably, his professional poise severely shaken as Madame Dumont directed him to roll up his pants leg while his colleagues looked on with undisguised interest.

"Quarantined? No, shot!" said Giselle darkly. "These dogs. And the dog people, who are worse. Does that hurt?"

Gabler hissed slightly as she dabbed iodine on his shin, and replied that it was nothing. Giselle rewarded him with a smile that caused Charlie Trinkam to clear his throat meaningfully.

"And, as you see," Madame Dumont continued, abandoning her patient, "we can give you only these three little rooms, here in the annex. But at least, you are away from the dogs. . . ."

"Nicolls and I can get to work on these papers," said Gabler, "and we'll try to get hold of Withers later tonight."

Thatcher felt a twinge of compunction as he abandoned his two minions and joined Madame Dumont, who seemed to be reaching an excellent understanding with Charlie in the hallway. Gabler, of course, would do his best to re-create the sixth floor of the Sloan no matter where the wind took him, but young Nicolls? Well, it would cure him of the mad urge to travel that Thatcher had observed in so many businessmen. Let him learn that it isn't all expense accounts and skittles.

Unaware of the extreme injustice of this, he listened to Giselle's confidences as she led them through the maze of twisting stairs that connected annex and main building. "Ah, he will not see Mr. Withers tonight . . . watch your head, here . . . Mr. Withers and Olivia are in conference . . . and have you gentlemen dined?"

Unhesitatingly, Charlie Trinkam sank the sandwich wrested from the New Haven.

"Then you must have something to eat," Madame Dumont decided. "In my dining room, since the public dining room is now closed. We will send something to M'sieur Gabler . . ."

"Shredded carrots," suggested Charlie happily.

Thatcher, a gentleman and a sportsman, would have abandoned the field to him if he had not been hungry. His presence was not noticeably dampering.

"What a week we have had!" said Giselle, leading them to her quarters. "First Peggy—then Donald! You cannot imagine the excitement! We have had meetings about it, you understand. But still, Mr. Withers and Olivia insist that we go on with the dog show! But they are no help"—and a distant paroxysm of barking brought a long-suffering look to her eye—"so it is all left to me. Gil, of course, stays at the inn and he does what he can with these dog people. But Olivia—no! Myself, I think that with two murders—it is not the nicest thing to have a dog show—but they insist . . ."

"Can't Brad help?" asked Charlie sympathetically, little realizing, Thatcher thought as he took the chair that Giselle indicated, that he was referring to a rival made formidable by propinquity if by nothing else.

"Ah, Mr. Withers," said Giselle from the doorway where she was giving instructions to a waitress. Her tone was modulated to convey a good deal of information.

"Ah," said Charlie, completing a remarkably effective exchange.

"Mr. Withers is worried," Giselle continued briskly. "They have the police at Ridge Road Farm all the time. Then there is the *affaire* of the antlers that we will never hear the end of. And in the village, there is bad feeling. People do not like it, you understand, that there are two murders and that nobody knows who killed Peggy or Donald. I do not like it myself," she went on matter-of-factly, "but of course business must go on."

It was a sentiment approved by both bankers. Giselle poured wine with a steady hand, and appeared to be listening for further barking while Charlie applied himself to the roast chicken which had just arrived.

"Do the police seriously suspect Olivia?" Thatcher asked.

"Who knows?" Madame Dumont replied. "But many people do, let me tell you. Since that poor little rat Donald is found murdered on the Withers place, they ask about the fight that Donald had here with Olivia. And they talk about Donald, who ran to the police with the story about his sister. It makes everybody wonder, you see?"

Charlie looked a trifle startled by this Gallic realism while Thatcher pondered. What eccentricity on Bradford Withers' part—what oddity on Gilbert Austin's part—would a serious threat to Olivia provoke?

He determined to find out only after a good night's sleep. Accordingly, after excusing himself from his companions— and contenting himself with an icy glare at Trinkam who remarked that he was looking a little tired—he removed himself to the public telephone, waited for a fat woman and a fox terrier to vacate it, and then dialed the Withers place.

"Thank God you're here," said his harassed superior. "Olivia's here. Listen, John, why don't you come right up? For that matter, why not stay here?"

Uncompromisingly, Thatcher refused the invitation to "discuss things" with Mrs. Austin. "And, it will be easier for me to . . . to coordinate things if I stay here at the inn."

Withers sounded disappointed. "You know best, John.

Now, Gabler called me with some damned nonsense about a contract. At a time like this. . . ."

The Flinders contract represented four million dollars, Thatcher did not remind Withers. Untimely it might be; damned nonsense it was not.

"You'd better see him and sign the thing," he suggested, idly brushing dog hairs from his sleeve.

"Oh, all right!" Withers grumbled. "I'll see him at noon tomorrow . . . but John, I want to talk to you . . ."

"I'll be up there at nine o'clock tomorrow morning," Thatcher told him firmly. He rang off, and congratulated himself on his decision to remove to Shaftesbury. With all its discomforts it was going to be productive of something—witness the Withers signature on the Flinders contract. These self-satisfied communings were interrupted by a tap. Thatcher turned. A Dalmation looked in at him challengingly. He was apparently eager to use the phone.

On Tuesday morning, John Putnam Thatcher breakfasted very early in the Shaftesbury Inn's pleasantly sunlit dining room. Not, however, early enough.

The whole dog crew, including a surprisingly efficient-looking Gilbert Austin, were already milling around the hallway, ready to remove to some distant meadow for preliminary judging, obedience testing or some such momentous activity. There was a great heaving of crates, loading of station wagons and crying of "Here! Spot!"

Austin grinned briefly at the banker as he became entangled in a matched team of Maltese and earned a furious look from a small man brandishing a box of talcum powder. "I have just brushed them, sir!" he said accusingly.

"Try leaching them, as well," said Thatcher, escaping.

In the dining room, Everett Gabler and Kenneth Nicolls, the latter a trifle groggy, were deep in technical conversation.

"Charlie," said Gabler, "isn't down yet."

"I didn't expect him to be," said Thatcher, taking his place.

"Tsk," said Everett. "Well, once we've got the Flinders papers cleared up—and Nicolls and I are going to see Withers at noon—we'll check with Charlie about the annual meeting that Withers wanted to attend. . . ."

Thatcher listened to these optimistic remarks, but spared

Gabler the knowledge that he himself was to have access to the Sloan's president sooner.

". . . and put through a call to Walter Bowman," Gabler said, quaffing a glass of warm water and lemon juice with every evidence of gusto.

Thatcher and Nicolls shuddered.

Thatcher left Gabler and Nicolls at the breakfast table, deep in plans and stratagems designed to circumvent Bradford Withers' congenital indifference to the business side of banking, and strolled into the lobby. There remained only one basset hound, regarding him with an expression that reminded him of his chief. All of the dogs, and it was to be hoped the dog people, were elsewhere.

Madame Dumont, sitting at the registration desk, greeted him with an enigmatic smile just as Gilbert Austin materialized from the sitting room.

"Going up to the farm," he announced, keys dangling. "I'll have to get up to the show in about an hour, but I have to stop at the farm. Do you want a ride?"

"I do," Thatcher replied economically, wondering what was leading Austin to visit his home as he followed him to the Mercedes parked around the corner. He should have known it was dogs.

"Want to see Roger," Austin told him. "Bold Baron isn't well. We're worried about him. One of our entries . . . then we have this damned kennel tour . . ."

"Yes," Thatcher said.

". . . had to call off the cocktail party, of course," Austin continued, pulling out of the parking place and sweeping around the corner at a smart pace. "But we still have to take the exhibitors through the Austindale Kennels on Wednesday. I think that means we have to give them coffee, at least, don't you?"

"Absolutely," said Thatcher. Much as he admired a man who could rise above personal tragedy to fulfill his civic commitments, he felt that Austin's current interest in dogs—and there was no doubt that the man was looking more alive than he had since the whole wretched Peggy Lindsay affair boiled up—argued a certain heartlessness.

". . . worried about Bold Baron," Austin was saying.

"How's Mrs. Lindsay?" Thatcher asked brutally. He had not liked the woman, but her losses seemed great enough to merit the sympathy that the rest of Shaftesbury wanted to lavish on sick dogs.

Austin was taken aback by the tone of voice. "She's collapsed," he said. "That is, Dr. Cooper says she's all right, but she says that she can't trust herself to get out of bed."

"You've seen her?" Thatcher demanded.

"Of course," said Austin, rather austerely. He drove in silence. "It's awkward, you know."

"I do indeed," said Thatcher.

"I mean about Donald wanting to talk to me before he was murdered. It made the police wonder."

"No doubt. They heard about it?"

"Everybody did," Austin said briefly. "Well, I didn't see him and that's all I can say."

If nothing else, Thatcher had diverted him from Bold Baron. "Thatcher," he said, turning to negotiate the turn off Ridge Road. "Do you think that the police seriously suspect Olivia? Giselle was telling me this morning . . ."

Thatcher looked at the sleek black car in front of the Withers' portico. "Why don't you ask them? They appear to be on the premises."

"They always are," said his companion. Nevertheless, he did not drive across the road to confer with Roger Kincaid about a sick dog, but followed Thatcher up the steps.

"I think," he said resolutely, "that it's time to clear this up. I can't let people go on suffering because I was weak." He sounded, Thatcher thought uncharitably, rather like his son.

The white-coated houseman ushered Thatcher and Austin into the library. No signs of disarray appeared in the well run house, Thatcher noted in passing. Fresh flowers filled the great copper bowls in the hallway while the staff went on its rounds with a quiet efficiency that was testimonial to the absent Mrs. Withers. Certainly Bradford Withers had nothing to do with it.

"Now, Parker," he was saying to the quiet policeman who looked impassively at him, "let's be reasonable about this." He made his voice heavily reasonable. "We've been cooperative—surely you can't deny that. Now, if only you'd be a little more cooperative . . . oh, hello there, Thatcher! Gil, good to see you! Juan, do you want to bring us some coffee. . . ."

His social instinct, probably the most developed of Bradford Withers' faculties, did not falter in the face of Parker's unresponsive silence, the air of determination with which Gilbert Austin looked around—or the dismay that John Putnam Thatcher could hardly hide.

Had they interrupted Withers in some labored and inept attempt to suborn the police? Sitting down, Thatcher felt that strong Shaftesbury-induced yearning for a train to New York; yet, as one in duty bound to the absent Stanton Carruthers (and the Board of Directors of the Sloan Guaranty Trust, for that matter) he steeled himself to enter the conversation, when all was made clear.

"Just telling Parker here that I appreciate his difficulties," Withers said chattily, his confidence augmented by the sudden enlargement of his audience. "But I feel that it's only fair to return those antlers. Don't mind for myself, you understand, but they were a gift to Giselle—Madame Dumont, you know —and you know how a man feels . . ."

"The Governor's Office called," Parker said without undue emotion. "I was just explaining to Mr. Withers that we still don't understand why Miss Lindsay was wrapped around them."

Austin winced but Brad nodded. "But, you've measured them and photographed them, haven't. you? What more do you want?"

Thatcher applied himself to the coffee produced by the admirable houseboy. Bradford Withers' natural insulation spared him two facts; the first, that Captain Parker no doubt regarded his desire for the return of his antlers as extremely suspicious; the second, that the enterprising Charlie Trinkam was currently rendering the antlers devoid of meaning. Charlie would no doubt be the straw to break the camel's back.

Meanwhile the camel had not finished his peroration when Gilbert Austin, ignoring the coffee, unceremoniously interrupted him.

"Parker," he said with a quiet authority that completely eclipsed his brother-in-law, "is it true that you're seriously concerned about my wife Olivia's story?"

The question transformed the farce to stark realism. The temperature in the room seemed suddenly to drop. There was no shift in Parker's expression or voice when he turned to Austin, but he was clearly a different man.

"Peggy Lindsay was killed after she had a fight with your

wife," he said choosing his words. "A fight that Mrs. Austin claims had nothing to do about the girl's pregnancy. A fight, she says, about the farm. Then, after she denies having seen the girl, the fact slips out, and Donald Lindsay reports it to us. And on Friday night, Donald Lindsay's head was bashed in. Your wife was at home, asleep, alone." He stopped. "Yes, Mr. Austin, we're interested in Mrs. Austin."

Gilbert Austin was unmoved by this recital. "You don't believe that Olivia is telling the truth about what she and Peggy were fighting about, is that it?" he persisted.

Wondering what was coming, Thatcher suddenly noticed that, from the fireplace, Bradford Withers was watching his brother-in-law with open-mouthed anxiety.

"I don't say I don't believe it," Parker replied. "It's unconfirmed . . ."

"I can confirm it," said Gilbert Austin, quietly triumphant. "I was there. I saw and heard part of the fight."

Parker looked at him; Thatcher put down his coffee cup; but the silence was broken by the noisy sound of relief from the fireplace. "Thank God," said Brad. "I saw your car, Gil. I didn't want to say anything but when I was on my way to Winsted, I saw your car parked outside of the farm . . ."

Austin looked up at him. "Is that why . . . by God! Brad! I thought you've been acting strangely."

Brad's relief was almost tangible. "You can't blame me for thinking . . ."

Nothing, Thatcher thought instantly, was less desirable than that Parker should hear whatever vagrant thoughts had crossed Withers' mind. "You didn't go inside?" he asked, incurring a look from Parker that told him how clearly his motives were apprehended.

"Yes," said Austin, sounding like a man relieved of a burden. "Yes, I wanted to talk to Olivia. I knocked, then I went inside—and there was a fight going on in the living room. Frankly, I just turned on my heel . . ."

"Can't blame a man for that," Withers confided to an unresponsive Parker. Whatever qualms had been raised by seeing Austin's car parked in front of Ridge Road Farm— about his brother-in-law, or possibly even Olivia Austin—he was now palpably and enormously relieved.

Thatcher watched him exchange a confident smile with Austin. Both of them belonged to that class of men who believe not only that truth prevails, but that it shines by its own light.

Austin, indeed, looked puzzled when Captain Parker broke his silence. "I have," he said, admirably unsarcastic, "just a few questions."

"Yes?" said Austin courteously. Thatcher immediately reminded himself to find out if any Sloan customers utilized the services of Austin and Austin, Engineering Consultants.

To Thatcher's sincere admiration, Parker did not snarl. Instead, with unwearied patience, he reviewed Austin's story. Peggy Lindsay and Mrs. Austin had been engaged in a bitter quarrel on Sunday afternoon when Austin arrived on the scene. They had been fighting, so far as Austin had been able to grasp, about Ridge Road Farm. No, no—here his color heightened but he sounded very firm—no mention had been made of the fact that Peggy Lindsay was expecting a child. "It was," Austin concluded repressively, "extremely unpleasant."

It accounted for Gilbert Austin's bad temper on Sunday night, Thatcher thought. He had been shocked by seeing the girl he was going to marry transformed into a virago. Or had he been shocked by Olivia Austin?

For that matter, did Austin, now earnestly replying to Parker's probing questions, have the remotest idea of how extraordinary this tale sounded? Did he realize that it suggested a motive for killing Peggy Lindsay?

He did not, because he was absorbing something else.

"That's interesting," said Parker, rising unhurriedly to take his leave. "You confirm your wife's story in all its details— the story she tried to hide, the story you didn't mention earlier. Then Mr. Withers confirms *your* story although he swore earlier that he hadn't seen a thing . . ."

"Now look here," Withers harrumphed.

"*And,*" Parker continued, "that would seem to be a neat confirmation of Mrs. Austin's story. Very neat. It's a shame none of you mentioned it earlier. Well, thanks for the coffee Mr. Withers . . . oh yes, the antlers. We'll probably take them back to the inn. The Governor can put enough pressure on us to get those antlers back to you. Not much more, though."

With this Parthian shot he exited, bearing, Thatcher conceded, the honors.

"What did he mean by that?" Withers demanded when he returned from escorting the policeman to the door.

"He thinks that both of you are lying," said Thatcher baldly.

"Lying?" said Gilbert Austin, flushing. From a man with his record of recent activities, this self-righteousness impressed Thatcher unfavorably.

"Good God!" said Withers, deeply shocked.

For the first time, John Putnam Thatcher felt deep and genuine pity for Olivia Withers Austin.

16 "...with varied scope for activities"

AFTER DINNER THAT EVENING, THATCHER joined his staff in the bar and cocktail lounge of the Shaftesbury Inn (labeled the "Montmartre Bistro" in the inn's advertising brochures) for a progress report.

"It's a mess," said Charlie Trinkam without noticeable sorrow. "I tried to talk to Withers this afternoon but he had that kid with him . . ."

"Bud," Ken supplied gloomily.

"It would be," Charlie said. "Couldn't get near him. So I just slipped away and improved the afternoon . . ."

"I'll bet you did," said Ken. To himself.

Everett Gabler signaled a passing waiter for a refill on his glass of celery tonic and announced that he had managed to get Withers' signature on the Flinders contract. "It's on its way to Philadelphia," he announced. "It wasn't easy . . ."

Thatcher looked at him inquiringly.

"Mrs. Austin," said Gabler. As he and Nicolls waited in the hallway, the sound of voices raised had reached them from the Withers living room. Then Olivia Austin was at the door, drawing gloves on rather jerkily. "That, Brad," she said calmly, "is one of the silliest things I have heard in my life. Hello, Mr. Nicolls."

It was enough to shake anybody.

"I can't convince myself," Gabler said, "that Withers had the slightest idea of what he was signing."

Thatcher listened to this rather irritably. His own afternoon had been unparalleled in horror. After accepting a ride back to the village with Gilbert Austin, who was still enraged to think that the police should doubt his veracity, he had decided to get a newspaper.

This, it developed, was a mistake.

As he walked briskly toward the railroad station, he became aware of a stately figure preceding him down the street. An incautious step around it—and he found himself looking into the face of the bereaved Mrs. Lindsay.

"Ah, Mr. Thatcher," she said, in failing accents. At her side was Elvira.

"Be brave, Margaret."

Hideously embarrassed, Thatcher murmured something about loss.

"Only a mother can know what I feel," she replied, groping for a handkerchief. "I have been simply prostrate, of course, but Elvira—dear Elvira has simply insisted that I rise from my bed . . ."

Elvira clucked.

". . . and go on. Although what I can live for . . ."

Elvira then contributed her mite. "Margaret, we have to see Mr. Bewley, you know . . ."

A slight tightening of Mrs. Lindsay's mouth answered this. She sniffed again, raised tragic eyes to John Thatcher, and allowed herself to be led away.

He found he had lost all appetite for *The New York Times*.

"Who," he asked Giselle Dumont whom he found hurrying into the Montmartre Bistro on his return, "who is Mr. Bewley?"

"Bewley?" she said. "He has an office on Central Street. . ."

"What kind of office?"

"Real estate and insurance. George, we must be sure to bring up the beer. . . ."

She hurried away, and Thatcher cravenly spent the rest of the afternoon eluding his subordinates and superiors, barricaded behind an elaborate summary of the Handasyde report. Why, he wondered, turning its pages, did he find his mind wandering to Greek tragedy?

". . . very suspicious," said Gabler, rousing him from recollections.

"Who is?" Thatcher asked shortly. It was a foolish question on the face of it; Olivia Austin, Gilbert Austin, Bud Austin, Giselle Dumont, for that matter—half of Shaftesbury seemed to be behaving oddly.

"Withers," Gabler said crisply. "There's something a little evasive about him."

"He was, it develops, lying about having seen nothing the afternoon of Peggy Lindsay's death. He saw Gil Austin's car on Ridge Road," Thatcher reminded him. "In a way it's a comfort. I was afraid he might be involved with some imbecility with Madame that would make our lot with the tabloids even harder . . ."

"Withers," Charlie interrupted to ask, "and Giselle?"

"Yes," Thatcher said. "Why?"

"Waste," said Charlie censoriously. "Sheer waste. She needs a man of wide experience."

Thatcher was amused. "You're thinking of someone like Gilbert Austin, I take it." Even as the words left his mouth, he wondered why he hadn't thought of it before. With Austin resident in the inn, with the easy understanding he had reached with Madame Dumont? Perhaps that was what was bothering Olivia.

"I was not," Charlie retorted.

Gabler gazed at his colleagues. "I can see that we're going to get a lot of work done," he said with rather prim sarcasm. "Murders! Divorces! And to top it all—these dog people!" Gabler bobbed toward the bar.

The bankers were sitting in a small pool of isolation amidst the disruptions attendant upon the Housatonic Dog Show which had just triumphantly completed its first day. Owners, handlers and breeders had stormed into the bar like an invading army after the evening's final round of judging. Whiskey flowed like water while congratulations were showered on lucky winners, imprecations were defiantly hurled at absent judges, and odds were freely offered on tomorrow's events. Small clusters gathered in corners for serious discussions concerning possible trades, stud services and forthcoming litters. The largest groups were absorbed respectively in the problems of changing the American Kennel Club's breed standard for chows and maintaining the price of poodle clips. Price cutting had reared its ugly head in the latter field of endeavor.

"What they need is some Fair Trade legislation," announced Charlie, fascinated by the commercial aspects of this problem.

"I don't expect the discount houses will enter the field for some time," Thatcher pointed out.

"You never know," said Gabler darkly.

"Oh, come on, Everett, cheer up," urged Charlie. "If we have any free time, I'm going to take in the Doberman show tomorrow morning. It's always nice to have a change in pace."

"Hmph! I suppose that's what you were fixing up with Madame Dumont."

"That's right," admitted Charlie easily. "She's promised to explain the workings of dog shows to me. After all, you never know, we may want to underwrite a kennel some time."

Gabler was unmoved by a justification he had heard from Trinkam many times before—although not as enraged as on the historic occasion in Paris when Trinkam had suggested another activity that the Sloan Guaranty might some day feel inclined to finance.

"I thought you were eager to get Withers' OK on the Handasyde report," he said waspishly.

Charlie grinned unrepentently. "Nicolls can handle it," he replied, thereby justifying Miss Corsa's foresight. "If I get tied up, that is."

Thatcher intervened diplomatically. "Did you get Brad to read the Amesbury estimates, Everett?"

"I did not! I was lucky to get his signature. He didn't have the time to do a single thing more. So, tomorrow . . ."

Thatcher made soothing noises. Bringing Everett along had been a mistake, he had to admit. Never noted for his tact, the irritation induced by dislocation left Gabler in no mood to cater to Withers' self-importance.

A stocky man in a checked vest strutted past their table, spilling some bourbon in the process. His progress was impeded by shouts from each booth he passed.

"Nice work, Oldfield!"

"Congratulations, fella! Let's see you keep it up tomorrow."

"Come on, Oldfield, have a drink. You've got something to celebrate!"

"Listen, Chet. I want to talk to you about our entry at the Westminster if you've got a minute, fella. . . ."

Thatcher eyed the hero of the hour with disfavor. The bourbon had fallen on him.

"Who is that? Our latest astronaut?"

"That's Chester Oldfield," said Trinkam, already displaying the results of Giselle's tuition. "Until a short time ago he was the second best handler in New England. He got four

Best in Breeds before dinner. Seems to have added to his collection tonight."

"Oh?" said Thatcher, reflecting that here was yet another motive for the murder of Peggy Lindsay.

Trinkam followed his thoughts. "He was a beneficiary of the Lindsay girl's death, all right. I understand that he's raising his fee schedule tomorrow. But he's got a good alibi. At the critical time, he was showing a Chihuahua in Toledo . . ."

Thatcher nodded gravely. "Impregnable," he agreed. "And I don't really think that anybody would kill a dog handler—and her brother too—merely to raise his own fees."

"Might not be a bad idea," Trinkam countered. "Knock off enough dog handlers, and you'd have a nice little monopoly set up. You could charge what you wanted. We'd better keep an eye on this Oldfield."

Bringing Charlie to Shaftesbury had not been a mistake. He knew how to handle Withers and, as a by-product, the Sloan Guaranty Trust had gained an expert on the dog business. You could never tell when that might come in handy. The ability to orient himself rapidly in esoteric commercial enterprises is the hallmark of the good securities man; Charlie had simply chosen an unusual method of orientation.

The subject of their idle exchange was deep in spirited conversation when there was a rude interruption.

"Oldfield, I want a word with you." It was not one of the handler's admirers seeking an audience—the peremptory tone made that clear. Turning, Thatcher saw Roger Kincaid standing in the doorway. His face set in grim lines, Kincaid advanced into the room, shouldering aside several breeders who came up to greet him warmly.

"You looking for me, Kincaid? I tell you I'm a little busy right now. If it can wait . . ."

"It can't," said Kincaid shortly.

"Now just a minute, Kincaid . . ."

"Never mind that. I've got something to settle and we're going to settle it right now. Who's started all this filthy talk about Bold Baron having distemper?"

The words, which scarcely seemed catastrophic to the bankers, had the effect of producing a thunderous silence in the room. Like some incredible sequence in an old-fashioned Western film, the line at the bar swiveled to get a clear view while a space magically cleared itself between the two protagonists.

"Distemper! Good God, I had no idea," sputtered Oldfield. "Why I didn't even know that you had it at your kennel."

"We don't have it at our kennel!" shouted Kincaid. "And if this is how you intend to win the Doberman show tomorrow, let me tell you, you've got another think coming."

"Who the hell do you think you're talking to? And what do you mean letting a Dog Show come to a town that's infected?"

"There wasn't any talk about infection until today. And I don't believe it's any accident that it started just before the Dobermans are judged. Somebody's trying to get the Austindale Kennel disqualified. I don't know if it's you or one of the breeders, but whoever it is, isn't getting away with it."

"By Jesus, you've got your nerve! If you think I'm going to take Baldur von Schulenbach into any ring with distemper in it, you're mad! Why, you're probably carrying the stuff yourself!" Oldfield started to back away from Kincaid as if he were a leper. In fact the entire population of the bar showed a marked disinclination to come within spitting distance of the Austin farm manager.

"We're not taking this lying down," Kincaid snarled.

"I'll have every dog from your place disqualified!" Oldfield retorted.

"I don't doubt that's what you had in mind all along. The minute I heard the talk, I knew there was some dirty work behind it."

"This is the first I've heard of it but believe me it isn't the last you've heard of it. I don't need a lot of tricks to win blue ribbons. What's more . . ."

Kincaid slammed a fist down on the nearest table. "We won't let this stop here! We've got one sick dog in our kennel and that's all. Anybody can look at it. We've never had distemper and we don't have it now."

"That's your story," Oldfield said pugnaciously. "But you're damned right someone's going to take a look at the place. I'm calling the state veterinarian right now. And God help you if you've had distemper there and didn't stop the show from coming here."

"Go ahead and call the state vet," challenged Kincaid. "Call him right now. Get him down here as quick as you can.

We're only too damn willing to get this thing cleared up. And we're going ahead tomorrow, vet or no vet!"

But at this, a chorus of protest arose from the bystanders.

"No, absolutely not," sputtered a little white-haired man sporting a tweed cap. "If you bring any dog near the ring I'm loading up my collies this minute. I don't care if Tippy did take a Best in Breed." (Tippy was, of course, Macneil's Fione nach Machamnor.)

The consensus of the gathering was squarely behind the speaker. Dire threats of immediate withdrawal were hurled at Roger from all directions. A woman with bobbed iron-gray hair did not wait to see the result of the discussion but hurried from the room, apparently determined to remove her Scotch terriers from the perils of infection then and there. In the midst of the circle, Roger Kincaid held his ground, his face flushed, his jaw outthrust. "Listen," he said stoutly, "this whole rumor is a lot of nonsense. Somebody—I won't say who—wants to keep our dogs out to be sure to cop the Doberman awards tomorrow!" This provocation brought a low growl from several Doberman owners, and a hurrying forward of judges to act as peacemakers. Speaking with the authority of men who make momentous decisions, they urged Roger to look at their side of the thing. How could anyone in authority condone the entry of a single Austindale dog until the entire kennel had been cleared by medical report? The veterinarians at the show who had to examine all the dogs were, of course, out of the question. The hound judge, a lean cadaverous man, was misguided enough to suggest that the business manager of the Housatonic Dog Show undertake the task. Somebody reminded him that Gilbert Austin held the position. "No. No, I see that," said the hound man. "No, Austin won't do."

The uproar continued with Roger Kincaid maintaining his position. But where Oldfield's suggestions merely infuriated him, he was finally made to see that in fairness to third parties some solution must be reached. Finally, a party of four responsible dog fanciers was selected to contact the state veterinarian. "I'll be in on it," said Kincaid sharply. "Me too," Oldfield countered. Two judges, medical men by profession and thus uniquely fit to discuss disease in measured tones, completed the roster.

The committee retired to Madame Dumont's office to map

strategy, leaving behind them a conversational whirlpool that was far from measured.

". . . distemper! By God, you know what that means! I've heard of kennels that were nearly wiped out. Fellow up in Waltham lost twenty thousand dollars . . ."

"Kincaid may be carrying it. Better change your clothes before you go out to your dogs . . ."

". . . when I heard about the murders I didn't want to come. Just thinking of poor Peggy makes me feel awful. But Bill insisted and now look . . ."

"I wouldn't put it past Oldfield, to tell you the truth . . ."

"Can't believe it. I know the Austins . . ."

". . . in a case like this you can't afford to trust your own mother. I know them too. But I wouldn't let a dog of mine . . ."

Thatcher and Gabler automatically turned to Trinkam as their new-found expert.

"I gather that distemper is contagious," remarked Thatcher in a penetrating tone designed to pierce the hubbub which was shaking the bar to its rafters.

"Highly." Charlie assumed the air of a man prepared to lecture for some time. "One of the greatest hazards in dog breeding. The really terrible thing about it is that human beings, although they don't get it, can carry it. They're developing vaccines against it but they're not perfected."

Gabler struggled against temptation and fell. He had firmly intended that nothing should deflect him from a wholehearted commitment to the problems of the Sloan Guaranty Trust. "Is it fatal?"

"Not always. But the dog's worthless from a commercial point of view. There are a lot of aftereffects—and of course the stud stock is knocked out. You can see what's got these guys going. If any of them carries back distemper from this show, they may wipe out their kennel and their living too. It would take years to reestablish themselves. Another thing about distemper is that it infects a locality. Once you get it, it's hard as hell to get it out of the kennel, or even an apartment."

Thatcher remembered that the state of Bold Baron's health had been occupying whatever time Olivia Austin and Roger Kincaid could spare from their involvement in two murders during the past week. Their concern was certainly more justifiable—although Thatcher had not yet surrendered to his environment to the extent of regarding it as fully justified—if the entire future of the Austindale Kennels were at stake.

"What are the symptoms?" he asked, trying to remember if anybody had been the least bit specific about Bold Baron's ailment.

But Charlie had exhausted his small store of knowledge. "I've just had one lesson so far," he reminded them. "Ask tomorrow afternoon."

"I think we may all benefit by your next lesson," said Thatcher who saw Giselle Dumont threading her way through the tables.

"But is not this terrible?" she demanded as the men rose and Trinkam expertly negotiated a change in position which jockeyed Everett Gabler over to John Thatcher's side of the booth. "What has come over my poor Shaftesbury? Even Roger Kincaid now loses his temper. Never did I think to see him in such a furor."

"Now, what's all this about distemper, Giselle?" asked Charlie.

"I do not know the details, but for a kennel to have it is a social disgrace. Also," she said with an innkeeper's eye to the till, "if this is true, never will Shaftesbury have another dog show."

Shaftesbury, Thatcher pointed out, seemed quite capable of generating its own excitement without resort to institutional assistance.

"Ah, bah! You should have seen us before all this. As quiet and respectable and wealthy a community as one could desire. Now, I do not know what will happen. It seems that it is impossible for this state veterinarian to come before tomorrow. And Roger, though he is white with emotion, he agrees that the Austin dogs will not be shown tomorrow."

"That's hard on him," murmured Charlie with the easy sympathy that made him so invaluable in dealing with Brad Withers.

"Hard on him! Yes," said Giselle giving justice where justice was due. "But, it is hard on me too. You do not think for one moment that these dog people"—she glared about her unapprovingly—"will go to the kennel tour at Ridge Road Farm tomorrow. And risk infection? No! They will all stay here. And what will my staff say when I have assured them for weeks that they would have two hours free to prepare for the Grand Banquet. I shudder to think." Here Giselle suited the action to the word and gave a comprehensive shudder which Charlie watched admiringly. "And what if they all walk out? Everybody must be mobilized. Affairs have reached a crisis. I tell you, it is a tragedy we have here!"

But Thatcher could not repress the feeling that a staff which had weathered the crises of the past two weeks would measure up now that, in the words of Giselle Dumont, real tragedy had been achieved.

17   "...indoors and out."

THE *Wall Street Journal* ONCE RAN AN EDITORIAL constrasting the realism of the American businessman with the starry-eyed utopianism of the American bureaucrat: "When you push a businessman to the wall," the *Journal* pointed out, "he is likely to read the handwriting on it."

Those representatives of the Wall Street financial community temporarily resident in the Shaftesbury Inn justified that tribute on Wednesday morning. After breakfast, they were informally convened in the lobby of the inn; there, with the acumen born of years of hard-eyed scrutiny of prospectuses (not to speak of American businessmen) they faced the undeniable fact that, temporarily at least, attempts to corner Bradford Withers, to get contracts signed, to get reports cleared—in short, to transact business—were doomed.

This *Mene Mene* was bluntly and forthrightly articulated by Everett Gabler (years of dealing with the American Railroad had made him a specialist in handwriting on the wall) as four Kerry Blues, and attendant personnel, bustled past, the rear guard of the massive morning exodus of dogs and dog people to the show.

"There's no use wasting time, John," Gabler announced, more in sorrow than in anger. "I called Withers this morning and it's clearly out of the question to try to get anything out of him."

Silence greeted this observation. It was not Kenneth Nicolls' place to remark that the dicta of his superiors were miracles of the obvious, so he shifted his weight and tried to look respectful. John Thatcher's attention was momentarily attracted by Gilbert Austin, who came hurrying out of the dining room in the wake of the Kerry Blues; he looked every

149

inch a man whose entire attention was on dogs. Charlie Trinkam was never at his best early in the morning.

Gabler cleared his throat, looked around the lobby with dislike, and continued, "It was only to be expected that two murders in which Withers—or his sister or her husband—is implicated . . ."

This reminded Thatcher of his duties to the Sloan.

"Everett, things are bad enough," he said. "Our line is feudal loyalty in the teeth of the evidence."

Gabler bobbed his head, impatiently acknowledging the pleasantry. "At any rate," he continued, gathering steam, "deteriorations were to be expected. I don't approve of them, but I understand them . . ."

"But Everett, the Flinders contract is OK," Charlie pointed out unsympathetically. "It's the damned Handasyde report that's being held up."

Generally speaking, the Flinders contract was Gabler's domain while Trinkam was, officially, concerned about the Handasyde report.

Gabler looked as if he would like to venture a few strictures on the relative devotion to duty hitherto manifested by the Sloan's two trust officers, then decided not to let this tempting opportunity deflect him from the mainstream of his complaint.

"What I do not understand," he said, a disapproving eye on Giselle Dumont, who emerged from her quarters, bestowed a glowing smile on the Sloan contingent and disappeared toward the dining room, "What I do not understand, I say, is why the illness of a Doberman pinscher should be allowed to bring essential bank business to a halt—especially after we have all come here to Connecticut to accommodate Withers. No doubt, Charlie, you can enlighten us."

"What was that?" said Charlie absently. "Missed what you were saying, Everett."

Gabler controlled himself with a strong effort. Under the best of conditions, he was a faultfinder. John Thatcher suspected that this current peevishness might also reflect injudicious sampling of the inn's culinary delights. He looked dyspeptic; on the other hand, he always did.

Nevertheless, Thatcher had to admit that there was something in what Gabler said. The most detached observer would be forced to agree that the murder of Peggy Lindsay, followed by that of her brother—objectionable as he had been—was enough to shatter a stronger man than Bradford Withers. Donald had, in addition, been discovered in the midst of those much-cherished Anguses. And Withers had more than concern for his livestock to distract him; there was Olivia Austin's peculiar behavior, not to speak of her errant husband. Under the circumstances, only a zealot could expect Bradford Withers to give his best attention to the affairs of the Sloan Guaranty Trust. (Or a fool, Thatcher reflected, considering the president's normal performance.)

But precisely why the illness of Champion Bold Baron, a Doberman pinscher, made it impossible for Withers to give his much-tried staff the benefits of his counsel on important matters of business remained obscure despite the long explanations that Thatcher had been privileged to hear when he succeeded Gabler in the telephone booth.

". . . terrible thing, distemper," Withers had said, sounding heated. "There's real danger that the dogs won't recover, you know . . . and the whole kennel could be wiped out. Olivia feels it . . ."

"You certainly have our best wishes," Thatcher said, "but if we could just go over the Handasyde report, Brad . . ."

"Frankly, while we're waiting for the state vet to come," said Withers in man-to-man tones, "I don't think I'd be much use to any of you boys."

Thatcher fairly ground his teeth to repress a retort.

". . . very worried, very worried, I don't mind telling you. Roger insists that it isn't distemper, and he should know, but we can't help being worried. And none of the dog show vets will come up—agreed that the risk of infection was to much. So we're waiting. Of course, Austindale isn't going to show at the show," Withers continued with more concern than he had ever revealed for the Sloan Guaranty Trust. "But we'll have to face that. I tell you, if this is a rumor that somebody planted to keep Caroline of Brunswick . . ."

"Who?"

"She's that nice little bitch that Roger was going to show. Just needs four points. . . ."

Thatcher emerged from the telephone booth to find his subordinates eyeing him hopefully. Only Charlie Trinkam failed to find immediate removal to New York so appealing that not even the prospect of another bone-jerking journey on the New Haven could dim its luster. And, thought Kenneth Nicolls with the optimism of the young, there was always the Bank plane. . . .

"We're going to have to sit this out," Thatcher told them irritably. "We'll take this morning off and we'll tackle Brad this afternoon . . ."

"John," said Charlie enthusiastically. "I think you're absolutely right. Now's no time to abandon ship." He smiled at his colleagues and informed them that he had to see a man about a dog. The dog was, it appeared, in the dining room.

Gabler cast a disgruntled look after him, then told Thatcher and Nicolls that he was going to retire to refresh his knowledge of the details of the Handasyde report. It was already, as Kenneth knew, encyclopedic.

"I'll need Nicolls," Thatcher said, absentmindedly responding to the younger man's involuntary look of entreaty. Prolonged exposure to Gabler's working methods without the safeguards provided by the Sloan—secretaries, coffee breaks, conferences—was a tonic to be administered to junior staff members with discretion.

"Fine," said Gabler hurrying off.

Thatcher watched him. "Well, if nothing else, Nicolls, we can find out how the Sloan is getting along without us. Do you have any change?" Happily, Kenneth managed to dredge some silver from his pockets, but Thatcher's ebbing temper was immediately tried by the long-distance operator in Winsted. Some imperfection in the connection led her to insist that New York City was a figment of the caller's imagination. "I am afray-ud," she intoned, "we do not ha-uv that exchay-unge." The subsequent conversation caused Kenneth to back away nervously.

Thatcher was finally connected with the sixth floor of the Sloan. "Miss Corsa? Thank God."

Miss Corsa greeted her distant superior with calm, then unflatteringly reported that the Sloan was getting along swimmingly without him. ". . . and Mr. Withers."

"There is no need to be offensive," Thatcher said irascibly. "I suppose that Bowman is losing his mind over those trucking stocks now that there's nobody there to hold him down."

"We bought forty thousand shares, yesterday," said Miss Corsa.

"Good Lord!"

Bowman had the defects of his virtues. With proper control his researcher's vast enthusiasm was invaluable. But given his head? "Now Miss Corsa," Thatcher said severely, "I want Bowman to call me before he plunges the whole Investment Division into chaos. I want you to make that clear to him . . ."

"Certainly, Mr. Thatcher," said Rose Theresa Corsa. A lesser woman might have quailed at the prospect of controlling Walter Bowman, a large jovial dreadnaught of a man. On the other hand, Miss Corsa handled John Putnam Thatcher daily.

". . . and Mr. Hauser," she said.

"That insufferable ass," Thatcher muttered.

"He has a resignation ready," Miss Corsa said reprovingly. "But he wants to know whom he should sent it to."

Again Thatcher spoke forcefully, and at length. He emerged to find Nicolls prudently deep in conversation with Charlie Trinkam and Madame Dumont, who hailed him with a gaiety that argued forcibly for the proposition that love (or its cognate emotions) is blind.

". . . and we will not be busy here until this afternoon," said Madame Dumont, ignoring Thatcher's expression. "So, this morning we go to see this dog show about which there is so much fuss. You will come?"

"Why not?" said John Putnam Thatcher. His tone of voice made Kenneth wonder if perhaps Everett Gabler and the Handasyde report were not preferable.

Whatever disadvantages the Housatonic Dog Show labored under, it rejoiced in a fine October day, with a hint of late summer lingering to blur the brilliant outlines of autumn in the Berkshires. And it occupied a truly beautiful site. Covering the five-minute walk from the inn in ten minutes (in deference to Madame Dumont's footgear, inappropriate to Shaftesbury in general and dog shows in particular) the quartet passed the school on Seaward Avenue, then sighted the large tents pitched in the meadow that stretched toward the distant mountains. Pennants flapped bravely in the healthy breeze, but the sun warmed a gay scene and a large crowd surging in and out of the tents and about the grounds provided a festive air.

"One thing I must say," said Giselle, making a handsome concession as she looked critically at the spectacle. "They have arranged all of this very well. It is too bad that there is the filthy story of the distemper so that Olivia does not see her work. And Gil, of course, is always efficient. Ah, Mr. Wrenn!"

This was Thatcher's first dog show, and he soon discovered that visitors have a choice of activities. They may watch the mysterious, slow examination of canine hindquarters and stops, of paces and stances, of conformations and cuts that is judging. The judging of dogs is not without its own excitement although to the nonspecialist—the man to whom one boxer looks like another—it can seem rather extended. Nor do the elliptical, knowledgeable, ringside comments enlighten his ignorance. "Crotty's doing the judging and she's always liked the lighter brindles. Frankly, I don't think that it's fair."

The second spectator pursuit at a dog show—and certainly the most popular one at an outdoor event on an invigorating October day—is that into which Giselle Dumont plunged, dragging Charlie Trinkam with her. This is animated conversation with friends and acquaintances, frequently peppered with cries of "Oh look, Dick, isn't he adorable!" as large and apparently man-eating animals are led past.

The third activity, much favored by those Shaftesbury young too junior for Kent, Choate or Miss Madeira's, is looking at dogs. For the Housatonic Dog Show (like all the best shows) is a benched event; that means that animals entered must be displayed in the long stalls set up under the three canopies nearest the road both before and after their moments in the ring. The innocent bystander, observing them, often says, "Oh, the poor things." As usual, this is sympathy misplaced. Every self-respecting beagle enjoys the excitement; it is the beagle owner, whose pride and joy had been on Monday adjudged fourth (in a field of five) or Best of Opposite Sex (in a field of two) whose Tuesday is pitiable. Happily, most of these unfortunates tend to forget the rules and slink off rather early on Tuesday afternoon. But when Thatcher and Nicolls arrived the stalls contained dogs still waiting for the judging as well as dogs who had already been judged—and owners, some of them fortified with paper cups of coffee, protectively guarding LaFrance Beau Sabreur (a French bulldog named Charlie) or Bateson's Renard of Burgundy (an Irish wolfhound called Sean) from the public. Many owners had hooked their dogs in the stalls, provided water and food (in the trays that Bradford Withers had distributed) then departed to gossip with friends or to watch the judging. At a distant roped ring, they were part of the solid row of backs indicating that a popular breed was in the spotlight. The dachshunds, to judge from the noise they were making, felt such desertion keenly.

Leaving Giselle and Charlie Trinkam in animated conversation with the Wrenns, Thatcher and Nicolls strolled toward the tent, passing groups of villagers and dog handlers on the way. Conversation, Thatcher noted, was evenly divided between dogs and the Lindsay murders, with Peggy Lindsay's colleagues effecting a synthesis by discussing the dead girl in her role as dog handler.

"I've always maintained it was a tramp . . ."

"Well, no matter what it is, Shadybrook will miss Peggy. Nobody could handle boxers the way she could . . ."

"The police aren't saying anything . . ."

"If a man's too old to bend, he shouldn't judge!"

This last was delivered by a woman who had breakfasted near Thatcher at the inn. From beneath her arm, an Australian terrier grinned malevolently.

"Is that meant personally?" Thatcher inquired courteously but she had already disappeared.

"I hadn't realized the hazards of a dog show," he commented, immediately confronting another. Over the heads of a gaggle of youngsters, he sighted a group of people intent upon one of the stalls. Bud Austin, ignoring the din around him, was trying to make himself heard. "Dad, I want to have a word with you . . ."

But Dad, and a formidably fat woman were otherwise occupied. The Great Dane beside them kept Bud at bay.

"A sliver!" said the woman thrillingly. "I'm not going to risk Kristin in there!"

"No," Gilbert Austin agreed, straightening. He nodded briefly at Thatcher. "We'll put Kristin somewhere else, Mrs. Sibley. You come with me to the steward's office . . ."

"Dad!" said Bud indignantly.

"Sorry Bud," his father said, "I'm busy." He escorted Mrs. Sibley and Kristin from the tent, followed, Thatcher noticed, by some distinctly appraising glances and a few speculative remarks.

"You'd think that Dad cares more about these damned dogs than about me," said Bud furiously.

Thatcher was tempted to reply that the dogs were handsome physical specimens (which Bud Austin was not) and that Kristin, in particular, seemed intelligent and good-natured when he noticed a black-draped figure proceeding ceremoniously up the aisle. Mrs. Lindsay, supported as ever by Elvira, was smiling sadly at the embarrassed couple offering condolences.

"Come along, Nicolls," Thatcher ordered hastily. "I want to see what judging involves."

"Perhaps I should go back and help Mr. Gabler," said Kenneth, unnerved. He was spared Thatcher's comment on this pusillanimity by two collies whose leashes became entangled with his legs.

Their arrival at Ring Eight coincided with the end of a round of judging. Wooden chairs were being vacated; a large number of cocker spaniels on slip leashes were being led back toward the tents, while under the banner marked "8" another cocker spaniel struck a heroic pose. Chester Oldfield, grinning broadly, knelt by his side. A thin man held a bowl. A tall man held a ribbon.

"Hold it!" shouted a photographer, immortalizing the moment. The smile vanished from Oldfield's face, he transferred the cocker's leash to the thin man, and strode off. The cocker spaniel allowed himself the luxury of an unchampionly scratch.

"Will Old English sheepdogs please come to Ring Nine?" boomed a voice over the loudspeaker. It sounded rather like Gilbert Austin.

"Nothing seems to be happening at Ring Eight now," Kenneth pointed out nervously.

"Splendid," said Thatcher, settling himself in one of the wooden chairs. "And Nicolls, why don't you go watch some judging?"

Being no fool, Nicolls fled, leaving John Putnam Thatcher, senior vice-president of the Sloan Guaranty Trust, head of its Trust and Investment Divisions, sitting beside an empty ring.

"English sheepdogs to Ring Nine!" the loudspeaker said crisply. "And will the parents of Donnie please come to the steward's office?"

If Donnie's parents weren't idiots, Thatcher thought sourly, they would abandon him. But the voice was not Austin's. As the voice pleaded with Donnie's parents, Thatcher looked toward the steward's tent to see Austin emerge, a sheaf of papers in his hand. A woman wearing an armband rushed up to him and spoke urgently. He listened, then followed her to the farthest tent.

"English sheepdogs," the loudspeaker commanded testily.

One of these immense creatures jogged past, followed by his owner, a miniscule man, quite ashen with nervousness. "You're going to be great, Honey," he said audibly, patting an enormous rump as he hurried toward Ring Nine.

Thatcher was forced to admit that in a clear sunny meadow nestling at the foot of the mountains, the English sheepdog (as distinguished from his owner, handler, hanger-on and admirer) is a handsome sight. Then, as another lumbered along toward Ring Nine (followed by a harried looking young couple and four children) he reflected that they looked remarkably alike.

He crossed his legs, and determined to give no dog fanciers an opportunity to explain how purebred canines are distinguished from each other. Already he knew more about dogs than he wanted to; Charlie Trinkam could be trusted to devote himself to the problem.

Resolutely, Thatcher ignored the pleasant tableaux around him; a large English bulldog backing deliberately into a tiny boy who roared with laughter then rose to pummel the dog while the man in charge of both animals lit a cigarette and ignored them; a Norwich terrier startling himself, his besotted owner and everybody in the vicinity by attempting a suicidal lunge at a supercilious Borzoi.

"But he never fights," protested his owner tearfully when the little ruffian was hauled from the jaws of death.

"He'd better learn," said the Borzoi owner shortly.

The Borzoi sneered.

Even this did not change the tenor of John Thatcher's thoughts. He found himself wondering what the police were doing while Shaftesbury enjoyed itself at the dog show. Somewhere, they were pressing inquiries about the murder of Peggy Lindsay and Donald Lindsay. Was it at Ridge Road Farm?

Shaftesbury was not, as the New York papers insisted, in the grip of a wave of hysteria. The Wrenns, Miss Finchley the librarian and the other familiar faces that had come Thatcher's way looked quite normal. On the other hand, it was not to be assumed that Shaftesbury was absolutely calm about double murder.

"They are wondering," Giselle Dumont had said. About Olivia. Presumably, they were also talking. Thatcher sighed.

A sudden yapping of human and canine voices behind him announced another crisis; no doubt a dog was displaying great strength of mind while his owner went to pieces. Thatcher was not surprised to see Gilbert Austin half-running toward the second tent. Devoted to duty was Gilbert Austin. A man of principles. Thatcher wondered if the police thought that he and his wife together had conspired to remove Peggy Lindsay from the landscape. Or, for that matter, if Austin knew that Mrs. Lindsay was on the premises.

He decided to refresh his spirits with contemplation of the distant mountains, emptying his mind of all thought of dogs, murder and, most insistently, of insurance. He had, in fact, begun that contemplation when he became aware of something cold and wet in his hand. It was a dog's nose, belonging to an extremely amiable golden retriever.

"Come here, Goldy," said an elderly man sitting four or five chairs from Thatcher.

"Goldy?" said Thatcher with pleasure, noting that Goldy gave him a friendly look but obediently returned to her master and sat down to look around with a nice blend of affability and dignity.

"Well, actually, Greenmountain's Proud Princess," the elderly man said with a smile. "But Goldy's easier. I'm Green, by the way. Greenmountain Kennels."

Thatcher cautiously introduced himself, feeling that similar identification would serve no useful purpose. To his surprise, Green said, "The Sloan?"

Thatcher admitted it. Green was, it developed, president of a small bank in Poland Springs, Maine. The showing of golden retrievers was his hobby.

"Actually, just do it as an excuse to get out," he confided. "Can't hunt as much as I did . . ."

"Age?" Thatcher inquired sympathetically.

"Hell no," said Green crisply. "Hunters. Woods aren't safe anymore. Six of them killed each other up home last year. I wouldn't take Goldy into the woods in hunting season." He ruffed her neck affectionately.

A man of sense, Thatcher saw immediately. He had not met many in Shaftesbury.

Green pulled out a big round watch. "They're judging the

Dobermans here in about a half-hour," he said. "Figured I'd hang around for that, then start home . . ."

"Did you show Goldy?"

Green frowned momentarily. "That damned fool judge said she was a little too big for what he likes—oh, well." He and Goldy were both convinced of her superiority; the idiocy of a judge was not going to bother him. "Still, I like to look at the Dobermans. They're an efficient-looking breed, you know. I always like a dog who gets out and does some work instead of just sitting around waiting for food like some lazy loafer."

This neat inversion of the sentiments of Secretary Charles Wilson pleased Thatcher. He listened courteously while Mr. Green described the number of small animals Goldy was capable of flushing, pointing and retrieving—when the woods were safe. Green however justified Thatcher's instincts. He broke off with a chuckle. "There," he laughed. "Getting to be as bad as a mother hen. Goldy's a good dog but of course no one's ever going to pay fifteen hundred dollars for her pups . . ."

"What?" Despite himself, Thatcher was roused.

Green looked at him. "Why certainly. Some of the fancier kennels and some of the popular breeds. And for an outstanding champion, the price can go higher."

"That makes last night's scene clearer to me," said Thatcher softly.

"You mean about the distemper?" Green asked. "I heard that there was some sort of ruckus. It's a serious thing . . ."

"So I gathered," said Thatcher. "I had not realized that it was also a major financial threat."

Green considered this. "For a lot of us, dogs are a hobby," he said, "but for a lot of people here, dogs are business." He scratched Goldy's ear affectionately.

Thatcher weighed his words. "Why didn't anybody object to Gilbert Austin's continuing here as business manager? Surely he can transmit the disease?"

Green looked amused. "Well, in the first place, who would do the work? Then, the chances of his transmitting distemper are fairly remote. He hasn't been at the Austindale Kennels lately, you know. Then, nobody wants to add to the troubles he already has."

Thatcher looked up quickly as Green continued: "There's been a lot of talk about Peggy Lindsay's murder. Most of the

159

people here knew her fairly well, you know. But Gil Austin is a pretty popular guy—and nobody wants to make it hard for him."

Acting on an instinct that told him he could trust Green's judgment, Thatcher asked a question that had been bothering him. "Could this rumor about distemper be just that—nothing more than a rumor? Something that one of the competitors of the Austindale Kennels started to keep them from showing?"

Green frowned into the distance at the implications of the question. Then, with a crinkle around his eyes, he said, "Let's put it this way: nine out of ten people here wouldn't do a thing like that . . ."

"But the tenth?" Thatcher persisted.

"It wouldn't surprise me out of a year's growth," said Green.

It was always, Thatcher reflected, a pleasure to meet a banker.

18   "Refreshment of spirit for the discriminating..."

FIVE O'CLOCK IS, DEPENDING ON YOUR POINT of view, an hour of triumph, defeat, preparation, tribulation or vindication.

For six impassioned dog fanciers, eligible for the Best in Show competition which would take place after the Grand Banquet and bring the Housatonic Dog Show to a ringing close on Wednesday night, it was unalloyed victory. Exhibitor, respectively, of the best working dog, nonworking dog, sporting dog, terrier, hound and toy dog, each now had documentary proof of a long-felt superiority over various despised rivals. A special bench had been erected in one of the outbuildings of the Shaftesbury Inn where a Saint Bernard, a bulldog, an English setter, an Afghan hound and a Yorkshire terrier were receiving their admirers in lordly seclusion from the common herd. The Yorkshire terrier was making a cake of himself with his front hair up in curlers. The sixth dog, a haughty Airedale apparently born in perfect show position, was effortlessly maintaining an air of aristocratic detachment right in the middle of the inn's lounge by the side of an owner unwilling to be separated from his paragon and proudly displaying a clutch of blue ribbons to all and sundry.

This conduct could not be expected to commend itself to other Airedale owners or indeed to any exhibitor for whom the Martini he imbibed was washed down in the bile of defeat. Feeling their disappointments most keenly were those who had come within a whisker of being included in the magic inner circle. Comment flowed freely among those who placed second.

"Masters has always been a setter man. Everybody know that. Breeds Irish setters himself. So what chance do I hav with a cocker? Might as well show a mutt . . ."

"You think that's bad?" inquired a handler obviously ben on detailing his own atrocity story. "Did you see wha McCormack did to me? That minnie schnauzer is the bes damn dog I've ever handled. Trouble is, McCormack is pa: it. Blind as a bat for one thing. What's more," he adde darkly, "I wouldn't be surprised if someone got to him. Yo know what they said about that show in Goshen . . ."

"Now I've had a lot of experience," pronounced an em bittered Chet Oldfield, who was not winding up in a clou of glory. His fee increases might have to wait a while. "Bu never have I seen anything to beat this. An Afghan, fo Chrissake! A beautiful coat, he said. Of course he's got beautiful coat. Caxton's no fool. You can imagine what th hindquarters are like underneath all that fluff. I've said before and I'll say it again. Give me a judge who know bone. Now, that otterhound of mine. . . ."

Maintaining an imperturbable course amidst this moanin and lamentation were the great majority of professionals. grueling two days, disruptive of all canine discipline an health habits, were over. Some were already leaving. Fc most, there would be the relaxation of drinks and dinne followed by dutiful attendance and applause at the ultimat event. And then, anxious to release their charges from th unnatural confinement of bench and crate, they would begi the laborious business of packing and loading in preparatio for a drive lasting half the night. They would leave it to th amateurs and gentleman breeders to feel they could afford night of respose for themselves and a night of further restrai for their dogs. For the professional, tomorrow was the da to start reckoning up the real results of the show—to lay ou the blue ribbons and the red ribbons and calculate just wha they meant in terms of next year's profits. Because the rea breeder—unless he resorts to the more esoteric byways c commercial traffic and supplies canine stars for television c attack dogs for the suppression of race riots—is dependen on the proved worth of the blood lines of his puppies an this worth is measured in terms of championship points.

To John Thatcher, always interested in the ways of money it was a fascinating insight into yet another form of busines enterprise. He had already spotted the handlers as the virtuo of this trade. No inventory, no cost of production, just a highly personal characteristic. All they had to sell was the fact that with them a dog looked more like a champion than without them. It didn't seem like much. But, he reminded himself, it could apparently be worth twenty thousand dollars a year. No doubt there was more to it than met the eye.

Picking up his glass and removing himself from too close proximity to three men interested solely in the field trial performance of Labrador retrievers, he skirted a welter of activity centering around a pile of crates. The confusion, he finally decided, stemmed from the juxtaposition of two activities. From one set of crates, ceremonial china (bearing a large heraldic crest composed of dogs *rampant* and *couchant*) was being unloaded. Into another set, Pomeranians were being manhandled by a grizzled elderly couple remarkably inept at overcoming the spirited resistance of the tiny animals. Yapping filled the air. The maids involved with the crockery stepped warily.

For the inn staff, of course, this was an hour of tribulation. Peering into the dining room Thatcher caught sight of Giselle Dumont, who had spent the afternoon radiating that aura of managerial competence in domestic crisis which seems to come so naturally to the French. She was hovering over the table in a posture of uncharacteristic indecision with a pile of place cards in her hand. Thatcher suddenly remembered Peggy Lindsay's prophetic comment on the day of her death.

Giselle, she had said, would not know how to handle the place cards.

Not, Thatcher thought as he recalled the unending confidences of Dr. Cooper with regard to compost heaps, that Peggy's technique had been above criticism. Probably she had been too exercised with the problems of arranging Austins and Lindsays in a manner calculated to avoid conflict to have any attention left for a mere noncombatant of a Thatcher.

Giselle Dumont was not alone. Leaning against the mantelpiece and examining an old pewter tankard, Charlie Trinkam was contributing erratic suggestions scarcely designed to aid Madame in negotiating the no-doubt intricate considerations of protocol attendant upon seating the luminaries of the Housatonic Dog Show.

"Spread those judges around," he urged cheerfully. "Give everybody a crack at them. They've been protected so far."

Giselle frowned in thought. "This Mr. McCormack," she said doubtfully. "To place him next to Mr. Yeats would, I fear, be a mistake. There has been some disagreement about a miniature Schnauzer."

As Yeats was the handler last heard expressing doubt about McCormack's eyesight, probity and ancestry, Thatcher could only feel that Madame Dumont's fears were fully justified.

"Hullo, John. Come in out of the crowd," said Charlie, shifting to one side of the mantel companionably.

"Not at the moment, Charlie. I've been looking for Austin. Have you seem him anywhere? He's not at the bar."

"Nope," said Charlie. "Haven't seen him."

"Poor Gilbert," said Giselle looking up from her task. There was enough feeling in her voice to make Trinkam narrow his eyes speculatively. "He works all the day at the dog show—and tonight he will also work—and now, he cannot relax. No, he must go up to have the discussions with the state veterinarian."

"Oh," said Thatcher. "Gone up to the farm, has he?"

"Yes," said Giselle, returning to the place cards. "And it is hard for him. Olivia . . . Olivia is not kind."

It suddenly occurred to John Thatcher that Giselle Dumont might be the proper person to explain what remained, to him, the inexplicable behavior of Olivia Austin. No doubt she understood why a woman who had been, as all accounts agreed, so sensible about a divorce should suddenly develop unmistakably vehement feelings upon learning that her husband had substantial reasons for remarriage.

Unless, of course, Olivia Austin were merely showing the wear and tear of . . . what? A guilty conscience? Conviction that the father of her son was a murderer?

Still, Giselle might be enlightening. He reminded himself to ask her—in Trinkam's absence, if that could be engineered. In the meantime, he made a passing comment.

"I'm eager to see this vet," he said. "Seems to be a peculiar and little known branch of the civil service."

Charlie grinned understandingly and pointed out the window. "I don't want to raise your hopes, John, but it's either the vets or the AMA descending right now."

Thatcher followed his glance. Up the path was coming an ill-assorted group. Leading, with heads held high and the width of the path between them, were Gilbert and Olivia

164

Austin. Some paces behind them came two spare, sandy-haired men equipped with black bags and professional demeanors. They interrupted their progress every now and then in favor of animated discourse until they were shepherded forward by Roger Kincaid, who was bringing up the rear in much the manner of an alert border collie. An *eclaircissement* of the distemper situation was clearly in the offing.

The bar was the place for information and Thatcher abandoned the dining room to find Gilbert Austin already in full flight.

". . . not the slightest doubt. Dr. Mallory will be here to tell you so himself. He has already told us that he doesn't see how this rumor could have got started."

From across the room he was ably seconded by his wife. "Obviously someone who doesn't know the first thing about distemper symptoms," she said in a voice that suggested practice with committees. "But we wanted you to know that you could all be easy in your own minds."

Gratitude for this fine display of consideration was voiced. Several exhibitors expressed regret that the Austindale Dobermans had not been shown—although not the winner of the Doberman blue ribbon. One thoughtful soul inquired after Bold Baron.

Olivia graciously smiled her thanks. "We're hoping that colonic irrigation will solve the problem," she said bravely.

It is not every woman who can be noble on such a subject. Surely, Thatcher decided, Gilbert Austin would have found Peggy Lindsay very flat.

The entrance of the veterinarians commanded the attention of the entire room. There was a nice display of professional courtesies. Dr. Mallory, the state veterinarian, reminded the assembled dignitaries of the Housatonic Dog Show that he had come to deliver his official report as required by law. He must emphasize, however, that his findings merely reiterated and supported those of Dr. Greenfield, the Austins' private veterinarian. He and Dr. Greenfield were as one on the delicate question of diagnosis. Insofar as treatment was concerned, the state laboratory had a new prescription, not yet on the market, which Dr. Greenfield might find of some use. It was an interesting case but absolutely, oh absolutely, minor.

Dr. Mallory was enthusiastically toasted. Dr. Greenfield was toasted. The Austindale Kennel was toasted. By the time that glasses were being raised to Bold Baron—"May his shadow never decrease!"—Thatcher felt almost reconciled to dog people. Giselle Dumont put her head in the door, surveyed the room with one experienced glance and ordered the dinner to be put back one hour at the risk of alienating her chef forever. It was worth it. This was the sort of thing that made a great inn.

Opportunities to toast the American Kennel Club's new breed standard for chows do not come one's way every day. On the strength of this reasoning, Thatcher decided to have another Scotch. Gallantly he fought his way to the bar to find himself shoulder to shoulder with Bud Austin. A disapproving Bud Austin.

"It's pretty silly, all this fuss about dogs," he said austerely. The offensiveness of the young left Thatcher untouched, but he resented the implication that he too belonged to an elite which would infinitely prefer to have a good solid discussion of the management problems at Raytheon.

He fixed his companion with a baleful eye. "Young man," he said in a voice that had intimidated brash graduates of many a professional school—although, to be honest, a brash young veterinarian had yet to come his way—"when you are a good deal older and wiser you will realize that no event which makes adults feel this good is silly."

"Good for you," applauded Cynthia Kincaid, watching Bud's huffy retreat. "I've been waiting two weeks for someone to tell him he's a brat."

By her side Kenneth Nicolls stood transfixed. What does a rising young trust officer do when his mentor is obviously well on the way to being pickled? The answer seemed obvious.

"What can I get you, Cynthia?" he asked, prepared to hold a watching brief. The sign of a good banker is flexibility in the face of the unforeseeable.

Half an hour later, after Cynthia Kincaid's spirited imitation of two distinguished veterinarians at the bedside of an ailing and irritable Doberman, they were the center of a crowd.

"My sympathies," she concluded to the accompaniment of cheers, "were with Bold Baron from start to finish."

"That's my girl," crowed Roger appearing from nowhere and wrapping the arm which was unimpeded about his wife. "A great dog with a great future." He raised his glass.

After refreshing himself, he continued, "I told Oldfield where he could get off."

"Oh Roger!" said Cynthia, a worried frown appearing. "You shouldn't have." She placed a hand on his arm; apparently Roger Kincaid, mildest of men, was capable of wrath when Doberman pinschers were in issue.

"He raised Bold Baron from a pup," a stranger explained to Thatcher. "Hell, the Austindale Kennel *is* Roger Kincaid. Couldn't have gotten off the ground without him. Can't blame him for taking it hard . . ."

His wife's admonition had touched Kincaid. "No," he said thickly. "I guess I shouldn't have. Oldfield's Doberman wasn't any good. Didn't stand a chance."

Olivia Austin, very much the great lady, had stayed for part of the festivities, ostentatiously stationing herself at a distance from her husband while she exchanged greetings with acquaintances and friends. Now, however, she went up to Bradford Withers, said something in his ear which it was apparent he did not hear, and prepared to take her leave.

"Too bad about this, Mrs. Austin," called a tall man. "We'd like to have seen the Baron but we'll wait for the Westminster."

"We'll be there," she said, moving toward the door as a country squire in checked jacket added his congratulations. "Beats raising beef every time, doesn't it, Liv?"

Mrs. Austin laughed.

"Edmonds," Thatcher's informant wheezed. "Great Danes."

Gilbert Austin had watched his wife take her departure without moving toward her, Thatcher saw. Mr. Edmonds had to repeat his jovial comments to rouse him. ". . . don't you think, Gil?"

Austin shook his head. "You don't have to raise beef to lose money, Tim," he said, drawing a laugh from several exceedingly prosperous-looking men.

"They're all worth a fortune," Thatcher's friend told him. "Gentleman farmers. Dogs are just a hobby with them."

"Mmm," said Thatcher, busy with some vagrant thought. Something in Gilbert Austin's manner struck him. Something about the way he had looked at his wife. The whole scene seemed very important suddenly; rather muzzily Thatcher groped for its implications but they eluded him.

Meanwhile Kincaid's limited fund of irritability was being given ample scope for operation.

". . . and so," a thin weedy man was saying to him, "I thought you wouldn't mind showing me around tomorrow morning. Luckily I wasn't planning to leave till noon."

"Well, I would," growled Roger ignoring the placatory hand of his wife.

The thin man assumed a mulish expression. "But we were given to understand that the Austindale Kennel would be open for dog exhibitors," he said angrily.

"Fundheim," hissed Thatcher's informant. "Scotties."

"I don't care what you understand. The tour was postponed."

Thatcher's informant waxed expansive. "Terrible Scotties. Don't know why he bothers. Pest to everyone."

"I don't see what difference the day makes," said Fundheim, who seemed to specialize in an exasperating obtuseness.

Roger became heavily reasonable. "I expect you don't know our problems, Fundheim. We've got a couple of murders to cope with, a farm going to hell and a sick dog. We don't have time for guided tours."

"Then you shouldn't make indiscriminate invitations," said his tormentor waspishly.

"Oh, for heaven's sake, Roger," said Cynthia, "I'll show him the kennel."

"Like hell you will! You've got too much to do already. Look, we expected to exhibit a fine lot of Dobermans. So we've all got our disappointments."

"But what difference . . ."

"Don't you understand English?" Kincaid demanded owlishly. "We're not showing the kennel. I'm sick and tired of a . . . of . . ." He lurched unsteadily to his feet, drunker, Thatcher saw, than he had first appeared.

"Of course, Roger," Cynthia rose swiftly and deftly removed her husband's glass. "Do you want to come outside with me for a bit?"

Fundheim, about to pursue the subject, was quelled into silence by a mass glare.

"It's final, you hear?" Roger flung over his shoulder.

Giselle Dumont, quick to sense any deviation from the atmosphere of bonhomie which prevailed throughout the room, left Bradford Withers to move near Thatcher.

"Poor Roger," she said, neatly signaling the waiter to remove the glass and ashtray that were sole signs of his dissipation. "When he drinks, his temper becomes undependable."

Mr. Fundheim looked rather frightened.

"Roger?" asked Austin, appearing beside her. Giselle nodded.

Austin looked decisive, and Thatcher thought, prone to good works. "Cynthia will take care of him," he said. "He'll be all right in the morning. Bud, I want you to go help Cynthia. . . ."

This seemed the height of folly to John Thatcher. He could not believe that a man rendered irritable by drink would be solaced by the company of Gilbert Austin's son.

"I take it," he heard himself saying with a freedom he would not have assumed in more sober company, "that this is not unusual." But Giselle Dumont had been borne out of earshot by the ingenious Charlie Trinkam.

"Now, see here," Bradford Withers protested.

They were not denied the presence of Bud Austin for long. Within a few moments, he was making his way back to the bar to report to his father.

"They're in the parking lot, Dad. Cynthia says she can get along without me. I'm afraid," he said gravely, preparing his audience for a blow, "I'm afraid that Roger has been drinking."

Thatcher's informant rose to the occasion. Flagging a passing waiter for refills, he again raised his glass. "To drink! May its powers never decrease!"

Shortly after that, for some reason or other, they all began to sing.

19 "... close to the beauties of nature."

THURSDAY, WHICH WAS TO BE A NOTABLE DAY,
started sedately enough. Kenneth Nicolls, drawn into temporary alliance with Everett Gabler by virtue of moral superiority, waited with him at the breakfast table for the arrival
of John Putnam Thatcher. The other diners were lingering
dog show types, all clearly the worse for wear.

". . . a disgrace to the Sloan," Gabler said, brandishing
his warm water and lemon juice.

Kenneth, who had just sighted a bleary-looking Chester
Oldfield tottering to a table in the corner, looked inquiringly
at Gabler who continued, "These . . . these peccadillos, I
suppose we may call them . . . are certainly a violation of
the canon of ethics of the American Bankers Association."

Gabler had been a pained observer of Charlie Trinkam's
notable tango with Madame Dumont at one point in last
night's proceedings. His remarks must be in connection with
that, Ken realized, looking around cautiously. Charles was
nowhere in evidence. Nor was Giselle.

Had Gabler retired before or after John Putnam Thatcher
led a spirited rendition of *Crimson in Triumph Flashing*?
("Harvard! Harvard! Harvard! Harvard! Harvardharvard
HAR-VARD!!") Had he been present when Bradford Withers
countered with rival and appropriate claims? ("Bulldog! Bulldog! Bow Wow Wow!")

Deplorable.

The virtuous element of the Sloan finished breakfast and
was on its way to corner Bradford Withers when Thatcher
encountered it in the lobby. He looked, Kenneth noted cen-

soriously, the picture of rude health and well-being. Hardened, no doubt.

"On your way up to Withers?" Thatcher said cheerfully. "Good luck to you. Oh, Nicolls. I believe I recall suggesting you as a speaker to the Black Angus Cooperative Society last night. You may have to do something about it."

The Frenchman, Thatcher thought contentedly as he proceeded into the dining room, is right; the best defense is attack. He felt so reconciled to Shaftesbury, the dog show and the world in general, that he spurned a solitary table in the bay window to join the hero of last night's festivities, Dr. Mallory, the state veterinarian who was just ordering breakfast.

Like the good professional man that he was, Dr. Mallory was powerfully discreet. He acknowledged an earlier meeting without tactless comment on its nature.

"Beautiful place, Shaftesbury," he remarked with his orange juice.

"It is," Thatcher replied. Why couldn't the bank develop this kind of spirit? Furthermore, the man was accurate. A faint mist hung over Shaftesbury green, rendering it idyllically calm. Its delicate pastoral charm was enhanced by two burnished collies who trotted toward the monument. "Do you get around much in your job?"

The state veterinarian's office, said Dr. Mallory, was a fascinating place to work. If it wasn't mastitis in New Haven, it was the threat of psitticosis in Hartford. Kept him on the go.

"And hoof-and-mouth disease?" Thatcher inquired, a vague notion that this afflicted cattle.

"Not in Shaftesbury," said Dr. Mallory, shocked. "These Black Anguses are pampered, petted. . . . Let me tell you, Thatcher, if the people of Connecticut were treated as well as these Black Anguses, this would be a happier world."

Thatcher was considerably entertained by this reverse anthropomorphism. "What about the Dobermans?" he asked, pouring coffee from a silver pot. "Surely those Dobermans are just as pampered and yet there was this danger of distemper."

Dr. Mallory put down his fork. "In a way you're right, Thatcher. I don't deny it. There was Bold Baron . . ."

It was an index of Thatcher's sense of well-being that Bold

Baron's unfortunate symptoms in no way impaired his appetite for blueberry pancakes.

". . . but how anybody could have thought it was distemper, I do not understand," Mallory said. "They've got a beautiful kennel with all the latest improvements. Kincaid knows his business." He paused in thought. "You know, as a realistic businessman . . ."

Thatcher braced himself.

"As a realistic businessman," Mallory said, allowing himself a realistic businessman's smile. "I think I would suspect an Austindale competitor. Those are beautiful creatures up there. . . ."

"Morning!" It was Mr. Fundheim, the little man who had tormented Roger Kincaid. "Mind if I join you?"

During the subsequent exchange, with Dr. Mallory assuming an oracular manner, Thatcher found himself looking idly out at the green. He remembered something mysterious that had become crystal clear to him last night, during the little man's baiting remarks. Possibly, however, it had been the Scotch.

". . . wanted to see Austindale," said Fundheim pettishly. "But I guess I'll start home. I understand they've got those new inside blowers . . ."

"Oh, they do," Mallory confided, with that approval of the rich that is the hallmark of the medical man.

The conversation turned to fluorescent lighting just as Thatcher noticed that the serenity of Shaftesbury Inn was about to be disturbed. A sleek black Ford, ruthlessly shining, came gliding up to the inn, braking sharply as a sassy little roadster with two women and a Bedlington shot under its nose and sped away down Ridge Road. The driver started the car with a roar and completed his approach to the inn; furious, no doubt. From what he had seen of the police, Thatcher felt that they were inordinately proud of their mastery of the automobile. It boded ill.

Having completed a smooth landing, the Ford halted. A door was flung open and Captain Parker, looking sour, clambered out. He turned, and from the back seat of the car, a uniformed man emerged, turned, and carefully withdrew a large, cumbersome article. A familiar article indeed.

"Excuse me," Thatcher murmured to his companions. Bradford Withers' antlers were, in a remote way, a concern of the Sloan Guaranty Trust. It was only fit and proper that a bank official should witness their return to the site of Peggy Lindsay's murder. Only Everett Gabler could claim that Thatcher was yielding to overpowering curiosity; and fortunately Gabler was chasing after the president.

The lobby was a scene of wakening activity. Giselle Dumont, now at her post at the registration desk, was dealing with Mrs. Sibley and Kristin, both of whom were leaving. A Pekinese man was peering into a crate while he waited.

"She's mad," he told the world sadly. "Always gets mad when I don't scratch her stomach before I put her in there. But my head. . . ."

Parker strode into the lobby, followed by a pair of blue legs, a large stag's head with two yards of antlers wobbling above them. A dachshund, plodding peacefully along, looked up and promptly went out of his mind.

"Liebchen! We're going home, baby. . . ."

Liebchen allowed himself to be dissuaded from launching an all-out attack on this savage beast and was led out to the air-conditioned Cadillac that would bear him home.

"What are you doing with those now?" asked Madame Dumont, her work with Mrs. Sibley finished. This was the question that interested Thatcher. Giselle, he noticed in passing, reserved her playful ways for those whose annual salary was considerably above that granted by the state of Connecticut to police officials. "Never," she said imperiously, "do I want to see them again. When I close my eyes, I see poor Peggy. . . ."

Thatcher did too, now that he thought of it.

Parker looked quietly disgusted. "Put it down over there, Dooley," he said, ignoring Madame Dumont's comments.

Dooley staggered over to the table and deposited his burden.

"No, I do not want it," Madame Dumont cried. "It reminds me . . ."

"Lady," said Parker with offensive evenness. "This is an important bit of evidence. We still don't know why Peggy Lindsay was jammed into it when she was killed in your inn . . ."

"Now, really . . ."

". . . and we would like to hold on to it. But Mr. Bradford Withers is a friend of the Senator, a friend of the

Governor, a friend of the Mayor. He wants you to have it—and when you've got friends like that. . . ."

Withers might number those officials among his friends, but not Parker. Nor Everett Gabler, Thatcher saw, as he turned to see that much-tried banker stamping into the inn, followed by young Nicolls. Ignoring the altercation at the desk, and two cocker spaniels who were docilely awaiting their master, he bustled up to Thatcher.

"Wild-goose chase," he said. "Brad's not home."

"You surprise me," said Thatcher. "I expected that he would still be in bed. Oh, Nicolls. It appears that I did not commit you to the Black Angus Cooperative Society. . . ."

Nicolls closed his eyes in a brief prayer of gratitude for blessings rendered, while Gabler slammed some papers on the table, glared down at the majestic antlers and said: "Dammit, this whole thing is impossible. First Charlie . . ."

"Good morning, all!" said Charlie jauntily from the stair-case.

There was a brief truce; Giselle abandoned her heated exchange with Parker to smile at Charlie; Gabler glared at him. Charlie unhurriedly crossed the lobby and entered the dining room and hostilities broke out anew.

"His houseboy said he got a telegram," Gabler said fussily. "And he dashed out. Seems Mrs. Withers is due to arrive. Now John, this Handasyde report has got to be cleared. I suggest that we all get on the afternoon train . . ."

"Again," said Giselle, "I do not care who knows Mr. Withers. These antlers, I do not want . . ."

"Listen, when the Governor calls . . ."

". . . now at the Sloan we can get Lancer's signature. . . ."

The strong opinions passionately enunciated in various corners of the room were beginning to vibrate in the low-ceilinged room. Thatcher felt that he should do something to quell the various scenes raging when there was a sudden, shocking interruption.

From outside of the inn, distant but audible even over the uproar within, came the sound of metal smashing metal, of glass broken on glass. This was followed by silence—indoors and out—then there was a clear, ghostly scream, its urgency positively paralyzing the lobby of the inn. Then, as they stood there immobilized, pandemonium broke loose. There was a fusillade of barking, and a crescendo of human voices, shouting, commanding, pleading.

Down the stairs from the second floor pelted a tall man with soap still on his face. Without a word, he galloped to the door and rushed outside, just as Dr. Mallory, his face working nervously, came roaring out of the dining room to join in the hunt.

"Come on!" Nicolls cried. Broken from their spell, the inhabitants of the lobby rushed to the door, momentarily becoming entangled with two other men who had joined them.

Shaftesbury green was no longer pastoral; on the contrary it strongly suggested a field of battle. But even Thatcher, a veteran of the Marne, was taken aback by the nature of the conflicts. Across the green, tipped drunkenly across Central Street, was a station wagon that had grazed two parked cars before skittering to a peculiar halt. And in front of that distressing sight, two thin bespectacled men were ineffectually squaring off at each other with weak jabs. Both were in an uncontrollable fury. Nobody was paying the slightest attention to them.

The collision had released a matched team of four Norwegian elkhounds from durance vile; seizing the opportunity they had abandoned the station wagon to cavort on the green when challenge reared its ugly head. The shock of the collision had caused the owner of two collies to slacken his grasp. From nowhere, two Shaftesbury regulars, amiable if undistinguished animals who had been relegated by the Dog Show to oblivion on the church porch, hurled themselves into the fray.

The results were indescribable. Near the monument, one of the elkhounds was locked in a vicious fight with the two collies. This was the center of attention for most of the doggy types who rushed out of the inn to try to halt something that must surely have a bloody if not fatal conclusion.

"Get a bucket of water!" shouted somebody as a snarling tangle of fur and claw writhed angrily around. At that very moment, Chester Oldfield brushed past Thatcher and Nicolls unceremoniously, two large buckets of water in his hands.

"Get that mutt out of there," he shouted, running toward the fight. One of the Shaftesbury regulars, a tall rangy setter, had been circling the fight, snapping and ready to join. The human spectators were trying ineffectually to separate the dogs without getting cut to ribbons.

Meanwhile a second elkhound was engaged with the other

plebian canine whose intentions, it was painfully clear, were the reverse of hostile.

A thin woman was chasing the third elkhound, who gamboled playfully just out of her grasp. Attracted by the noise, a number of people started to the green.

This gave the fourth elkhound his opportunity. He bit the Shaftesbury postmaster.

"Nature red in tooth and claw," Everett Gabler said.

"I wonder if we can do anything," Nicolls said, when he noticed that Parker had finally turned his attention to the sparring match by the cars. "Simpler to cope with than the dogs," Thatcher replied.

Charlie Trinkam, his head appearing over that of the waitress in the dining-room windows, called out to his chief. "Never a dull moment in Shaftesbury, is there?"

"Oh, this is terrible," cried Giselle. "How brave! Look!"

And indeed, with an exhibit of bravery that Thatcher was the first to salute, Chester Oldfield, who had given the buckets of water to seconds, gave a signal; just as the streams were thrown, he propelled himself into the midst of the slavering animals, took a firm grasp on the elkhound's chain collar and staggering slightly from the shock of the water, dragged the beast away from the collie's neck. A red-faced man had secured the first collie, and the second was secured by the man with soap on his face. Breathing hard and exhausted, the late combatants, champions all, were thrown unceremoniously onto the green.

"I've got him," shouted a small man, leading up the second elkhound.

To the third, the worst was happening.

The fourth elkhound was located two days later.

Peace returned to Shaftesbury green. Casualties of course were extensive, Chester Oldfield having suffered a deep gash in his arm, the postmaster a superficial bite. "Better come along with me," Dr. Cooper said. He had materialized from his office. "I tell you gardening is a lot safer."

Mr. Basil Slotman, and Mr. David Heimert, were charged by Parker with disturbing the peace. They left under the guard of Sergeant Dooley.

Dr. Mallory finished an emergency examination of Champion Campbell of the Isles. "A nasty wound . . ."

"Will it be an honorable scar?" demanded an anxious voice

from the crowd behind Thatcher which was clustered around the doctor.

"I'm afraid," said Mallory sadly, "I'm afraid his show days are over."

During the subsequent lamenting, Thatcher turned back to the inn, Giselle Dumont beside him. "Dogs," she said. "But what is this!"

"This" was the staff of Shaftesbury Inn, neglecting its duties to peer out of doors and windows. They hastily deployed.

The lobby was, for the moment, cool, dark and peaceful.

"I'm tired of dogs," said Giselle. "Very tired. No doubt I will have to house the dogs whose owners are in jail. And I am tired of antlers, as well, I tell you. Look at them. How ugly."

They looked. There on the long table were Everett Gabler's unread papers. But of antlers, there was no sign at all.

John Thatcher took advantage of the subsequent convulsions—and he could find it in his heart to sympathize with Captain Parker who was virtually incoherent from rage and suspicion—to retire to the dining room for a second cup of coffee.

"John, I'm going to want to talk to you," said Everett.

"Not now," Thatcher said shortly. Gabler had been an employee at the Sloan for almost twenty years. One look at Thatcher's face convinced him that it was indeed a case of not now.

"Well, I'll try to find Withers then," he said, taking himself off.

Charlie Trinkam and Ken Nicolls respected Thatcher's desire for solitude as well, remaining to form appreciative spectators to the exchange between Captain Parker and the owner of Shaftesbury Inn.

"What do you mean, stolen?" he roared. "Where are they . . . ?"

Giselle was at the end of her tether. "Look!" she shouted. "When we are out looking at those dogs. Somebody comes in—no doubt a madman—and takes them. It is easy . . ."

Suddenly she broke off.

"Why would anybody want to steal them? Tell me that!" demanded Parker.

Giselle did not seem to hear him.

The thought that had just come to her, had come to Thatcher some five minutes earlier. While everybody at the inn was concerned with dog fights, somebody had entered the inn and removed forty pounds of stuffed head and antler.

Thatcher stirred his coffee abstractedly. Unlike Captain Parker, he had a fair notion of who had done it—and why. The Captain, already a victim of Brad Withers' influence in high places, did not know that he was beginning to feel the effects of Caroline Withers' influence on her husband. Presumably Brad had some all-powerful reason for desiring the presence of those antlers in his house before his wife's arrival.

But the important thing was not the antlers. It was the ease of their removal. When everybody was looking out at the green, or rushing out to it, a large and heavy object could be removed from the inn. Presumably this meant that a large and heavy object could be brought into the inn.

During a parade, for example.

A body.

"Of course," said Thatcher aloud, cursing himself for a fool. "She wasn't killed at the inn at all. She never got to the inn. Somebody made it look that way."

He thought of place cards, suddenly, and of Dr. Cooper, the gardener. Then he thought of Goldy, and the banker from Poland Springs.

For a moment, he sat without moving, a feeling of tiredness spreading over him. Then, with the quick decisive movement that was characteristic of him, he went to the doorway that led to the lobby.

"Captain," he said. "I'd like a few words with you."

Parker broke off his savage indictment of Madame Dumont. After one look at the banker's face, he followed him.

"He too, he knows," said Giselle staring straight ahead.

"What is this?" Charlie demanded.

Giselle looked at him, then without another word left the room.

Thatcher did not talk to Captain Parker for very long. The sun was just a little past its midday zenith—touching the glowing hillside with a color that gleamed through the mist—when the police car left Shaftesbury Inn to drive out to Ridge Road. It came to a smooth halt beside a field where a small, compactly built man was working competently with his hands over the barbed wire fence.

Roger Kincaid did not protest when he was arrested for the murder of Peggy Lindsay and her brother Donald.

20   "Inquiries invited."

ORDER AND BEAUTY AGAIN REIGNED IN THE Sloan Guaranty Trust. The muted hum of administrative efficiency pervaded the entire building. Weekly reports were initialed at the proper place and at the proper time; appointments were kept; contracts were signed; portfolios were reviewed. The guiding hand was at the helm. Bradford Withers was back.

More to the point, so were John Putnam Thatcher, Charles F. Trinkam, Everett Gabler and Kenneth Nicolls. Watching them hurl themselves into their work with renewed zeal, the sixth floor of the Sloan breathed a collective sigh of relief and decided that the good old times were back again. The shock troops had gone forth into enemy territory and returned unscathed. But this was an oversimplification. Not one of the four bankers returned to pick up his personal life exactly where he had left it.

Kenneth Nicolls, sitting in conference in Thatcher's office, his attention nominally centered on the Handasyde report, realized that he had entered on a new and even more mystifying phase of his progress toward parenthood. An unnerving experience, he admitted to himself, as he automatically nodded agreement to Thatcher's concise summation of their discussion.

"What about the tax credits?" asked Charlie Trinkam, more adept than Nicolls at keeping his mind functioning with oiled precision on two completely disparate trains of thought. No automatic responses for him. Discoursing fluently on the subject of investment guaranties, he came to a firm decision. He would not take the train to Shaftesbury next weekend. A car would give them more mobility. (Charlie could not know that a change in the schedule of the Rochester Symphony

180

Orchestra was going to deliver a certain cellist to Shaftesbury over the operative time period. As he himself had remarked, there is rarely a dull moment in Shaftesbury.)

That Kenneth Nicolls and Charlie Trinkam should find preoccupation outside the four corners of the Handasyde report was regrettable but predictable. John Thatcher, who knew full well that he had not captured his audience's whole-hearted attention, could measure the insidious aftereffects of the Sloan's sojourn in Shaftesbury only in terms of Everett Gabler. That devoted servant of Rails and Industrials was, indisputably, abstracted. This was unprecedented in the memory of man.

When, at long last, the Sloan plane had arrived yesterday to bear Thatcher and his subordinates from Shaftesbury, embarkation had been unaccountably delayed by Gabler's unusually solicitous inquiries about the care and handling of the luggage. It was gradually borne in on his colleagues that Everett's personal baggage upon arrival at the Shaftesbury Inn (one small valise, three overflowing attaché cases) had been augmented. Displacing the attaché cases in their owner's affection was a small wooden crate with a wire grill. From it issued suggestive noises.

Three interrogative glances flew to Gabler who had the grace to blush.

"A Welsh terrier," he admitted. "Llewellyn ap Llandanagh."

Three pairs of eyebrows ascended in silence.

"Remarkable blood lines," he said defiantly.

Charlie snorted. The terrier barked. Eventually, they were all loaded, the crate at Gabler's feet. His reference to blood lines had not been idle chitchat. The flight to New York was enlivened by exhaustive itemization of Mickey's genealogy. "His great-grandmother," said Gabler happily, "was Champion Matilda of Llanelly."

The loving care which for fifty years had been lavished on the American Railroad had found a new outlet. In view of the condition of the American Railroad, Thatcher was inclined to approve.

This morning Gabler had reported to work armed with literature about obedience training which he fingered during the Handasyde discussions. Thatcher sighed heavily. What with Nicolls turning moony over the mystery of birth and Everett enrolling his dog at good schools. . . .

But Thatcher's own involvement with the affairs of Shaftesbury had yet to run its full course.

Miss Corsa entered the office to announce: "Mrs. Withers."

"Show him in," said Thatcher absently.

"*Mrs.* Withers," enunciated Miss Corsa with crystal clarity and no interest. "She would like to see you."

"Of course, of course," muttered Thatcher hastily.

However unwelcome the wife of the Sloan's president normally might be at a business conference, John Thatcher had realized for some time that explanations would have to be made to some member of the Shaftesbury community. And when all was said and done, Carrie Withers was easily the most detached—and probably the most intelligent—representative of that group. Thatcher's hurried attempts at explanation to Gil and Olivia Austin on the evening of Kincaid's arrest had not been notably successful. Gil, with more vigor than civility, had flatly branded the accusation a falsehood and announced he would see Roger himself. As they were leaving Olivia had stepped back to press Thatcher's hand. "You mustn't mind Gil," she whispered so that her husband could not overhear. "You see, all along, he was afraid I did it and that somehow it was his fault. Now he's terribly ashamed at feeling relieved, especially when it's at Roger's expense." Sensitivity is all very well, but it was a relief to know that one could confidently rely on Bradford Withers' wife being totally devoid of all guilt feelings.

Miss Corsa's announcement had brought all four men in the office to their feet. Thatcher, blessed with a large desk, accomplished his ascent with relative grace. The other three clutched to their chests the folders, loose-leaf binders, writing pads and dog school brochures with which they had equipped themselves.

Carrie Withers entered. Resolutely blued hair made a startling contrast with skin weathered to the technicolor hue which off-season vacationers in the sunshine bring home with them. Brisk and energetic, she acknowledged introductions and allowed herself to be divested of a mink coat.

"I know I'm interrupting, John, but I couldn't leave without thanking you for all your help in Shaftesbury."

Thatcher made modest noises. It was nothing. Brad had never been a serious suspect.

"Oh, that's not what I mean." Carrie waved impatiently.

"But you stopped him making a fool of himself. Or anyway," she added judiciously, "as much as possible."

Hurried suggestions of departure sprang to the lips of Thatcher's remaining guests. Gabler, his attention wrenched away from contemplation of Mickey's forthcoming victories in the ring, looked disapproving.

But Carrie would have none of it. "No, no, you musn't go. I'm grateful to all of you." Her glance lighted on Charlie. She beamed. "And you're Mr. Trinkam. Giselle Dumont has told me all about you."

Charlie, a man of wide experience, contented himself with a cheerful grin. He was beyond the age where this phrase opens up bottomless pits of horror. Giselle didn't know that much. Nicolls wondered uneasily what Carrie was thanking them for. Better not to ask.

Thatcher, paling at the thought of exposing his staff to a wave of Carrie Withers' frankness, said firmly that they had all been delighted to do what they could. They had all been shocked and appalled at the murders in Shaftesbury. His diversionary tactics worked.

"And of course I want to hear all about that too," Carrie said. "Roger Kincaid! I could hardly believe it when Brad told me. Why in the world should Roger go around killing the Lindsays?"

"Money," said Thatcher succinctly, happy to find solid footing on a topic which did not involve them in a spirited analysis of the ineptitude of the Sloan's president.

"But," said Carrie patiently, putting her finger unerringly on the core of things, "Roger doesn't have any money. Neither did the Lindsays."

"No, Roger doesn't have any money in the Shaftesbury scheme of things," said Thatcher a little sadly. "That's what confused things all along. The Shaftesbury view of life."

Carrie, who tended to forget that there was any other view, was bewildered. "What do you mean by that?"

"Shaftesbury thinks in terms of capital and tax losses. So we all accepted two facts which were completely untrue. First, the Kincaids, Roger a farm manager and Cynthia a minister's daughter, have no money. They just happen to live like the rest of Shaftesbury. And second, all farming in Shaftesbury is unprofitable. That's its chief purpose."

Carrie sniffed. "What do you mean, live like the rest of Shaftesbury? Why, the Kincaids don't have a place!"

"No, Carrie, but they just happen to send their children to the same schools as Shaftesbury, drive the same cars as Shaftesbury, take part in the social life of Shaftesbury. On top of all that, Roger is a drinker, which happens to be a very expensive habit. You don't do any of that on a farm manager's salary. Good heavens, if a teller in one of the Sloan offices did any of that, we'd have his books audited instantly! But in the atmosphere of Shaftesbury, if you're not raising prize beef at a loss, you're maintaining the standard of living of a working man."

"Now," said Trinkam with a certain professional gusto, "there is where Kincaid used his head. Capitalizing on loss farming in a totally new way."

"You can't tell me that anybody could raise beef in Connecticut at a profit," said Carrie as one who knows her ground. "That's not possible!"

"Of course not," agreed Thatcher. "But the reason you can't is because commercial beef ranching requires large tracts of cheap pasture land. You go to Texas for that, not suburban Connecticut. The Austins were so indoctrinated with that concept that they never stopped to ask themselves why that reasoning should apply to raising Doberman pinschers. It doesn't. You buy the same feed for your kennel no matter where you are. The Austindale Kennel was being run at a very handsome profit and it was all going into Roger Kincaid's pocket."

Carrie was impressed. "Brad didn't explain that," she murmured.

This surprised no one.

Nicolls, overcoming the nervousness aroused by finding himself closeted with the wife of the Sloan's president entered the conversation. "You have to hand it to Peggy Lindsay, figuring all this out."

"Yes," nodded Thatcher. "The contemplated marriage between Gilbert Austin and Peggy was a deathblow to Kincaid. No wonder he was so upset by the divorce and worked so hard for a reconciliation! The last thing in the world he wanted was to have Peggy Lindsay around Ridge Road Farm."

"But she'd already been around. She used to show some of the Dobermans."

"She'd been around as a handler earning a fee on a piece-work basis," corrected Thatcher. "Now suddenly she was taking a proprietarial interest. You've got to remember that Peggy Lindsay was as much of a wage earner as Roger Kincaid. And what was much more dangerous, her business was dogs. I noticed very early that while Gil and Olivia referred to Ridge Road Farm as the house or my home, Peggy always called it the property. And I made the mistake of attributing this to the difference in monied status. Giselle Dumont said some sensible things to me the night of the murder. She said we all thought of Peggy as the 'other woman' when really she was an acute businesswoman. But I was too blind to see the implications. When Peggy said property, she meant it. She didn't see a house, she saw an income-producing kennel. Of course, she wanted the house too, and for all the reasons Olivia mentioned. But what infuriated her was Olivia trying to hold on to the house by denying the value of the business."

Everett emerged from his surreptitious study of obedience trials. "Then she didn't know Roger Kincaid was in back of it?"

"Not at first she didn't. From what Kincaid has told in his confession, it's pretty clear that that didn't come to her until the last day."

Kenneth had been too busy with domestic details to keep abreast of the telephoned communications from Connecticut. "Oh, has Kincaid confessed?"

"Oh, yes. He was never built to be a premeditated murderer, you know. He just had fallen into the lifelong habit of taking the easy way out. When he drank too much for city life, he moved to the country. When he couldn't make as much money in the country, he stole. When somebody found him out, he murdered."

"Peggy," prodded Trinkam. "You were telling us about how she found out about Kincaid."

"That's simple enough. She went up to have her big scene with Olivia at Ridge Road Farm. While she was screaming denunciations of Olivia, it came over her that Gil and Olivia were genuinely innocent of the money-making qualities of their kennel. After all, Gil was just as much in the dark as Olivia. Olivia had roused her to a white-hot pitch of fury in the course of their quarrel, and she was always a girl who flung herself at things when she was worked up enough to overcome her basic lack of self-confidence. You know what happened next. She realized that the profits had been diverted before they ever reached the Austins and flung out of the house, leaving Olivia in mid-sentence, to have it out with Roger. Remember, Cynthia said she was boiling with rage when she passed the Kincaid house. So she was. Roger in his first statement just pushed her farther along the road to the village. Of course she was murdered right there. Roger says he had no idea of what he was doing and I believe him. She charged up to Roger, still in fury, and started abusing him as a thief, stealing from her Gil. Roger, who had been living on his nerves for days anyway while Peggy complained loud and long to the entire village about the valuation of Ridge Road Farm, just lost control and struck her. The next thing he knew he had a body with a broken neck slumped over the barbed wire in his field."

Trinkam's eyes lit up in appreciation. "Barbed wire," he said softly. "So that's how the antlers got involved."

"Exactly."

"Now just a moment," protested Ken. "I don't see that at all."

"You've got to put yourself in Kincaid's position," said Thatcher, making yet another unreasonable demand on his subordinate's activities as a banker. "There he was with a body that couldn't possibly have acquired a broken neck accidentally in its present position. So he had to move it. All he really wanted to do was find some place in the fields with a hill and rocks and briars where the marks on the body could reasonably be explained. Particularly the damage done by the barbed wire getting entangled with Peggy's arms. So he loaded the body on the back of the pickup truck he had in the field with him, covered it with a tarp, and was about to set off when Cynthia appeared, demanding that he immediately drive to the parade. There wasn't anything he could do but drive into town, drop his family, and then go about his disposal activities. It was at this point that the antlers entered the picture."

"I'm interested in those antlers," said Carrie, frowning mightily.

"Brad," said Thatcher sacrificing something to diplomacy, "wanted them at the inn for the dinner that night. He was just ahead of Kincaid in the traffic jam by the village green. Roger, you realize, was just about frantic by that time. He didn't really dare leave the truck for a minute with that tarp loosely concealing its contents. Then what does he see? The entire staff of the inn out front and Brad depositing the antlers inside and then going off to the parade. He just drove around back and walked in with the body. We all saw the other day that when everybody's attention is riveted on some spectacle on the village green, you can walk in and out of the back of the inn carrying anything you want and nobody will notice. As soon as Kincaid got the idea to leave the body draped around the antlers, he realized it would be to his benefit to make it seem that Peggy had been killed at the inn. So he left her purse and gloves in the front hall. He had to get rid of them anyway. Then, in a moment of inspiration, he took the place cards out of her purse and put them around the dining room. He was careful to separate the Lindsay-Austin factions, but didn't pay much attention to anything else. That's how I ended up with the garden enthusiasts. Actually he didn't get back to Cynthia until the last section of the parade was passing. All the business at the inn took some time. He could have parked in much less than half an hour."

"And Donald Lindsay?" asked Carrie. "I suppose it was the same thing that Peggy figured out."

"Yes, but Roger didn't give him as long to work on it. Donald was used to thinking of his sister in economic terms and he was sure that money was in back of her murder. That may have been good sense," said Thatcher in the tone of one giving the devil his due, "but personally I think it was congenital bias. Anyway he clearly intended to keep things stirred up, probably in the hope that he could exist on blackmail in the future. He put pressure on everyone and by the time he made a few significant remarks to Roger about the valuation of Ridge Road Farm, Roger agreed to meet him at night. You recall that Roger was sitting up those nights with Bold Baron. When he met him, he killed him."

A thought came to Kenneth in the ensuing silence. "My God, I actually sat and watched him hose off the pickup truck!"

Thatcher smiled grimly. "Yes, Roger Kincaid had plenty of troubles after the murder. With the police continually tramping around the Austin place, he had to undertake his clean-up operations in the full blaze of publicity. I sat and watched him remove the section of barbed wire against which Peggy Lindsay fell. But barbed wire isn't easy to dispose of. Particularly in a countryside where no one else uses it. The police found that section he removed in the shed. There were still fragments of Peggy's tweed jacket and dried blood on it."

Carrie sat bolt upright with renewed interest. Discussions about relative incomes in Shaftesbury left her cold, but barbed wire, pickup trucks and Doberman pinschers she could understand. "What's all this about the distemper rumor? Brad said he could believe Roger might commit a murder but not that he could slander the Austindale Kennel."

Three bankers sat in respectful silence. The fourth was more responsive.

"Disgraceful," muttered Gabler.

"That's what I meant about Roger having plenty of other problems. Much against his wishes, Gil and Olivia foisted a dog show in Shaftesbury on him and then invited all the participants to a kennel tour. With everybody speculating about possible motives for Peggy Lindsay's murder, he certainly did not want some sixty dog experts wandering around his kennel making loud estimates of its profitability. Kincaid would know," said Thatcher with feeling, "that you could count on their talking nothing but dogs and kennel profits throughout their stay. So he went to work. The first thing he did was act as peacemaker between Giselle Dumont and Olivia Austin and have the cocktail party at Ridge Road Farm cancelled. But that wasn't enough for his purposes. So he did a very obvious thing. He went down to the inn when he knew it would be crowded with exhibitors and demanded to know who had started a rumor of distemper with a great show of righteous indignation. Remember, nobody had ever seen him so upset before? Now, you know what kind of furor was caused by the word 'distemper.' Is it likely that there could have been a rumor before Roger started it? Of course not. We would have had people howling for the state vet. So at one blow, Roger accomplished two things. He got the kennel tour called off in such a way that no one would come near the place, and he got the Austindale Kennels disbarred from the ring. A very economical operation," Thatcher concluded with indulgent approval.

"And when did you catch on to this?" asked Trinkam.

"Nothing was clear until Brad walked off with the antlers and I realized how easy it would have been to bring a body into the inn. But I think I began to wonder the night before. Gil said something about it's being as easy to lose money on dogs as on beef and that didn't make sense. Then there was

Roger's display with that miserable little exhibitor who wanted to upset all Kincaid's plans by going up to the kennel the next day. For an easygoing man Kincaid was remarkably offensive."

"He was drunk, you know," said Charlie. "After all, we were all a little sozzled."

"There's a difference. Everyone was a little tipsy, true. But Roger acted as if he were drunk enough to be taken home by his wife. Drunk enough to become disagreeably quarrelsome. Then we're told he's a problem drinker. Now a good practiced, hardened drinker doesn't become heavily drunk to the point of slurring his words and reeling on his feet when everybody else is mildly tipsy. No, Roger was putting on a show. And for a very good reason, too."

Carrie sighed. "Really extraordinary," she said. "It hardly seems possible that we can all settle back to the same old lives in Shaftesbury, now."

In Shaftesbury, the same old life *was* extraordinary, but when Thatcher involuntarily raised an eyebrow, he was not thinking of the domestic manners of the wealthy. "All?"

Carrie, who looked like a wise old Samoan chief (it was the mahogany glint of her skin and her white hair), understood him. "Of course," she said impatiently. "It took me about ten minutes to fix *that* up."

This was instantly intelligible to John Thatcher and Charlie Trinkam, totally incomprehensible to Kenneth Nicolls, and uninteresting to Everett Gabler who was sneaking surreptitious glances at "Showing Your Own Dog."

"Men," Carrie said crisply, "are fools."

No one had the temerity to protest.

"Everything is all right?" Thatcher asked, feeling his way.

"Well of course it is. I sympathize with Olivia, of course. But years ago I warned her that marrying a Quaker was going to be no bed of roses . . ."

"Carrie," said Thatcher firmly, "will you please tell me what Olivia was so angry about? It's the one thing that eludes me."

She looked up at him. "Why, Gil's perfectly asinine behavior, of course. For heaven's sake, John. Here she is—her life totally disrupted—she didn't go to Paris this year, you know—because Gil wanted a divorce. . . ."

"Yes, I understood that much," Thatcher said rashly.

"I doubt it," Carrie told him. "Well, of course Olivia was

189

wonderful about it. Naturally she wondered what the man saw in poor Peggy Lindsay . . ."

"Naturally," murmured Thatcher.

". . . but of course Olivia's a great romantic, you know, so she told herself that Gil was in love. At his age! Hah!" Carrie bleated sarcastically, diamonds flashing.

"Why did she get so upset, then, when she heard about the baby?"

"Well, how would you feel?" demanded Carrie unanswerably. "She discovered that Gil proposed to disrupt a perfectly happy home, to drag them through the divorce courts *not* because he was desperately in love—but simply because he felt the gentlemanly thing to do was to marry Peggy Lindsay! Really! Olivia hadn't really grasped what I meant about Quakers, you see. She was utterly outraged by this . . . juvenile attitude!"

To Thatcher and Charlie Trinkam this explanation was reasonable; Gabler, had he been listening, might have expressed his habitual doubt. He rather thought that Olivia Austin was simply another hysterical woman. Kenneth Nicolls, on the other hand, deeply in love with his wife, was shocked to his core.

"And?" Thatcher prompted.

"I had a long talk with each of them," said Carrie briskly. "And I made Gil promise never to stray again. He won't of course. He's not really the type. All of this was a mistake at the Canandaigua Dog Show, I understand. But it makes him feel better to think he's undergoing a penance of some sort. Particularly when he feels so wretched about Roger."

"Has anybody succeeded in convincing him of Kincaid's guilt?"

"Oh, Roger didn't make any bones about it when Gil went to see him. But Gil was always very fond of Roger so now he's managed to convince himself that somehow he's responsible. It's just the sort of thing he would do. I'm sure that poor Peggy never had any idea that Gil didn't want to marry her. He would have made it a point to hide his feelings from her. Really, he is perfectly infuriating. Or, he would be," she amended conscientiously, "if he weren't so attractive."

"And Olivia?" asked Thatcher. "Is she wretched about Kincaid too?"

"Olivia," replied Carrie, "is far too happy to think about

anybody but Gil. Real happiness, you know, is a very selfish business. She even promised me that . . ."

"What in the world did you make her give up?"

Carrie smiled. "Just a few of her cultural activities. A man can take just so much polished perfection. Actually, in spite of everything, they're happy as children to be together again. They're taking off for the Bahamas—it will do them good to get away from Shaftesbury . . ."

"Splendid," said Charlie heartily.

"Oh, that would have never come to anything," said Carrie, answering the thought rather than the word. "Giselle doesn't have much patience."

They exchanged knowing smiles.

It was youth that led Ken to rush into hasty and ill-advised speech.

"And Mr. Withers has back that fine stag head he shot, so everything's all right."

Carrie stiffened into a figure of outrage.

"The head that *who* shot?"

"But Mr. Withers . . ." began the unfortunate Nicolls.

"Do you mean to tell me that Brad has had the gall to maintain that he shot that stag? The stag that I stalked for four hours? He's been going around saying . . ." The lady paused for breath. Wrath descended on her brow. "Well," she continued in the fortissimo tones of strong emotion, "I'm going to have it out with him right now!"

Her departure left Nicolls squirming under the silent reproach of his superiors.

"But," he finally stammered, "it's not that important who shot those antlers."

There was a moment of heavy silence.

"I don't think, Nicolls," said Thatcher gently, "that you've fully absorbed the Shaftesbury view of these things."

Keep Up With The BESTSELLERS!

_____ 80409 LOOKING FOR MR. GOODBAR, Judith Rossner $1.95

_____ 80720 CURTAIN, Agatha Christie $1.95

_____ 80676 TALES OF POWER, Carlos Castaneda $1.95

_____ 80588 FOREVER, Judy Blume $1.75

_____ 80675 THE MASTERS AFFAIR, Burt Hirschfeld $1.95

_____ 80445 SECRETS, Burt Hirschfeld $1.95

_____ 78835 THE PIRATE, Harold Robbins $1.95

_____ 80763 WEEP IN THE SUN, Jeanne Wilson $1.95

_____ 80762 THE PRESIDENT'S MISTRESS, Patrick Anderson $1.95

_____ 80751 JULIA, Peter Straub $1.95

_____ 80723 SEVEN MEN OF GASCONY, R. F. Delderfield $1.95

Available at bookstores everywhere, or order direct from the publisher.

POCKET BOOKS
Department FB-2
1 West 39th Street
New York, N.Y. 10018

Please send me the books I have checked above. I am enclosing $_____ (please add 35¢ to cover postage and handling). Send check or money order—no cash or C.O.D.'s please.

NAME_____

ADDRESS_____

CITY_____STATE/ZIP_____

FB-2

POCKET BOOKS